"Not that the st
will take a long

— Henry David Thoreau

Dinner Along the Amazon

Timothy Findley was born in Toronto and now lives in the
country nearby. His novel, *The Wars*, was a winner of the
Governor-General's Award and a winner of the City of
Toronto Book Award, establishing him as one of Canada's
leading writers. The book was acclaimed throughout the
English-speaking world and has already appeared in eight
translated editions. Findley wrote the screenplay for the film,
The Wars, directed by Robin Phillips. *Famous Last Words*, his
best-selling novel of gripping international intrigue, was
published in 1981 to rave reviews, and in 1983 Penguin
reissued *The Last of the Crazy People*, his brilliant first novel

DINNER ALONG THE AMAZON

Timothy Findley

Penguin Books

Penguin Books Canada Ltd., 2801 John Street, Markham, Ontario, L3R 1B4, Canada
Penguin Books Ltd., Harmondsworth, Middlesex, England
Penguin Books, 40 West 23rd Street, New York, New York, 10010, U.S.A
Penguin Books Australia Ltd., Ringwood, Victoria, Australia
Penguin Books (N.Z.) Ltd., 182-190 Wairau Road, Auckland 10, New Zealand

Published in Penguin Books, 1984

Reprinted 1984

Copyright © Pebble Productions Inc.,1984
All rights reserved

Manufactured in Canada by Webcom Limited
Typesetting by Jay Tee Graphics Ltd.
Series design by David Wyman

Canadian Cataloguing in Publication Data

Findley, Timothy, 1930-
Dinner along the Amazon

(Penguin short fiction)
ISBN 0-14-007304-3

I. Title.   II. Series.

PS8511.I573D56 1984   C813'.54   C84-098289-5
PR9199.3.F548D56 1984

For Marian Engel

We will sit in a circle longing for the lights of Moscow. We will bite each other's fingers, to see the blood. We will continue to clean our houses. We will make artifacts.

And the morning will come, and so will the night again. Won't it?

The Honeyman Festival
Marian Engel

Acknowledgements

"Lemonade" first appeared in *Exile*, in a slightly different form and titled "Harper's Bazaar."

"War" was read on CBC's "Anthology."

"About Effie" first appeared in *The Tamarack Review*, Autumn, 1956.

"Sometime – Later – Not Now" first appeared in *The New Orleans Review*, 1972.

"What Mrs Felton Knew" first appeared in *Cavalier*, April, 1970, under the title "E.R.A."

"The People on the Shore" was read on CBC's "Anthology."

"Hello Cheeverland, Goodbye" first appeared in *The Tamarack Review*, November, 1974, in a somewhat different form.

"Losers, Finders, Strangers at the Door" first appeared in *75: New Canadian Stories*, 1975, Oberon Press.

"The Book of Pins" first appeared in *74: New Canadian Stories*, 1974, Oberon Press.

"Daybreak at Pisa" first appeared in *The Tamarack Review*, Winter, 1982.

"Out of the Silence" first appeared in *Ethos*, Summer, 1983.

Contents

Introduction

It came as something of a shock, when gathering these stories for collective publication, to discover that for over thirty years of writing my attention has turned again and again to the same unvarying gamut of sounds and images. They not only turn up here in this present book, but in my novels, too. I wish I hadn't noticed this. In fact, it became an embarrassment and I began to wonder if I should file *A CATALOGUE OF PERSONAL OBSESSIONS.* The sound of screen doors banging; evening lamplight; music held at a distance — always being played on a gramophone; letters written on blue-tinted note paper; robins making forays onto summer lawns to murder worms; photographs in cardboard boxes; Colt revolvers hidden in bureau drawers and a chair that is always falling over. What does it mean? Does it mean that here is a writer who is hopelessly uninventive? Appallingly repetitive? Why are the roads always dusty in this man's work — why is it always so *hot* — why can't it RAIN? And my agent was once heard to moan aloud as she was reading through the pages of a television script I had just delivered: "Oh God, Findley — *not more rabbits!*"

Well. Yes. . . .

More rabbits; more dusty roads. I'm sorry, but I can't help it. I seem to be stuck with these obsessions and perhaps they simply go hand in hand with those other obsessions all writers have: the kinds of men and women they write about; the way they bring their people together and tear them apart; what sort of names they give their characters and whether they give them cats or dogs to live with. Or rabbits. More than likely, it is these obsessions which signal, as much as anything else, whose world you are in. In the world of Alice Munro, for instance, there tend to be a number of visiting aunts or aunts in residence or aunts *"we're just going to drop by and see."* In Chekhov's gallery there are all those wonderful portraits of the doctor who fails his calling and who makes a profession of disillusionment. In Maugham, there is always Maugham — the perfect narrator, hovering at the story's edges but never in the story's way, (obsessed with being there — and nothing more). In Cheever there is always infidelity, which is always futile, always sad — always a part of the growing up process, the inevitable discovery that youth is not a gift for life. And yet, we never tire of Munrovian aunts, Chekhovian doctors, Maughamish Maughams or of Cheever's wistful losers. Why? It strikes me the answer must be that we never tire of them precisely because the writer never tires of them, but finds them always freshly seething with possibilities whenever another aunt, another doctor or another man in love with his neighbour's wife hoves into view.

When you come right down to it, the pursuit of an obsession through the act of writing is not so much a question of repetition as it is of regeneration. Each of Chekhov's doctors begets another, whose tics may be reminiscent of his forebear, but whose person and condition are quite, quite different. And the regeneration surely is a sign, a signal that something remains to be done with this person, that the writer instinctively recognizes everything hasn't been said about him: all the questions have not been put, including the most important question of all: *why* am I obsessed with you? One day this question — all the questions — may be answered and when this happens, the character disappears. No more disillusioned doctors. This is

what happened with Chekhov. All those doctors in his stories
— and in every full length play but one — his last, *The Cherry
Orchard*. This suggests there may be hope — that all your obsessions do not track you to the grave.

On the other hand, writers are never through with the world
they see and hear. Even in the silence of a darkened room, they
see it and they hear it, because it is a world inside their heads,
which is the "real" world they write about. Of course, this interior world is fed by the world we all share — the one we all
move around in every day of our lives. But the writer tends to
feed it selectively — a little of this, a little of that; none of some
things and a lot of others. This process of feeding the world inside your head goes on from the moment you are first aware
there are not only things to see and things to touch and things
to hear — but also things to record. Don't ask why. There isn't
any reason. It is simply something required of a person, the
way you are required to go to bed at night and get up in the
morning. Your body — or something in your body demands it:
an obsession like any other.

The stories in this book are arranged chronologically, by
decades. "Lemonade" (which was published as "Harper's
Bazaar") got started in a flat which I shared with the actor,
Alec McCowen, and was completed in an old hotel where I
shared rooms with an actress, Sheila Keddy. Later, it was
altered and finalized on the dining room table in the home of
my agents, Stanley and Nancy Colbert. I don't know how it
has any unity at all, since my flat with Alec was in London,
England and the old hotel where I lived with Sheila was in
Washington, D.C. and the Colberts' dining room table was in
Hollywood, California. Needless to say, I was glad when I
finally settled down.

Some of these stories, or incidents within them, are drawn
from real life — either my own or the lives of others. This has
no real importance, it seems to me, since all of the people
would fail to recognize themselves — even Ezra and Dorothy
Pound or Tom and Vivienne Eliot, who appear towards the
end of the book. It was simply that something about them —
about these real people — something overheard or spotted

from the corner of my eye, caught at my attention and worried me until I had it on the page. The Eliot story is the best example of this. It is fairly safe to say that no such confrontation as the one depicted in "Out of the Silence" ever took place — and if it did, it more than likely only took place in Vivienne Eliot's mind. What caught me — the thing with which I became obsessed — was the thought that two people could live together for so long, endure the same history and the same painful experience of marriage, and yet the same history and experience could produce madness in one of them and poetry in the other. It was also intriguing to me that Eliot had put so much of Vivienne into that poetry — that he had even put her there before he met her, before he knew her and married her. It was as if he had willed a fictional lady with whom he was obsessed to come all the way into real life. And what could *that* mean. . . ?

This provides the perfect place for me to invite you into this book, and into the world with which I have been obsessed for so long.

Dinner Along
the Amazon

Lemonade

For Ruth Gordon

Every morning at seven o'clock Harper Dewey turned over
and woke up. And every morning he would lie in his tumbled
bed (for he slept without repose even at the age of eight) until it
was seven-thirty, thinking his way back into his dreams, which
were always of his father. At seven-thirty he would get out of
bed and cross to his window where he would stand for a
moment watching his dreams fade in the sunlight until there
was nothing in the garden save the lilac and the high board
fence.

And the birds.

Robins and starlings and sparrows flowed over the smooth
lawn in great droves, turning it into the likeness of a market-
place; and the raucous babble of their bargaining (of dealings
in worms and beetles and flies) poured itself, like something
distilled or dehydrated, from the jar of darkness into the morning air, which made it swell and burst. This enormous shout of
birds at morning was always a delight to Harper Dewey.

Presently, over this sound, there would burst the first indication of an awakening household: Bertha Millroy's hymn.

Bertha Millroy was the maid — and a day, to Bertha, wasn't a day at all unless it began with a hymn and ended with a prayer.

She lived — Bertha — in the attic, in a small room directly above Harper's room and she sang her hymn from the window which opened over his head. When it was finished she would say the same thing every morning — "Amen" and "Good morning Harper." Then they would race each other to the landing on the stairs. Harper never cheated, although he could easily have been dressed long before Bertha if he had chosen to be, because he was always awake so much earlier than her. But this every morning race had never been specifically agreed upon and if Harper had ever said to Bertha at the window "Let's race," or if Bertha had ever said to Harper below her "Beat you downstairs," the whole procedure would have been off. Neither of them could remember when this habit had started — it just had.

Well, one morning early in the summer, (in fact it was hardly more than late spring), Harper and Bertha met on the stairs' landing — Bertha won — and after they had scanned the note they found there, they looked at each other and then quickly looked away. They descended to the first floor in their usual fashion — Harper going down the front stairs to collect the paper from the front porch — and Bertha going down the back stairs to light the stove and to bring in the milk.

This morning, Harper didn't open the paper, although he usually read the comics sitting on the porch step. Instead he returned inside, letting the screen door clap behind him and leaving the big oak and glass door open so that the air could come through, into the still house. He went straight out to the kitchen and sat down at the table, slipping the still folded paper onto the breakfast tray which was laid out for his mother.

In the kitchen, Bertha Millroy behaved in the same morose fashion, as though touched by the same hand. And indeed their mutual despondency was based upon a kindred misgiving. And Mrs Renalda Harper Dewcy was the instigator of that misgiving.

Mrs Renalda Harper Dewey, widow of Harper Peter Dewey the First (killed in the battle for Caen, August 1944, the year after Harper P. Dewey the Second's birth) was a lady who lay in bed till nine o'clock every morning because of the night before. It used to be that she would lie abed until eight and then it became an occasional night before — but now the lie-abed was until nine and had ceased to be occasional.

This morning there had been a note on the flat top of the balustrade on the landing. On the note were written the words "Ten o'clock — thank you" in rather indistinct watery blue ink. "Ten o'clock, thank you" and that was all.

Bertha put on the kettle.

"I don't want any tea," said Harper Dewey.

"You don't drink morning tea because you want to, Master Harper Dewey," said Bertha Millroy in her flat voice, "you drink it to assist nature."

The kettle boiled.

Bertha warmed the teapot.

They were silent.

Bertha threw out the water into the sink and put tea leaves in the pot.

The robins moved across the lawn outside the kitchen window.

Harper watched them.

Bertha poured boiling water over the tea leaves, turned off the stove and put the lid on the teapot. One, two, three, and sat down.

"Ten o'clock indeed," she muttered — and then she poured tea into their cups.

One of the robins was listening to a worm under the dew. Harper watched. The robin's head was cocked to one side as it listened. Then it ran a few steps on tiptoe and caught the worm noise again — this time nearer to it. The robin waited. Harper waited — Bertha Millroy waited — and then the robin stabbed the ground with its beak — caught the worm and tossed it into the sunlight. Harper shivered.

"I don't want to assist nature," he said, and he pushed his teacup away.

The thought of having to wait until ten o'clock to see his mother was unbearable to Harper. He had never had to wait that long on any other morning that he could remember.

There was a procedure — one which took place every day — which they followed, commencing with the preparation of Mrs Dewey's breakfast tray. Bertha would serve up the eggs into the plate and pour coffee into the silver thermos bottle and Harper would butter toast. Then Bertha would take the tray and Harper would take the paper and they would mount the stairs to the second floor. Outside his mother's door Harper had placed, long ago, a small chair with a cushion on it, where, at this stage of the procedure he would sit, while Bertha went into the bedroom to awaken his mother.

Then he would listen to all the sounds which came from his mother's room. First of all Bertha Millroy pulled the curtains after which, every morning, she would say, "It's nine o'clock, Mrs Dewey," (this morning she would say "ten o'clock") — and Harper's beautiful mother would reply in a sleepy voice, "Thank you Bertha, let me have my wrapper."

After this he would count to himself the various stages of her awakening which he had trained his ear to recognize, although in his whole life he had never witnessed them.

First of all his mother rolled over from her side onto her back. Then there was the sound of Bertha mincing to the bedside. The sitting up came next. This was a combination of three sounds. The plumping of pillows, a slight voiceless sound which his mother uttered as she was helped into a sitting position (simultaneously there would be a grunt from Bertha) — and finally Bertha saying pleasantly "There."

After the sitting up came a pause. "Now," Bertha would inevitably say, "here we are." And she could be heard mincing across the room to where she'd lift the breakfast tray and mince back again to the bed, accompanied on the return journey by the tinkle of ice against the walls of the orange juice glass and sometimes a harsh clank when the coffee thermos hit the plate of eggs. "Thank you" followed that and then silence.

Next, coffee being poured and the paper being opened and Bertha stepping to the dressing table to get the brush and then, sometimes but not always, a few listless strokes of the brush through his mother's hair.

Then Bertha would emerge from the room, somewhat triumphantly, and she would say as she appeared, "Call if you want — don't if you don't," and then she went downstairs.

At this juncture Harper's turn came.

"Good morning, mother."

"Good morning, Harpie. You sit there like a good boy 'till I'm ready — then you can come in dear."

"All right."

He knew that he wasn't allowed inside until she'd gone into the bathroom and shut the door behind her, he knew this explicitly, but for some reason or other she felt she must tell him again and again every morning and so he let her.

After she had gone into the bathroom he would go into the bedroom and sit on the bed and look at the pictures in the paper and listen to the bath water running into the tub. Afterwards, when he heard the water running out of the tub he would go to the highboy (it had been his father's) and open the middle drawer.

Inside the middle drawer there was always the Colt revolver lying on a white tea towel — and beside it lay two boxes of cartridges. But the Colt revolver held no interest for him at all. He knew what it was there for and he respected this, but aside from respect he felt nothing. It guarded a treasure, which lay under the white tea towel, contained in two boxes — one which had velveteen on the outside and another which was leather. These were his mother's jewel cases. This was the treasure.

Although Harper had no idea, had no conception of the value of these jewels he believed them to be the most beautiful objects he had ever seen. Actually their value was enormous (but Harper wouldn't have understood the meaning of value — he only understood that they were beautiful).

There were earrings and finger rings and necklaces and brooches. There were strings and strands of pearls and an emerald on a golden thread. There was an opal ring and a sapphire ring of such gigantic proportions that Harper wondered always how his mother ever wore it. And there was a diamond set in the midst of emeralds and yellow sapphires that truly dazzled the beholder with its radiance.

Every day, Mrs Renalda Harper Dewey wore either one piece or several pieces of this jewelry and Harper every day would take out the two boxes and stare at the contents trying to guess which piece or pieces she would choose. Very often he was right in his choice because he had a certain insight into the inflection of his mother's voice which she employed when she called to him in the hallway.

However — in the last two months this had become a source, not of pleasure to him but of anguish, for something was happening — an extreme mystery — which no one could explain to him no matter how often he asked about it. Certain of the smaller pieces of jewelry were disappearing.

The first piece had disappeared over six months before, just after Christmas. It had been a small brooch of silver, studded with tiny diamonds. It was in the shape of a spider's web and the diamonds had represented dewdrops. Harper had been especially enamoured of this piece and when he found it gone he was panic-stricken and searched the entire room for it. But then his mother said to him: "I sold it," in a cold beautiful voice, and he was heartbroken. She said she'd sold it to finance a gift for her own mother. But she didn't tell him what the gift was and he had never heard his grandmother mention it.

Since then, other pieces had gone — none without immediate notice from his loving eye — but, as they went the cold beautiful voice delivered credible reasons as excuse — Granny's insurance — Mary Flannagan's wedding present — old Aunt Alice's silver anniversary — and more.

During the last two months there had been a marked increase in the loss which could not be ignored or brushed aside as more "expenses for gifts." And since it was two months since the first note, which read "Nine o'clock please" had appeared on the landing, Harper Dewey with a sinking heart (but with a mind that could not prompt him to an exact reason) somehow, perhaps instinctively, put two and two together and made four.

As for Bertha Millroy, there was no mystery to her — whatever it was — she knew.

So that now, when there lay between their cups of tea — between their two pairs of moving hands which drummed with speculation on the kitchen table — a note, which read "Ten o'clock, thank you," their eyes could not meet and they could not voice their distress for they were filled with fear.

Bertha Millroy wondered just how Harper would discover and she said a word to God asking him "not to make her do the telling."

At nine-thirty Harper Dewey was in the back garden with his pet guinea pig when he heard Mrs Jamieson, the lady from next door, knock on the side door of the house.

He heard Bertha shut off the taps at the kitchen sink and a moment later Mrs Jamieson's voice.

She sounded angry and at once had to be subdued with an admonition from Bertha.

"M'am, you must be quiet. Mrs Dewey is asleep."

"Asleep, is she? Well that's more than I can say for myself thanks to her last night."

"Come in m'am and explain your trouble. Can I give you some tea Mrs Jamieson?"

The side door slammed.

Harper went inside through the sunroom and stood listening in the dining room to what was being said beyond the kitchen door. He still had his guinea pig in his arms.

"That woman!" expostulated Mrs Jamieson — who had grey hair and an enormous Norman nose. "That *woman*!!"

"Now, Mrs Jamieson, you must quiet down and explain yourself. There's nothing we can do until you say your piece. Here's a cup of tea. Here. Now say it."

Mrs Jamieson clanked a teaspoon around the inside of the teacup.

"She came to me last night. Last night at *two* o'clock in the morning!"

She paused, relishing her role as informer.

"Last night at two in the morning? That don't even make sense," said Bertha.

"You're darned tootin' " — Mrs Jamieson was of the old school — "You're darned tootin' it don't make sense. That

woman.'' She made a clucking noise in her throat. ''Drunk!''
she pronounced. ''Drunk and disorderly and all unkempt. . .''
She left off as though the spectacle was too much for her
meagre vocabulary to deal with.

Bertha heaved a deprecating little sigh. ''Oh dear me,'' she
muttered.

''You should have seen her, Millroy — I can only tell you.
Why she didn't even know where she was at. Drunk! Why I've
never seen anyone so drunk. She had her hair all down around
her ears and her lipstick all smudged and them pretty earrings
of hers — why she'd lost one. You know the pretty ones of
pearl? Well, almighty, if one wasn't gone and the other hanging there like it'd drop any minute. And she smelt so of liquor I
had to hide behind the door. She couldn't focus neither. And
the things she was trying to say. I could barely make them out
but they was insults I wouldn't like to think that boy of hers
would ever hear. She thought I was a stranger, see? She
thought she had her own house and that I was some fool
prowler that'd gotten in to steal her things. Why, she behaved
just like some — Well — I hardly like to say it Millroy — but
she was talking and — she looked just like some harlot from
over to New York City.''

There was a short, empty pause.

''Oh I felt so sorry for her,'' murmured Mrs Jamieson in
genuine distress. ''I felt so sorry for her — but I just had to say
it.''

''Say what?'' asked Bertha.

''I told her to go to hell,'' said Mrs Jamieson. ''And I
slammed my door.''

Another pause.

''I never used such language in my life. It was just awful.''

''Well, what happened?''

''Oh, then she staggered down the walk and I watched to
make sure she got the right house and then I went to bed. But I
never got to sleep.'' Her voice rose. ''And there she is — sleeping up there — almighty it's enough to make *anyone* curse.''

''Mrs Jamieson, she's sick, you mustn't get angry with her.
She's sick.''

"Well, what's she got to be sick about anyway — any more than any of us. Any more tea?"

"I guess she grieves her husband. I don't know."

Harper listened while Bertha poured out more tea for Mrs Jamieson.

"I guess I grieve my husband — but I don't tell the world that I do. No, Millroy, she's not got the right to. . ."

Harper went upstairs.

He listened from the top step to make sure that Bertha was still busy with the neighbour woman and then he tiptoed down the hall to his mother's room.

The door was closed and he had to shift the guinea pig in his arms to open it quietly. Just before he went in he said "shh" to his pet and muffled it against his thin chest.

The light coming through the chiffon curtains was dense and murky and at first he could only see his mother's shape roughly hewn out of bedclothes and shadows.

All that Mrs Jamieson had said in the kitchen had not made sense to Harper. All of it he had not understood — but he had fathomed that his mother was sick and that she had been bad and he knew that he had to see her to set his mind at rest.

He stepped to the bedside — but just as he did he heard Bertha's feet upon the stairs.

He went and stood in the corner.

Bertha came into the room. She set the tray down on the highboy and smoothed her apron out like crisp brittle armour and, as she did every day, pulled the braided cord that sprung the curtains from the windows. The sunlight leapt into the room, and pounced, like a beast of prey, onto the big double bed — onto the candy-pink sheets and onto the figure that lay beneath them. Harper, who at that moment was frozen with terror at being discovered in his mother's room, gave a startled cry — like a mouse being caught in a trap.

Bertha took the situation in hand immediately.

"Shut them eyes," she said, stepping briskly to the side of the bed (like a nurse Harper remembered when he was in hospital, like a nurse going to save someone from falling out of bed, like a nurse going to pull the sheet off a corpse so that the doctor could look at it and tell why it had died). "Shut them eyes and don't say a word."

Harper left the room. And all the while he sat in the hall, holding his guinea pig — all the while his mother was being helped into a sitting position — all the while the hair was being brushed and the lipstick spread and the tea poured out — Harper Dewey saw what he had seen — like a vile photograph forced before his eyes. His mother's face pressed against the sheets — his mother's mouth all open and showing where she had no teeth — his mother's eyes which had no brows — and all of this, all of this 'face,' was the most insipid colour, a horrid yellowy white — pressed against the pink sheets like an advertisement for sickness.

It was much longer that morning before Bertha Millroy left the room on her mincing feet, and shut the door with a click behind her. And after that there was a longer pause than he could ever remember before his mother said to him: "Good morning, Harpie."

And when she said it he didn't reply. Instead he went back to the garden where he locked his guinea pig in its cage and put it out of the sunlight under the lilac trees.

There was a morning a week or so later that pronounced the coming of summer with the vehemence of heat and the clarity of a clap of thunder.

There was no sign of rain — there being not a single cloud in the sky — and yet the thunder came and went sharply, somewhere beyond the horizon of trees and rooftops. Harper had never heard thunder in the morning and he sat in the kitchen listening to it while Bertha went about brewing their tea as though nothing unusual was happening at all.

"Thunder is clouds bumping," said Harper looking out the window.

"That's right."

"What clouds?"

"I don't know, Harper. Must be one somewhere."

"Two."

"Two then. Just 'cause you can't see them doesn't mean

they ain't there. Drink it up." She put his cup of tea on the table.

"I'm going up today," he said.

"That's right, honey, she'll be glad you did that."

"It's been over a week," said Harper.

"She'll be glad to have you back then. But I wouldn't say nothing. You know that every morning you ain't been there she still went on saying 'Good-morning' to you? Went right on saying it just hoping you'd reply. It'll do her good to hear you say it back today."

"Did she mention me to you?"

"No, honey, she didn't say a word."

"But she said hello each day?"

"Uuh-huuh."

Harper fell silent.

"I hope I don't scare her by saying it back today."

Bertha laughed.

"She'll be delighted to be scared so. Just pipe up with it — don't worry."

So at ten o'clock they went up and Harper said "Good morning" from his place in the hall.

When she was gone into the bathroom and the noise of the bath water being run began and when she began to sing in there so that nothing could be heard through the door from the bedroom, Harper got off the little chair in the hall and tiptoed in to the highboy.

He moved his hand towards the middle drawer.

The key was gone.

Gone.

Everything was suddenly motionless.

Never before had the key not been there. The drawer had from time to time been locked, but the key had never been removed. In fact, in the whole house there was nothing shut away behind locks. If they were, there was no key. And if there was, the key was always in its place.

The moment of cataclysm passed, and there was a faint movement beyond the windows and the chiffon curtains parted as the breeze pushed its way gently into the room. Harper's first sensual awareness was of scent — a light, almost itchy smell which came from his mother's perfume bottles. He moved — and he began to wander, completely without direction, from one object in the room to the next — testing its openness with his eyes, and sometimes touching the handle of the drawer to see if there were any give to it. At the dressing table he lifted the tops from the bottles of scent. He stuck one of his fingers into the powder bowl and watched the faint pink dust explode into the air and settle in circular signals about the little round spheres and towers of glassware. It came into his mind that his mother would know by this that he had been there, where he wasn't allowed: but it passed out again: he didn't care: she had locked him out, and he had found his way in, as the wind had found its way back in through the windows.

Harper went over to the bed and sat on it like an Indian. He pulled the covers up behind him so that they made a teepee over his head. He drank the milk out of the milk jug on the breakfast tray and waited.

The door from the bathroom jerked open and a cloud of steam rolled into the bedroom. Out of this cloud, like a floating figure in a Japanese print, stepped Renalda Dewey, with the silence, the intensity, of a mime.

She went towards the dressing table, trailing little licking tails of damp chiffon negligee, her dark Italian head held like something beautiful on a stick above the collar of her gown inclined towards the objective of her progress. After, in a trance of perfect silence, she sat before the mirror and let her eyes fall upon the compromise arranged before her. The manufacturer's labels, of gold and silver, out of deference to expense, had numbers on them, one and two and three and four — with instructions for their application — and a touch of this, a daub of that, a trace of the other, finally a deft indication with a brush dipped in the fourth. She sat there, working, for a half-an-hour, but it seemed like a full hour or more to Harper sitting on the bed. Finally, however, she was finished and sufficiently clothed to let Harper see her.

"You can come out of your tent now dear."

The teepee fell back from his head.

She was pinning artificial roses onto her suit coat, three of them, grey and yellow.

"Come along, dear, I want you to tell me how I look."

He stood up.

"I think they're very pretty, don't you?" she said touching the roses.

"Yes."

"I think I'll wear flowers all this summer."

She looked into the mirror. It was as though she couldn't find herself there. She had to go very close to it and lean one hand against the table to steady herself and she had to almost close her eyes before she found what she was looking for.

"Yes. And later on I can wear *real* roses."

"Mother?"

"Harpie, look out the window, dear, and see if the car is there."

They passed each other in the middle of the room. He looked — but she didn't look back — she seemed, instead, intent on finding something — something, he sensed, that she wouldn't allow herself to see until his back was turned.

"Yes," he said from the window, "it is." He stood watching the chauffeur, who was smoking a cigarette. His mother was in the bathroom running the taps at the sink.

In a moment she came out.

"Good-bye, dear."

"Mother — aren't you going to wear. . .?"

"You have a nice day with Bertha, dear. And don't upset her. Oh — and if you play the piano for heaven's sake close the dining room windows. I don't care how hot it is, you mustn't disturb Mrs Jamieson."

"Yes'm."

She was suddenly in the hallway — then halfway downstairs — then in the kitchen saying something to Bertha to which Bertha replied "I'll try m'am" — and then she was at the door, where she called out:

"Good-bye, dear!"

She stepped along the red bricks of the front walk towards the car.

"Mother."

She stopped.

The chauffeur threw away his cigarette.

She looked at the budding roses in the flower beds. She picked one and held it to the artificial flowers. For a second a look of displeasure crossed her face, and she made a gesture to throw the real rosebud away — but then she reneged and put it inside her handbag. Then she smiled.

He had never seen such a smile and he knew suddenly that she was smiling because she was escaping him.

She said something to the chauffeur and got into the car. Sitting in the rear seat she gave her attention entirely to the yellow rosebud which she had removed from the handbag — putting it this way and that in the air and holding it to her nostrils to catch its embryonic perfume.

The chauffeur got into the front seat and started the engine. It gave a roar.

"Mother."

She was —

"Good-bye!"

— Gone.

One morning, a month later, Bertha Millroy got up from the kitchen table, tucked the paper under her arm, picked up the breakfast tray and said:

"You're not to come no more."

Upon which she fled, under the protection of shock, into the newly forbidden reaches of the upper floor.

So it was that later in the summer, when the heat came down into the city like a flood from the hills, that Harper Dewey didn't see his beautiful mother for days on end. And although it was obvious that she was still in the house (sometimes he would hear her call out, but never for him), her presence was not made visible to him.

Sometimes at night he would be awake in bed when she came home — and he would listen to her clicking up the brick walk and turning the key in the front door. Then he would sit up on the edge of his bed and she would be heard talking downstairs in the front hall. He never caught the words, neither what they were, nor their significance — he surmised that she was alone because of the form of intonation. They had a hollow sound, as words do which are not caught in the shell of an immediate ear; and they seemed to have been cast adrift, like pieces of foam from the edge of the sea and they had disintegrated and drowned long before they reached his bedroom.

At night, his bedroom was his cave, where it was dark and he sat or slept like a secret unspoken in someone's mouth.

While she moved about in the lower regions of the house he would follow her footsteps as she went from room to room and through the passages between. This walking about lasted for a long time and he determined that she must do it in the dark because there was — on most evenings — a constant shuffle, which accompanied the wander, as though she were bumping into things, or only just avoiding them and stepping aside in that sudden startled way of people in the dark. And her voice would go with her through the dark, calling out when she fell and whispering in satisfaction when she cleared some obstacle which had been in her dark path and when she found what she sought (and he did not guess what this was) she would sigh and mutter and then be silent.

It was the silence which followed each of these nightly preambles which frightened him and mystified him the most. Her very breathing and indeed his own as well, would appear to have stopped and in the whole house nothing would stir, not even Bertha Millroy in her attic room, not even she in the midst of all her dreams, would stir.

In the silence Harper set his mind upon the repose of things in the dark and he would see the Lilliputian heads of the pearls strung on a gargantuan string and he would begin to cry at the sight of their ghostly faces.

Finally he would lie down on his back and the silence would break, but no one would hear it break. He would be long asleep before she would turn out the lights below and climb the stairs and lock herself in her room.

Summer became itself on the street where Harper Dewey lived with his mother and Bertha Millroy. There were elm trees on

the boulevards on either side of the street and beyond the
boulevards wide sidewalks bordered with fences and low stone
walls. All of the homes had a Victorian flavour about them,
which most of the residents had had the sense to disguise. Thus
the houses were mostly of painted brick and refashioned façade
— of fronts stripped bare of ornament but still retaining high
pointed convergences of line and many had little turrets and
false gables.

All the houses were confronted with wide long lawns and
most attempted to hide their Victorian manner behind screens
of ivy vines and a profusion of trees and bushes, so that the
whole length of the street was a vision of green mottle, relieved
with floral colour and the rich red of the brick walks which, like
the many courses of a maze, wove in and out of the gardens up
and down either side of the street.

The residents were of varied stamp but all within the
category of what is known as the 'professional' world. There
were doctors, and one of the city's prominent lawyers; also an
ex-mayor, a retired colonel, two university professors, a clergy-
man, an author, two widows (Mrs Dewey and Mrs Jamieson),
also a Mr Robertson whom no one knew anything about except
that he was enormously wealthy and drove about in a Rolls
Royce car and that he had two boxer dogs of whom everyone
stood in distant respect (Mr Robertson never spoke to a soul
and no one ever spoke to him); there was also an architect and
a witch. The witch was Miss Kennedy.

She lived in a tall dark house at the end of the street, the one
house that had not been stripped of its Victorian vestiges. It
stood closer to the street than the rest, its tall façade looming
darkly in the unrelenting shadow of the only oak tree on the
whole street — a tree reputed to be two hundred years old,
which meant, to Harper's delight, that it had stood there in the
days of the Indians. It was also said that in the early days of the
city, when there was a stockade built about its periphery,
renegades and witches (perhaps Miss Kennedy's own fore-
bears) were hung from this tree. In that time the burning of
witches was forbidden, so that they were hung, as common
criminals were, deprived of the dignity of a heretic's martyr-
dom, traditionally fire.

One day in early August Harper went down the street to speak to Miss Kennedy.

He stood outside her gate, hesitant only for a moment, and then went into the shallow garden, in which nothing would grow because of the thick shadow of the oak tree.

Miss Kennedy hovered in an upper window, dressed in a dark Victorian wrapper. Harper pulled the chain which rang the doorbell.

Inside he could hear Miss Kennedy's Pekinese dog snuffling excitedly at the space between the floor and the bottom of the door.

There was the sound of steps within and a gentle admonition to the little dog before the door opened to reveal Miss Kennedy — wrapper clutched at the breast, her red hair piled high upon her thin bony head, her eyes snapping, her mouth pursed, her ears dragged down at the lobes by the weight of elaborately long earrings. She smiled.

Harper was amazed. It had not occurred to him that a witch ever smiled. Leer, she might, but smile, never.

"Well, Harper Dewey. Is that right? What is it?" she said.

"I — I'd like to speak with you. I'd like to have —" he turned and looked back at the street, wondering if he should run off now while he could, but before he could remedy the situation, Miss Kennedy spoke.

"Come inside," she said, "I'll fix some lemonade."

Harper imagined the contents of the lemonade and blanched.

"Thank you m'am," he gulped, and stepped inside, never, he was sure, to return.

The Pekinese immediately flung itself at his toes.

"Stop that!" squealed Miss Kennedy. "That's Harper."

The dog wagged its tail and backed away, voicing a high pitched greeting.

"Hello," said Harper, nervously.

"You sit in there, dear, while I fix the lemonade."

Miss Kennedy gestured, with a long arm, to a sitting room to the left of the dark hallway.

Harper went in. It was cool in the sitting room and there was an organ in the corner, with dust on the keys.

"Hasn't she got a maid?" Harper asked the dog, touching the keys. There was a loud noise. Harper was so startled that he sat down on the horsehair sofa, the leather of which felt cold and comforting against the back of his legs.

There were pictures on the wall of people who wore strangling, old costumes and who all looked as though life had been extremely painful for them. He concluded that they well might have been Miss Kennedy's 'victims.' Not one of them smiled. Harper sat very near the edge of the seat.

In a moment Miss Kennedy returned. She carried a tray on which she had placed two tall glasses with long-handled spoons in them and a squat cut-glass pitcher filled with lemonade.

"Let's sit outside, shall we? You take the tray."

With great relief Harper rose and bore the tray outside.

They went onto the front porch where he set the tray on a table and Miss Kennedy sat down in a high-backed rocking chair. Harper stood facing her formally. Miss Kennedy pointed to a wicker chair and told him to sit down.

She poured lemonade into the two glasses and pushed one of them towards Harper, and then, taking up her own glass, she sat back in the rocker and smiled. Harper left his lemonade on the tray, and watched it closely to see what would happen.

"Here in my lap I have two Chinese fans," said Miss Kennedy. "You may have one of them — but you must choose which one you like. I assure you, I'm equally fond of both of them, so you mustn't worry about which one I like the best. Here."

She offered him two silver bars.

"How do they open?" he asked.

She opened one of the fans ceremoniously and demonstrated its use.

"It's very pretty," remarked Harper.

He opened the second fan himself with a little difficulty and imitated Miss Kennedy's floating gesture perfectly.

"You're a born orientalist," she said, obviously pleased with the grace with which Harper manipulated the Chinese fan.

"Thank you," said Harper, unaware of the meaning of orientalist. He wondered if it was another word for witch — perhaps a definition of 'male witch.'

He sipped at his lemonade delicately. It tasted fine.

The Pekinese jumped into her mistress's lap and sat with her tongue dangling out towards Harper.

"What a funny face she has," he thought.

Miss Kennedy read his mind and said:

"Her name is Ming Toy."

"That's very pretty. Hello Ming Toy."

Ming Toy smiled and shook herself delightedly.

For a moment they sat fanning themselves and drinking their lemonade. Miss Kennedy regarded Harper patiently and with pride. Children never came to call on her. In fact no one came to call on her, and it pleased her that someone, especially someone so fine as Harper Dewey, whom she regarded as the most interesting child on the street, should be her first summer visitor.

"You said you wanted to speak to me, Harper. What is it, dear?"

Harper blushed and set aside the sweating glass of lemonade.

"Well, it's about the oak tree."

"About the oak tree, Harper? What about it, dear?"

"I want to live there," said Harper bluntly.

"You want to *live* there. Mercy me! Whatever for, dear?"

"Only for one night, Miss Kennedy. Just for one night." He began to lie. "You see, some of the other children — we had a sort of bet."

"A bet?"

"Yes."

"About the oak tree?"

"Yes. We bet that I was afraid to stay in the oak tree all night."

He waited vacantly for her reaction.

"And of course you bet that you weren't afraid at all."

"Yes'm. That's it."

"And your mother? Does she know about this?"

"Oh yes'm. She knows *all* about it. And she said 'why certainly' I was to go ahead and do it."

"I see, and so you want to have my permission to stay there. Well — so long as your mother says it's all right I guess I can't say no. When do you wish to do this? Tonight, I suppose."

"Yes. If I can stay there all night then I just have to say so in the morning."

"And do I have to say so in the morning?"

"Oh no, m'am. That's the point of my coming here now, you see. You aren't supposed to know all this. But I sort of thought that, well, if you sort of heard me getting into the tree and all, well then it would be all off, unless you knew what I was doing there. But please, you're not to say anything, not to anyone, no matter who asks. It's meant all to be a secret."

Miss Kennedy pondered for a moment, her left hand poised on Ming Toy's tiny head, her right hand gently motioning the fan through the air a few inches from her nose. Then she stopped fanning and bit the silver tip lightly with her teeth.

Harper waited, apparently nonchalant, drinking his lemonade and looking out along the street.

After a moment, Miss Kennedy said "You'll want a blanket, I suppose. And how will you keep from falling out?"

"Well, I figured I'd tie myself in."

"That's wise. You know if you fall to sleep you're liable to tumble down and we don't want that."

"No m'am."

Miss Kennedy commenced to organize the whole thing.

"And Miss Ming Toy will have to sleep at the back of the house so she won't disturb you."

"Yes m'am."

"And I'll leave a sandwich and a thermos of cocoa on the porch so's you can sneak it off after it's dark. When will you arrive, Harper?"

"Well, I figured as soon's it's dark."

"Fine. And I'm not to say a word?"

"No m'am, if you please."

"Very well then. I'll expect you after dark." She stood up.

"This ought to be a great adventure," she said. "It's not the kind of thing we do every day, is it?"

"No m'am. Only once in a while."

"Yes. Only once in a while."

Miss Kennedy looked along the street. Sunlight fell amottle on her high red hair.

"I have been waiting for adventure all my life," she said distantly, "how lucky that you're so young."

Harper did not understand this so he said nothing.

"Perhaps it only comes to those who make it come. I've never been one to ask the world to enter my life — but oh — I've wanted, Harper, I've wanted and I've waited. Yes — it's lucky that you're so young." She glanced at the oak tree. "But look how long *he's* waited," she said. "Ah well." She sat down again with a sigh. "Thank heaven I can't expect to wait that long."

It got dark at ten o'clock.

Harper's bedtime was at nine.

At nine-thirty he crept from his bed and put on his shorts and a shirt and a heavy wool sweater, for in spite of the present heat he knew that by morning he would be cold. He put a flashlight into his pocket, together with his jackknife and twenty-five cents and then he put on his socks and a pair of running shoes.

Harper had planned to leave the house by climbing out of his window and crossing the rooftop to the front, where there was a drainpipe which he had climbed many times.

Bertha moved in the kitchen below his room. He crept to his door and locked it.

At ten-thirty, after despairing of his mother's arrival, and fearing that Bertha would soon return to the attic where she would certainly hear him crossing the roof, he went to his window and clambered out.

The stars were out too, and for a moment he stopped and stared at them and then quickly climbed to the roof's crest and down the other side. He had one brief moment of panic when a car drew up across the street and he feared that it was his mother returning — but it disgorged whatever passenger it wished and drove away into the dark, music blaring from its radio.

He went down, monkey fashion, to the ground, clutching the drainpipe with toes and fingers alternating his balance. At the bottom he waited, standing in the flowerbed and then he ran quickly down the lawn and through the gate of the driveway and along the street.

Once near Miss Kennedy's he slowed his pace and soon stopped at her gate, where he heaved a loud sigh and crept inside.

There was a light on in the upper floor and Harper guessed that Miss Kennedy had lain awake to make sure of his safe arrival. He was quite right, for at the sound of the gate clicking closed he saw her high-swept head appear in silhouette at the window and nod in his direction. To show her that he had seen her he gave a brief flash of his flashlight in her direction and a moment later her light went out.

He went to the porch and found on the topmost step, just as she had promised, a packet of sandwiches and a thermos of cocoa. He stuffed all of these into his sweater front and approached the oak tree.

In the dark it loomed huge and monster-like, holding out its many arms toward him. He reached up and grasped gingerly, just within tiptoed reach, an arm that felt sturdy enough to support him.

He swung up into the bowl of the tree and sat there, breathing hard, wondering how much higher he must climb to be safely out of view of anyone passing in the morning light.

He clambered carefully inch by inch into the tree's heart. A squirrel further up in the branches scampered away, giving him a moment of terror, but then everything settled into absolute quiet. On the whole street there wasn't a sound.

Harper suddenly remembered that he had forgotten to bring a rope to tie himself into his nest and he also remembered that Miss Kennedy had warned him to bring a blanket.

"Oh well, I'll just have to keep awake and forget about being cold," he said to himself.

He ate one of the sandwiches and listened for some sound on

the street. There was, at first, nothing to be heard; but gradually, almost imperceptively he became aware of whatever strange noises the night made when he was usually asleep.

Crickets and creakings, birds stirring in their nests and chirruping in their sleep; distant cars moving through the city on unknown missions; late streetcars electrically humming far away on the main street. Late walkers conversing seriously upon subjects utterly unknown to Harper; cats yowling in darkened yards; dogs dreaming of rabbit hunts; the poor, distantly arguing over money; a woman's mysteriously rapturous scream; a telephone's insistent ringing in one of the doctor's houses; music, mice and the hum of telephone lines — the crackle of street lamps and once, he even imagined, the tinkle of stars.

Eventually he began to doze and he dreamt that he was holding on to his father, who was carrying him across a field that was strewn with the bodies of the dead. His father was talking to him about a letter.

It was a letter which Harper knew as his 'Duty Letter' which he kept in his top bureau drawer at home. His father had written it to him from England a week before the invasion of Europe, in which he knew he must partake and in which he must, perhaps, die. It was a very serious letter. In it his father spoke of Mrs Dewey and of Harper's responsibility towards her — of his 'Duty' to obey his mother and always 'to love her more dearly than all the earth.' The letter also mentioned other things — some of which Harper understood had enormous importance: the future if his father lived — the future if he did not. But the main thing Harper clung to in the tree in front of Miss Kennedy's house that night was the part about his mother — and his duty to love her. And the fact that his father had underlined the words that came at the letter's end: *"While I am gone you are all your mother has. She loves you. As do I."* Then it was signed: "Your Father."

Over and over again those final words were repeated — "all your mother has." Harper awoke with a start, when his father stumbled and fell, pitching them both forward towards the ground.

He grabbed wildly at a branch and only barely managed to save himself. He hoped that he hadn't cried out.

He re-established himself in the heart of the tree and sat there pondering over his dream. "All your mother has . . ." his father had said — but Harper knew that his mother had escaped from that, and that now she had something else which had taken his place.

Toward morning a policeman walked along, boldly and noisily below him, singing under his breath.

Just before it began to be light beyond the rooftops Harper fell asleep again. This time he awoke before falling, however. He took a long slow breath. The morning air was cool and a breeze flurried the leaves and began to waken the other tree residents: squirrels and birds and chipmunks and mice. Soon, all about him there was action, which he did not disturb (his fellow dwellers obviously having investigated his presence in the night and endorsed it) for they passed in and out of their home as though it was the most natural thing in the world to have a representative of the human species in their treetop midst.

Harper began to wonder if his plan had worked. Of course, not until Bertha discovered his absence would any reaction be set in motion. He regretted having to incorporate her despair with his mother's, but he had to obtain some sort of notice and he felt that running away, even so near at hand, must bring some sort of attention to himself from his mother.

He only hoped that Bertha would hesitate for an hour or so before reporting his absence to the police. What he hoped for was that his mother would call out for him, find him gone and then take his absence into account and ask to have him back.

At what he judged to be about eight o'clock he climbed out of the tree and went to Miss Kennedy's front door.

He rang the bell.

In a moment she appeared carrying Ming Toy in her arms, still dressed in the Victorian wrapper as though she had not even retired following their conversation of yesterday afternoon.

"Well, did you fall out?"

"No, m'am."

"Did you sleep?"

"Not much m'am. Only for a moment."

"Well — you come in and we'll have a nice big breakfast."

She led him to the kitchen, where she had already begun to prepare breakfast and where the table was laid for two people and Harper smiled gratefully, happy that she had taken the trouble to be ready for him. He wondered idly why Miss Kennedy had never married. He decided that most probably no one had ever had the time to ask, she was so well organized.

He sat down and she served him some rolled oats.

He noticed with pleasure the absence of any sign of a teapot.

"So I guess you win your bet," said Miss Kennedy pleasantly.

"Yes'm. I guess I do."

"Were you scared, Harper?"

"No m'am. Only once when I nearly fell."

"People used to always live in trees. It must have been very pleasant, once you discovered just how to keep yourself in. Did your rope not help?"

"Well — I forgot the rope."

"Oh Harper!" she cried. "You might have been killed."

"Oh well," said Harper, "I wasn't."

Just as he was finishing his eggs Harper heard a police car going by outside, its siren blaring its urgent message down the length of the street.

His heart fell.

He looked at the clock.

It was nine-fifteen.

Bertha hadn't waited.

For a moment he panicked. He heard the car stop further down the street, just, he guessed, exactly in front of his own house. He glanced at Miss Kennedy, who seemed oblivious of the racket the siren had created.

"Well," he said, pushing away his plate, "I guess I'd better get home."

"Oh, don't you want some coffee?"

"No, no, oh no thank you — I'm not allowed coffee. I'd better go."

"Well, all right, I suppose it *is* getting late."

"Yes'm."

"All right. You run along. And good luck with your friends. And if you want me to speak up for you, you just come and say so."

"Thank you m'am. I will."

"Oh, and take your fan, dear. You went off without it yesterday. Here it is. I set it aside."

"Oh, thank you. It's very pretty."

They went to the front door.

Miss Ming Toy snuffled at his heels.

"It's going to be another beautiful day," said Miss Kennedy looking out at the sky. "If only, when it rains, it rains at night."

"Yes'm. I hope so too."

"Well, you run along dear. And please, do come and see me again."

"I will. Thank you." He bent down. "Good-bye, Ming Toy," he said.

"Say good-bye to Harper, dear."

The little dog barked pipingly.

Harper and Miss Kennedy both laughed.

"Good-bye."

"Good-bye."

"And thank you."

"Nonsense," said Miss Kennedy. "Thank *you*." There was a note of lonely finality in her voice. "It was nice of you to come."

"Sit down," said Bertha. "Now, where you been?"

"I ran off," said Harper, betraying nothing.

"You ran off, is that it? You just ran off? Where to? You can go now," she turned to the policeman. "I'll take care now."

"All right, Miss, just so long as he's home, I guess it's all right."

"Thank you for coming so quick. But I'll take care of him now."

The policeman tipped his hat at Bertha and winked at Harper and disappeared out the side door.

She poured two cups of tea.

"You had me absolutely dying here this morning. I just didn't know what to think."

"I ran away."

"Why?"

"I had to."

"Had to? No one has to do that. Now why?"

"I want her to notice."

"Who to notice?"

"Mother."

Bertha grunted.

"What's wrong? I suppose she didn't even notice it," said Harper in despair.

"Notice it?" snapped Bertha. "Notice it? I should think not. She done the very same thing herself."

"What do you mean?" said Harper. "What do you mean?"

"Just exactly what I said. She done the very same herself."

"Mother?"

"Yes, sir. She didn't come home here last night neither."

Harper stared blankly.

"Honestly," said Bertha. "The pair of you."

Harper went white.

"Now where was you?" she asked.

"In a tree."

"Don't joke. Don't joke; this is no time for that, honey. This is serious. Now speak where you was."

"In a tree," he reiterated. "At Miss Kennedy's in her oak tree."

"Well if that's true, then why was you?"

"I had to hide, Bertha. I had to make my mother take attention."

"So you hid in a tree," she paused — "You there all night?"

"Yes'm."

"You didn't do nothing wrong there did you?"

"No m'am. What could I?"

"Well — so long's you're safe then. What about breakfast?"

"I had it with her."

"With Miss Kennedy?"

"Yes'm."

"I thought you kids were all scared to the death of her."

"No m'am, she's all right. She gave me a Chinese fan."

"That's nice."

Bertha expressed no desire to see the Chinese fan, which Harper laid on the table between them as he mentioned it. Instead she reverted to the subject of his mother.

"Well, now, about your mother."

"Didn't she phone?"

"If she phoned would I be worried? No sir, I have no word of her, not a sign."

She fell silent.

Then, after a moment, in which Harper stared at her unblinkingly, she began to speak under her breath.

"Of course, I figure I know just about where it is she'll be and you are not to go and worry. I'm gonna go there and pick her up and then we'll come home. But —" she ran her flat fingers in rows over the oilcloth on the table. She was, for a moment, unwilling to declare anything further it seemed, for she shot Harper a sharp glance as much as to say that she hoped he hadn't heard what she had already said, but then she went on, even though it seemed to be against her will to do so. ". . . but I figure this has got to stop. An' though I haven't got it figured out how, I got it figured out that it's *us* that'll have to stop it."

"You mean my mother and how she drinks?"

"Yes. No! Be quiet. I'm speaking here now."

"Yes'm."

Bertha stared from the table out of the window before she went on.

"Now I come," she said, "to the end of my rope — the end of it and there ain't no more of it to pay out. That," she said, "seems to be that. However, I have here an expression in my mind which comes from something which I heard somewhere which goes like this."

She paused, recollected and went on, her voice going high into another register which Harper had never heard her employ before. She turned her eyes, which had been downcast, back out the window and looked into the cloudless sky, which was burning itself out, over the house.

"It went like this. When you come," she said, "to the end of your rope, and ain't got no more to go — *don't do it in* — but tie a knot and hang on." She paused. "An' that's it." Then she laced her fingers in a pattern on the table-top and whispered, more to the sky than to herself, "an' I just tied."

For a moment she sat there, with her starched face turned away and with her taut hands on the table, but then she swung around and Harper saw that she was crying and that there was nothing to be said, so he watched her cry.

Bertha finally let her head go down and she put one hand on the back of her neck, while with the other she sought out her 'hankie' — found it, and blew her nose into it.

"What are you going to do?" Harper asked her.

"Go an' get her."

"Now?"

"Soon's I'm ready," she said, getting up from her place at the table. She tucked the handkerchief back into her apron pocket. "An' while I'm gone you straighten your room."

"Why do I have to do that?"

"Because I said it. I want it all shipshape when I return."

"But it's not. . ."

"Listen! When I say clean up, I mean clean up. So get along now and don't argue."

"Well, all right."

Harper got up too and went upstairs. When she was sure that he was gone, Bertha went into the hallway and to the telephone, where she picked up the receiver.

She dialled, and was answered.

"Hello," she said, "have you got a Mrs Renalda Harper Dewey there? This here's her maid."

Twenty minutes later Bertha stood in Harper's doorway in her coat and hat and she was pulling on her white cotton gloves with the black stitching.

"I gotta go now and see about your mother."

"Where is she?"

"Nowheres. She's fine. I just gotta go and see her. I may not be back until after lunch, so I want you to promise not to leave the house. I'm telling Mrs Jamieson to keep her eye out for you."

"Yes'm."

Harper bent over his toy box. "She's not sick, is she?"

"No. I told you, everything is O.K. But I gotta go. I fixed you sandwiches in the icebox and a thermos of soup is on the table. Save some for me."

"Yes'm."

They looked at each other.

"An' be good."

"Yes, Bertha."

She smiled, tears respringing to her eyes. All of a sudden she bent down and kissed him — something she hadn't done since he was four years old.

"I'm just prayin' all the time I'm gone," she said, "you pray too."

She went.

A moment later he heard the front screen door bang shut and he ran to his mother's room to watch her going down the walk.

She was walking slowly and when she got to the gate she seemed unsure, for a second or so, of which direction she intended to step out in. Then she decided and was gone. Harper turned from the window and confronted the forbidden room. He hadn't been in there for such a long time that he was surprised at how familiar and immediate all the objects were to him.

He looked at the highboy.

"I've got to get back in here," he thought vehemently, "I've got to get back in this room."

About an hour after Bertha had left to find his mother, Harper was sitting on the floor of his own room, surrounded by a number of old comic books and funny papers. He had taken them from a hiding place, well known to Bertha Millroy's brooms and mops, under his dresser.

"What am I going to do with these?" he wondered. "I just can't stand the sight of them any more. Old *children's* stuff! I

gotta get rid of it now I'm so old. I should trade them with Sally
Davis, except that'd just mean more of the same and I don't
want any more of them. I ought to sell them.''

Sell them.

His mind began to turn upon the words. ''Sell them. Sell
them and get something else you'd rather . . .'' He stood up.

''Why I could buy back some of that stuff of mother's'' he
said out loud, ''I could buy it back and make her well again. I
could buy it back and then I'd get up into her room again —
that's all it needs.''

He faltered.

''Comic books aren't going to buy all that,'' he realized.
''How is it done?''

He went downstairs into the garden. he took the guinea pig's
cage from its place under the step and set it in the middle of the
lawn.

''Come out,'' he said. ''Come out and have some grass for
breakfast.''

He opened the cage door and the guinea pig snuffled its way
slowly onto the open lawn. Harper watched it head towards the
flower beds beneath the lilac trees and then he lay back on the
grass and looked at the sky.

''That stuff she drinks,'' he thought, ''now if she sold the
jewels to buy that stuff, it ought to be worth the same to sell it
back.''

He had guessed that whatever it was that his mother drank
was that same thing for which she wandered the house at night.
He had guessed that whatever it was would be in the sun room,
the dining room or the living room, and he had guessed rightly.
He found no less than eight frosted bottles in all — two in the
sun room, two in the living room, and four in the forbidden
bedroom. One of these was partially emptied and he decided
that it was safest to leave that one behind. The rest, he put into
an old shopping bag from the kitchen cupboard, and hid them
in the back of the garage under the tub that he used to wash the
guinea pig in.

Then he went back to the garden, where he remained for the
rest of the morning, nervously waiting for Bertha's return with

his mother, and frantically wondering what he would do with the seven frosted bottles he had just commandeered from his mother's treasury.

At twelve-thirty he put the guinea pig back in its cage, lodged the cage in its place under the step and gave up waiting.

He went inside and was sitting at the kitchen table, eating his sandwiches and drinking his soup when Bertha returned.

She was alone.

It was obvious that she was in great distress, but she tried not to let on to Harper that anything serious had happened.

"Where's mother?"

"She couldn't come yet," said Bertha, turning her back to him and removing her coat.

"Is she busy?"

"Sure, she's busy. You know she's always out every day like this. How's the soup?"

"Fine. You want some?"

"Yes."

She sat down. She was still wearing her hat and her white cotton gloves with the black stitching.

"I'll get a plate," he said.

Bertha studied the oil cloth.

"You still got your gloves on," said Harper, putting a soup plate and a spoon down in front of her.

"Oh."

She pulled them off listlessly.

"And your hat."

"Oh well."

She let the hat stay. It had flowers on it. Daisies.

Harper poured some soup into her soup plate from the thermos and presented her with the spoon, which she took without noticing what she was doing.

"What's the matter, Bertha?"

Harper sat down at his own place.

"Nothing, everything's fine."

Harper had always believed everything that Bertha said, but he didn't, of course, believe this. He fished his mind for something to say that would draw out the truth.

"Is my mother coming home tonight?"

"I don't know yet."

There was a long pause, in which Bertha dipped her spoon into the soup and drank without a sound. Harper watched her. Her eyes were staring with a fixed, faraway gaze at the tabletop just in front of the plate. One of the daisies on her hat bobbled every time she tilted her head to drink.

"Bertha?"

"Unh — huh?"

"When you grow up, do you have to drink stuff like my mother does? I mean, is it something you've just *got* to do, I mean, like going to the office and all that?"

"It's a choice," she said. "You do or you don't."

"Will I, Bertha? Am I going to do it?"

She looked at him.

She looked away from him.

She sighed and put down the soup spoon.

"Honey," she said, and she put one hand up to her face, the fingers massaging her left eye, "if you did, I can only tell you — it would break your mother's heart."

Just about sundown all the hoses were dragged onto the front lawns and boulevards along the street and the evening air was cooled and scented by their many spinning fountains.

The smell of wet grass at the end of a hot day was a particular summer pleasure to Harper Dewey. Tonight it mingled with the odours of the petunia plants and of the yellow roses that grew in the garden. Tonight, in fact, in every way was more sensuously beautiful than any other night he could remember. The sky seemed extra cool and to look at its distant blueness gave him a sense of well-being despite his growing fear over his mother's whereabouts. Everything seemed at his command. How many were the birds that sang and how peculiar that he should understand their song. Distance too obeyed him. He could bring the faraway sound of dogs close into the shell of his ear, and at the same time sounds in his own front garden could be dismissed into the highest places of the sky. He felt, oddly, for the first time in his eight-yeared life, that he finally had something to say about the ownership of the world and of the right a person had to take action in it. There was a personal knowledge inside of him which was entirely his own, based upon a losing and a seeking which he conducted with his own devices and from his own resources. Perhaps he was turning from childhood — although he did not feel it going from him. His sense of loneliness was to determine this, beginning to become the loneliness of an adult, the loneliness defined by remembrance.

Harper sat on the front porch and thought over his bazaar. He meant to be rid of the frosted bottles by selling the contents mixed with lemonade. In that way, he figured that whatever the strange drink added in zest and originality to his lemonade, would also add to its worth. He could then claim more than a mere nickel per sale — and thus use the contents of the bottles to buy back what had been sold to purchase them. It seemed to be an eminently well rounded plan and he was extremely proud of it.

Bertha came out with some ice cream.

"You gonna sit here for this, Harper?"

"Yes."

"I figure I will too, then."

Harper and Bertha sat with their legs stretched out and ate their ice cream from blue and white plates, the colour of the summer night.

"What're you thinking, out here?" Bertha asked him.

"Oh — nothing."

"Come on now — something's going on. What is it you're up to?"

"Well," said Harper, "I figured on a bazaar."

"Say it again. A what?"

"A bazaar."

"What's that?"

She ate and waited, slapping her feet together at the toes.

"It's where you sell what's no longer wanted by someone to someone who figures he can use it. Some call it 'white elephant'."

He looked at her to determine whether she had cottoned on to his meaning.

She hadn't.

"I propose," Harper said, "to sell them lemonade."

"Lemonade, eh?" Bertha's mind was elsewhere.

"I propose to sell them lemonade on account of this enormous heat-wave here in the city."

"Well, well," she said. "Lemonade. Think of it."

"Mother —" he began — and stopped.

She turned on him.

"What's this got to do with your mother?"

Harper blanched.

"Nothing," he said, "it's merely a diversion." Diversion was his new word. "I look forward," he added in clarification, just in case Bertha was unaware of his meaning, "to taking my mind off things." He stressed the final word with an odd vocal twist. He almost choked on his ice cream.

Bertha, for her part, still looked a trifle bewildered. But she consoled herself with the thought that if he kept himself busy selling lemonade he would indeed be diverted from all that would surely now happen as a consequence of his mother's errancy.

She looked over at him.

"You'll need lemons," she said.

"I'll go tomorrow when the store opens."

She smiled. "I thought you said a bazaar was where you got rid of what you didn't want."

He thought quickly. "Well —" he said at last. "*We* certainly don't want the lemons."

"Yeah," she said, with a twinkle. "Maybe we don't want 'em, honey, but we ain't got 'em."

"No," said Harper glumly. "Not yet, anyway. Once I buy them though — we won't want them."

"No — I guess we won't," said Bertha.

Just then, as they were sitting there, a big black car drew up to the curb at the foot of the brick walk.

Bertha stood up.

"Harper, you go inside. Here take this."

She thrust her plate of ice cream at him.

"Go in Harper — to your room."

Harper sensed that argument was useless — so he asked for no explanation. He had no idea who was in the black car or why their presence (for it was obviously this) necessitated his departure, but he wasn't fool enough to go to his room, where he might never find out. Instead, he went up to the top of the stairs and looked down, from the window there, at the scene below. He still held the two plates of ice cream in his hands.

Bertha moved down the walk and stood talking to a man who was dressed all in black. Several times this man directed a gesture towards the black car and Bertha would follow his gesture with her eyes and sometimes she would nod and sometimes she would shake her head — as though in sadness. Once she looked back at the house and almost caught Harper watching, but he ducked away in time to save himself from being seen.

When he looked again, the man dressed in black and Bertha had moved down into the boulevard near to the rear door of the car and it seemed that the man was giving Bertha some sort of instructions, for he gestured often into the air with his hands. Then he gave her something which she put in her pocket and he made a 'three' sign with the fingers of his right hand. Then he bent towards the rear door of the car as though to speak to someone inside. Bertha glanced nervously along the street and also looked towards Mrs Jamieson's house next door.

Now, the man in black opened the car door as though to let someone get out, for he stood back from it. Then Bertha went forward and held out both her hands.

First Harper saw feet and then he saw a hand extended, which fumbled to grasp Bertha's two. Then over the hands, a bowed head appeared of black and gray dishevelled hair. It was his mother.

She got out of the car and stood clutching Bertha; but she looked at the ground, not into Bertha's face, nor into the face of the man in black. Then someone else, from within the car, extended a white arm and handed out a purse and a hat, which

Bertha took, and a coat, which the man took. Harper knew this arm. It was the arm of a nurse. He didn't have to see any more than its starched white sleeve to know that.

The man in black put the coat gently around the shoulders of Mrs Harper Dewey and spoke, again, to Bertha. As he did so, he left one hand on Mrs Dewey's shoulder, very lightly and assuringly and Harper knew that he must be a doctor. Bertha nodded at the doctor, then, in a way she had of saying "thank you." After that, the doctor got into the back seat of the car and the car drove off, driven, Harper supposed, by the doctor's chauffeur. Of his mother's chauffeur and of their own car's whereabouts Harper could not guess.

Bertha and his mother came slowly up the front walk. They walked as though they had come from burying the dead — Bertha, as she would, with her head held high and his mother as she had, with her whole torso drooping as though gigantic weights had been tied to her shoulders. Suddenly, his mother did a very strange thing.

She stopped and she put her hands at her sides and stood away from Bertha, moving towards the flower beds at the side of the front walk. She knelt beside them looking at the roses that grew there — late, late roses just about to die — and she stayed there for a long time, touching them gently with her fingers. Finally her head fell forward and she put her hands over her face and wept.

Bertha stood quietly, still with her ramrod stance, behind her, looking off somewhere into the deepening evening sky.

At this juncture, Harper took the ice cream plates and locked himself in his room — just as Bertha had told him to do in the first place.

Later on I can wear real roses.

Quiet soon fell over the house, the deep quiet of loneliness.

Harper sat in his room and the ice cream melted, and it made two white pools in the middle of the blue and white plates. Harper set the two plates up on his bureau and put the wrong end of his spoon into one and stirred it around while he leant with his other arm on the top of the bureau, which was built low. He tried to make patterns, but they wouldn't remain.

He listened to the house. An old familiar feeling came to him. It was a feeling that this particular home was a house of the past. Through it now, went a sensation of quietness that he remembered from other times — times when the three presences were single and when one did not acknowledge by any show of communication that the other two were there. He listened for his mother but he heard nothing — he also listened for Bertha but again there was nothing. He tried to ascertain by indication that his mother or that Bertha was waiting too, somewhere in the house, listening for him or for each other; but he couldn't. It was as if he were entirely alone.

He made for the door of his room.

Just as he got there, however, he heard a sound. The sound came from down the hall and it was the sound of a key being turned with an effort towards quietness (he knew this because it was slow) and he guessed that it was his mother locking herself in her room. Then he heard footsteps. Bertha's.

She came to stand outside his door. She put her knuckles against the wood and rapped gently.

"Harper?" She called him very quietly.

"Yes?"

Bertha tried the handle.

"Unlock the door, honey."

Harper let her in.

"Come downstairs, baby, we'll finish our ice cream in the kitchen."

She went to the bureau and got the plates.

"It's all melted. Tch. Well, — we'll dish ourselves up some more. No reason we can't do that. Come along, baby, and *be* quiet."

It was as though someone in the house were sick and he was being given ice cream to make up for the attention being accorded to the sick person. Harper didn't care for these tactics and he didn't particularly admire Bertha for resorting to them. Also he distrusted and wondered at her return to naming him "baby."

They went down to the kitchen.

"Your mother's asleep," said Bertha, standing at the icebox.

"I don't want any more ice cream."

"All right then. Neither do I."

She shut the icebox door and came closer, intending to sit at the table, but they looked at each other.

"Let's have a drop of coffee instead," said Bertha, going immediately to the stove where she prepared the percolator. "I hadda give her some pill and this'll make her sleep. Doctor says she'll sleep all night and if she don't I'm to give her another. But she ain't to have more'n three all told. But one is best if it'll work, so we gotta keep it quiet down here."

Harper was silent, so she looked at him.

"You hear me, Harper?"

Harper nodded, looking out the window.

"There ain't nothin' I can tell you, baby. I don't know it myself." She sounded sad but it was as though he was the sadness.

Harper began. "When she wakes up. . . Will she be better, when she wakes up?"

"I surely hope so, baby. A good sleep is all she needs. She ain't had that for too long, he says, an' I guess you an' I don't hafta be told that one."

There was nothing more said then. They listened, Bertha standing by the stove, and Harper sitting looking out the window, to the coffee percolating in the percolator. It began slowly, like raindrops falling from the eaves on metal and then sped along as their thoughts grew in pace and confusion until this sound came to reach an unbearable climax — such a climax as had to be broken.

Bertha turned the stove off. There was a sigh into silence.

"Maybe I'll hafta stay in tonight, so I'll drink a lot of this," she said, "but you only gonna have a little bit in milk. Then I guess it'll be time for you to go to bed."

Harper said: "Bertha, where's she been to?"

Bertha poured coffee into a cup and then into a glass of milk before she answered, with Harper watching her.

"Nowheres."

"Then who was that man? And that nurse in the car?"

Bertha looked at him sharply, but decided not to press the charges.

"Friends."

"He was a doctor."

"That's right."

"But it wasn't our doctor. It wasn't Dr Peel."

Bertha nodded. "That's right. It was Dr Hamilton. Your mother's doctor." She looked away.

"But we've always gone to Dr Peel. Both of us — you too."

"Nonsense. That's only you an' I who goes to Dr Peel. Your mother is frequenting Dr Hamilton these days."

"I don't believe you. I think Dr. Hamilton found her somewhere. This somewhere you had to go to this morning."

"And where would that be, Mr Know-it-all?"

"I don't know. Maybe in the street somewhere. I don't know."

"Now I told you Harper. Your Mother ain't been nowheres bad and that's that. Now she's gone to sleep and so we'll hear no more of it. I'm tired, you're tired and it's time you went to bed. I gotta stay up. So you go now and I'll come up and see you in a minute."

And then — "Go on, Harper."

"You aren't the same as you used to be," said Harper after he had reached the doorway. "I don't like you anymore."

And then he ran, noisily all the way to his room, where he slammed the door.

In the kitchen Bertha pronounced the name of God.

The next morning, Harper went to the grocery store and bought lemons and sugar and paper cups. Bertha gave him the money.

As he was coming past Mrs Jamieson's house on his way home, loaded down with his purchases and practically staggering under their weight, he heard a voice calling him.

"Oh, Harper! Harper Dewey."

He stopped and listened.

"Harper, dear. I'm over here."

He looked around and saw Mrs Jamieson standing under a tree in her front garden. She held a trowel in one hand and wore a large sun hat that had a ribbon hanging down the back. She beckoned him in.

He set the parcel of lemons and sugar and paper cups inside her gate and walked over her lawn.

"Good morning, Harpie. What have you got there?" she said.

Mrs Jamieson was the only person, besides his mother, who called him Harpie and he distinctly rebelled against it, as it seemed far too personal a name for her to use.

"I'm selling lemonade all afternoon," he said.

"Oh! You're going to have a lemonade bazaar. How nice. I suppose you're trying to make some extra pocket money — is that it?"

"Yes."

"What for, dear?"

Mrs Jamieson went back to her trowelling, around the base of the tree.

"Just to buy something."

"Well tell me what, dear? What is it you want?"

Harper was silent.

Mrs Jamieson looked up, pushing back the brim of her sun hat.

"Oh, I see. It's a secret!" she said, "something for that naughty mother of yours? I'll bet that's it. You know, I saw her coming home yesterday. Oh, Harper, you must be a very brave little boy to put up with all that. You know, of course, don't you darling, that *all* grown-ups don't behave like that? It's just, I suppose, that your mummy is sick. But we *all* don't do that when we're sick. Some of us are brave. And you must be brave too. Not that you haven't been. As I said, dear, I think you must be *very* brave. Very, *very* brave to stand for it for so long; and so *well* too. But you mustn't get the idea that we're all like that or that anybody *needs* to be, dear. Drinking. . ." Mrs Jamieson droned on over the earth she was working, "is just an escape and only irresponsible people do it. It's only apt to show us how weak they are, my dear, and we must never think of them as being pitiful or sad. Your mother, Harper, used to be one of the most beautiful women you could see anywhere in the whole world. But she let herself go, you see, and that was naughty of her.''

She looked at Harper and smiled. He stood listening to her with his hands held behind his back.

''When you grow up, you won't do that will you, Harper? You won't let go and give in like that? God doesn't want us to be like that, you know. He wants us to be strong and brave.'' She went back to her work. ''Tell me, Harper. Tell me something. Does your mother pray, dear? Do you know?''

''Bertha prays,'' said Harper flatly.

''Yes, dear, I know — but does your mother? Do you know if *she* does?''

Harper looked off over Mrs Jamieson's head towards his own house beyond the hedge and the fence. He looked at his mother's window. Then he spoke, very quietly and almost with serenity, to Mrs Jamieson.

''I think God must hate having made anyone as silly as you are,'' he said.

He left immediately, without looking at her, without pausing to determine her reaction and without any feeling of fear or of remorse. He picked up his package at the gate and walked, sedately and evenly, all the way to the side door where he rang the bell, because he was locked out.

At three o'clock Harper went down the drive and set up the orange crate and the chair and put out the paper cups and put on his white sun hat with the green eye-shade and rang the bell. The bell was the little silver one that Mrs Dewey rang at table when it was time for Bertha to clear. In the thick air of the afternoon it didn't seem to make much noise — and for about half an hour there weren't any customers. Then the first one came. Jo-Jo Parkinson — five years old — from across the street.

''Howdy Harper,'' he said. He was all undone down the front and his hands were filthy.

Harper said: ''You have dirty hands Jo-Jo — get in an' wash.''

"I been in the sand pile at Sally's. She's coming across too
— with two dimes. So set up."

"When Sally Davis comes here I'm telling her to take you up
to wash over them hands. You look plain disgusting and your
pants are undone."

"I just went."

"Well do up."

Jo-Jo giggled and did up.

"I went in the sand," he confided. "Like our cat does. And
then you bury it."

Sally Davis came over.

Sally Davis was eight like Harper. They were both hard put
to it to make up who was the more adult.

"This child here," said Harper, "has got dirty hands and
face. I'm not gonna sell no lemonade to a coalman."

"He's been in the sand."

Jo-Jo giggled.

"I know," said Harper. "He said that. Are you gonna wash
him over?"

"No. I want two lemonades please. Why's it so expensive.
Ten cents is too much."

"It's gotta be ten cents."

"Why."

"It's just gotta be. That's all."

"Well — all right."

Harper eyed Jo-Jo. "But I'll remind you if he's sick it's not
my fault. It's those hands of his which are just purely
revolting." He dipped out two paper cups of 'lemonade' with a
long-handled saucepan — and handed them over on receipt of
Sally's twenty cents.

He watched them drink.

Jo-Jo was delighted and immediately asked for more. But
Sally was slightly suspicious.

"You call this here *lemonade*, Harper?"

"Read it on the sign."

Sally read out: " 'Harper's Bazaar of Lemonade 10¢.' Well
I don't know. Tastes peculiar to me."

"Jo-Jo likes it."

"Do you Jo-Jo?"

"Yes," said Jo-Jo. "I like it an' more thank you." He set out his paper cup on the top of the orange crate.

"It costs you ten cents," said Harper.

"Sally?"

"I already gave you ten cents. Don't come to me."

"O.K. G'bye then," said Jo-Jo and went off towards his own house at a run.

"I think maybe I would like another cupful please Harper," said Sally Davis, fishing in the pocket of her shorts for a dime, "the flavour sort of grows on you."

Bertha stood at the top of the drive and hollered out: "How's sales going, Harper? Hello there Sally."

Harper replied that sales were practically non-existent and Sally said "Hello."

Bertha went in. Sally drank her second cup slowly.

"Harper . . ." she said. "How about for a little free trade — I drum you up some business and you give me two more cups in exchange?"

"Just where do you expect to find this business. It's gotta be people off the street and there's no one about. I guess it's too hot."

"Jack Parker and Tim are over in Tim's back yard. I heard 'em. I could sort of provoke 'em over I guess."

"How provoke 'em?"

"All you gotta do is mention cold drink on a day like this."

"It ain't so cold right now" said Harper — poking his finger into a stone jug of lemonade. "But go ahead and try."

Harper had left the big pot in the garage out of the sun and brought down two stone jugs and the long handled saucepan to ladle with.

When Sally had gone Harper tipped back on his chair and looked both ways along the street. The high elm trees were like umbrellas up and down the sidewalks. Far away he could hear a dog barking at a car — and the car going away into the distance. He thought about his mother. He was glad, when he thought of her, that Sally Davis was going to drum up more business — because he wanted it all sold. After it had all been sold, he would take the money and buy back his mother's jewels. The jewels had bought the frosted bottles — now the frosted bottles would buy them back. He had comfort in his heart.

Soon he saw Miss Kennedy coming along under the elm umbrellas — carrying her coat over her arm and looking very hot and depressed — and he prepared to make a sale.

She came up.

"Hello Harper."

"Hullo Miss Kennedy."

She began to rummage about in her handbag.

"I don't seem to have a dime dear. But I have a quarter — can you change it?"

"Yes'm. I have fifteen cents here."

"Then I'd like some lemonade, please."

Harper dipped her out a cupful.

Miss Kennedy stood back and admired the view along the street.

"Oh Harper, how I do love summer. But for this heat I'd say that summer on this street is summer like nowhere else in the world."

"Yes'm. It's pretty."

Miss Kennedy finished her cup of lemonade.

"That is a remarkable concoction Harper. Let me have another cup."

Harper began to worry. If Miss Kennedy stayed too long the children might not come, they being so afraid of her.

"Were you going somewhere, Miss Kennedy," asked Harper — as he handed her her third cup of lemonade.

"Oh yes, but I have lots of time. I thought I'd seek out some nice air-conditioned movie house and relax this afternoon. But out here — thank you Harper — out here it seems so tranquil and still — it's very relaxing and this lemonade of yours certainly does help to take the edge off the heat. Oh dear — it was so *hot*. I thought I was going to suffocate up there in my house."

She had a fourth cup — and then a fifth.

Jo-Jo appeared on the other side of the street. He had apparently seen Miss Kennedy and had decided to wait until she had

gone. He sat down on the curb and stuck his dirty hands in the
summer-dried leaves in the gutter. Every once-in-a-while he
eyed Harper and Harper would smile and beckon him but he
turned his head away and pretended to look somewhere else.

"Harper?" said Miss Kennedy.

"Yes'm."

"How would it be if you set up a chair here for me on the
boulevard, under this tree —" She gestured vaguely towards
one of the elms — and he could see that she was slightly
bewildered.

"This stuff of my mother's," he thought, "certainly has a
powerful effect on people."

"— and you might do me the favour to bring me an umbrella from the house. I think I won't go to the movies after
all."

"Yes'm."

As Harper went up the drive he thought to himself that Miss
Kennedy "plonking herself down" right there would be the
end of business — but when he returned with the chair and the
umbrella it was obvious that precisely the opposite was to be
the fact.

Miss Kennedy was surrounded by children. They had made
a great circle around her and she was standing in the middle
smiling, but he could see that she was somewhat confused.
Popularity was strange to her. The children (Sally was there
and Jack Parker and Tim — and Annabelle Harrison, the terrible rich snob from round the corner — and several others)
were all silent. Jo-Jo still sat, immune to their curiosity of Miss
Kennedy, poking his fingers into the gutter across the street.

"Thank you Harper," said Miss Kennedy as Harper broke
through the circle to set up her chair. "That's just fine."

They set up the chair — (it was a deck chair with orange and
white candy-stripe canvas) — and Miss Kennedy sat in it and
put up the black umbrella over her head. She looked like someone in the middle of Africa — a missionary surrounded by
natives.

"Bring another cup of the delicious lemonade my dear."

Harper obeyed.

"Hey look," said Sally, "let's us all have lemonade. That's what we came for."

Harper was kept quite busy taking in the money and serving up and he had to go up to the garage to get more so that he didn't notice at first what was happening between Miss Kennedy and Jo-Jo Parkinson. What was happening between Miss Kennedy and Jo-Jo Parkinson practically amounted to a chronicled fairy tale. "The old witch" sat there eyeing him with one hypnotic drunken eye — her head slightly cocked, her gaze beaming from under the black umbrella.

Jo-Jo was fascinated and rooted to the spot.

"Little boy," called Miss Kennedy with her wistful voice, "why don't you come across that street and have yourself some lemonade?"

The hot afternoon beat its heavy wing over the elm trees and over the front lawns along the street — and over the group of people at Harper Dewey's front drive.

"Little boy," cried Miss Kennedy.

The birds were silent in the trees. The lemonade drinkers paused to listen.

"Little boy — put down that dirty stick and come across to me."

Jo-Jo put down the stick.

"Little boy — listen to me — I myself will buy you lemonade."

Jo-Jo came across.

Harper Dewey watched with the rest as Jo-Jo stood at the foot of the deck chair and looked sheepishly into the witch's eyes. Miss Kennedy smiled.

"Harper — bring this child a cup of lemonade."

With a look at the others — at Sally Davis and Jack Parker and Tim and even Annabelle Harrison the terrible rich snob from around the corner — Harper Dewey drew a cup of 'lemonade' for Jo-Jo Parkinson.

"Now bring it here."

Harper brought.

"Give it to him."

Jo-Jo accepted the paper cup without taking his eyes from

Miss Kennedy's smiling face.

"There you are, Jo-Jo," said Harper. "That'll be ten cents."

Miss Kennedy paid him — and when, instead of going back to his booth, he stood there staring at her — she said to him: "Go on Harper — Go away."

Harper went. He and the others grouped themselves in silence around the orange crate. Even Bertha came down to have a look.

"Drink it up."

Jo-Jo stood still.

"Don't you like it?"

Jo-Jo continued his position, like a stagnant pond about to have a pebble thrown into it.

"Who's got your tongue, little boy? Old cat?"

Jo-Jo very slowly stuck out his tongue to show her that he still had it in his mouth.

"That's right. Now put it back."

He drew it back in.

"Do you know how to smile, little boy?"

Jo-Jo nodded.

"Well then . . .?"

Nothing happened. Jo-Jo looked at the lemonade in his hand.

"Harper — bring me another cup," cried the witch.

Harper brought again — received his ten cents and dutifully returned to the selling stand, this time without being told. He was thinking of Mrs Harper Dewey — his mother — and how she had never wooed him.

"Now," said Miss Kennedy, "you and I will take this drink together — and then we'll have another."

She raised her paper cup and Jo-Jo raised his.

Miss Kennedy smiled.

They drank.

To herself Miss Kennedy said: "Afternoon children — dear God — never let them know what I have done."

Dim beyond the curtains, which hung like stagnant fog across the windows, Mrs Renalda Harper Dewey's bedroom looked,

if one could have seen it by daylight, like a stage-set at the close
of a slapstick battle that had employed everything from cream
pies to flower vases.

Her clothing was strewn from one end of the room to the
other and on into the bathroom. Three glasses had been
broken, a hand mirror shattered, a bottle of scent had been
splattered against one wall and the powder bowl from the
dressing table had been emptied all over the rug. The
telephone by Mrs Dewey's bed had been disconnected (after a
surge of anger at not being able to contact her lawyer), and the
lamp there had been overturned and an enormous hole burnt
in its shade by the light bulb.

Mrs Dewey lay on the bed face downwards with her arms
clutched around the pillows, her lipstick smeared on the sheets
and her negligee, all undone, caught around her waist in a
tangle.

At about four-thirty in the afternoon she awoke.

She lay very still. She had no idea where she was and no
recollection of where she had been. At first, she felt no sensation whatsoever, being almost numb from the effect of the pills
that Bertha had given her, but gradually she became aware of
her arms pulled tight around the pillows.

She mumbled something into the sheets and pulled the
pillows closer. "Peter?" she murmured. "Peter?" Suddenly
however her fingers became aware of the texture beneath them
and she pushed the pillows away with lonely disgust. Presently
she tried to lift her head but pain seized the back of her neck
and stopped her. She groaned.

She focused her eyes on the bedside table and she saw the
telephone and the lamp in their disarray.

"What on earth has happened?" she said out loud.

She rolled over painfully and dragged herself into a sitting
position with her back against the head of the bed. She reached
around behind her and pushed the discarded pillows into place
and sighed back against them.

She closed her eyes. Sitting so still, she began to feel a little
clearer and she reopened them.

The sight of the wreckage about the room drew a weak sound

of bewilderment from her which again touched off the pain in the back of her neck. She put her fingers against her forehead.

Nothing made any sense. She recognized her own bedroom, but she couldn't think why it was in such disorder nor why she was there at this time of day. Her bedside clock said four-thirty and she had never been still abed at such an hour in her life, unless because of sickness. She concluded that she therefore must be ill. She certainly felt ill — but she couldn't define what, exactly, was the matter with her.

The thick smell of the perfume, from the wall where it had been splattered, made her feel sick to her stomach and she rose further to sit on the edge of the bed. The motion of swinging her legs over the side made her even more nauseous and she nearly fell forward onto the floor.

She attempted to stand, but this was even worse and she knew that she would have to be sick there and then. She lunged towards the bathroom but couldn't reach the toilet or the sink and was sick on the tiled floor. "How disgusting," she said. "How revolting."

After a moment she recovered and took a towel from the towel rack and wet it under the taps in the bathtub. She wiped off her face and her hands and threw the towel into the corner, looking after it as though it were a discarded victim of the plague, then she took another towel, soaked it in cold water and returned to the bedroom, shutting the bathroom door behind her.

Back on the bed she put the cold towel behind her neck and lay back on the pillows. However, the smell of the perfume soon began to reattract her attention and she looked about her to see where it was coming from. Finally after scrutinizing the floor and the bed, and after holding her negligee sleeves up to her nose, she noticed the stain on the wall. She closed one eye to look at it, then she opened that eye and closed the other. But she couldn't focus her mind on it. She stared at it — opening and closing her eyes — but she could make nothing of it. Finally she just sighed its presence out of her mind and decided to open her window.

At the window, the glare of the afternoon sun stunned her

and she fell back into the shadows. In doing so she stepped on a piece of glass and cut the ball of her right foot painfully.

"Oh God," she muttered, "what is *happening*? What is *happening* to me?"

She limped into the middle of the room and stood there swaying back and forth, looking from corner to corner, trying to make sense of what she saw.

"I'm going to get blood on the rug," she thought. "There will be blood all over the rug. *A — ll* over the *ru — g*. All over this bea-u-ti-ful god damn rug." She felt oddly as though she were dreaming, and so, with the callous recklessness of a dreamer, without the responses of reality, she abandoned her bleeding foot with the same sense of useless incomprehension as she had the perfume stain on the wall.

From beyond the open window she heard laughter. Pulling her negligee around her she walked delicately across to the window, where she leaned weakly against the sill. She could only barely see through the chiffon curtain, but she was afraid to expose her eyes again to the flat glare of the sun, so that she peered almost blindly out through the gauze.

There was more laughter and at the end of the driveway she made out the black umbrella and the orange deck chair with Miss Kennedy sitting in it with Jo-Jo on her lap. Harper and the other children were gathered about her.

"What on earth is she doing?" she wondered. "What is she doing in my deck chair? And that umbrella — that's Peter's umbrella. No!" she cried out. "No. No. That doesn't make sense even. No one's ever touched that — that was Peter's — that was Peter's — that was his. No one has *ever* touched it."

Perhaps she only imagined that she was calling to them because no one turned in her direction and there was no sign whatsoever that she had been heard. "I guess they know," she said. "Of *course* they know."

Relieved, she tottered uncertainly back in the general direction of the bed, but she missed it and found herself suddenly sitting in the middle of the floor.

For a second she was too stunned to react to what had happened but then a spasm of tears burned up towards her eyes from her throat and she wept, with her legs stretched out before her and her hands caught in the disorder of her negligee. She looked like a broken doll.

After the tears a wild confusion of images appeared before her — some real, some flickering in and out of the picture from the past, some, distortions of the actual. She saw her own tears where they remained upon her husband's mute umbrella for a moment, and then she saw Harper as he stood with his back to her at the foot of the driveway. She saw the mess of powder and blood on the rug, a furious kaleidoscope of colour that was perhaps the drapery, perhaps an overturned vase of flowers, perhaps only the vaguery of madness, and then she saw her own prone self stretched upon the floor.

It occurred to her to wail, as a child would wail, from the midst of some self-created ruin of shattered glass or fallen cutlery, but suddenly anger rose in her, the anger of private degradation and the fury of her fallen pride.

She crawled in a splurge of remembrance to her dressing table and took from beneath it the half-finished bottle of gin, which was the bottle that Harper had left behind in deference to its near emptiness.

She took a mouthful straight from the bottle, which gave her the strength to rise and cross to the bathroom.

"Everything else is broken," she announced to herself.

In the bathroom the stench of vomit on the floor nearly drove her out, but she threw a towel over it, grabbed the tooth glass from its shelf and ran into the bedroom slamming the door behind her. "They were all broken, I had to," she said. "I'm sorry."

She poured a full glass of gin and crossed to the window. She swallowed two mouthfuls without stopping, and for a moment she thought that it would make her throw up again, but it gradually burnt its way into her bloodstream and her stomach relaxed. After a moment she felt better.

She watched Harper.

He was standing alone and silent, a little to one side of the group of children around Miss Kennedy, and he had his hands behind his back. He seemed not to be listening to them talking;

he seemed, instead, to be thinking of something private and sad of his own.

She smiled and spoke his name quietly to herself, "Harper." It gave her no comfort. "Harper Dewey," she said. "Harper Peter Dewey."

She pulled back the curtain with her free hand and shaded her eyes with the hand that held the glass of gin.

She blinked and looked at her son.

"Harper Dewey," she said, as though in conclusion.

After a moment she took another mouthful of gin and swallowed it slowly and deliberately, almost meditatively. Harper, below on the sidewalk, turned to look at the house and Mrs Dewey dropped the curtain slowly, hoping that he had seen her. He stared at her window for nearly a full minute, pulling at the green eye-shade of his sun hat.

"Harper Dewey," said Mrs Dewey and she waved at him. But she knew he hadn't seen her, because he shifted his stance and looked back towards Miss Kennedy and the children.

Desperately Mrs Dewey finished her glass of gin and poured another which emptied the bottle. She looked down at her bleeding foot and said, defeatedly, with a broken sigh, "Peter," and she lifted her glass. "Success! He's as blind as a bat."

She pulled the chair from the dressing table over to the window and sat down. The children were laughing again at something Miss Kennedy had said to them and they laughed for a long time as though it must have been something very funny indeed that she had said.

Harper, however, aloof from their amusement, walked over to the driveway and picked up a stone. He stood with his back to the house, with his feet apart, apparently listening to the end of Miss Kennedy's story. The others continued to laugh, but Harper turned around and gave his mother's window a long, slow, tearful stare. His hand went to his eyes.

"Harper Dewey," said Mrs Dewey. "Harper Peter Dewey. Blind as a bat," and she smiled.

After a moment she looked down at her glass and had just put her head back with it held to her lips, prepared to take a

long swallow of gin, when the window in front of her was shattered by a stone that fell at her feet.

She was holding it in her hand when they found her.

In his bed in the dark, no more a cave, no more a safe place
alone, he sat waiting.

What he was waiting for he did not know — but he felt that
there was action coming. This action, whatever it might be,
could, he began to suspect, come from any side, even from
some inanimate object right there in his own room.

The windows might fly open of their own accord — (they
were shut because the summer rain had finally come in a great
cloudburst) — or the bureau might topple, or the pictures fall.
God might put his hand into the room, even, and take him
away and leave him somewhere on a hilltop or in the middle of
some foreign and frightening field.

If only he knew, or if he could at least guess, what it was that
he was waiting for he might be able to prepare himself for
defence. He could barricade the door or hide in the cupboard.
He could even leave the room and ask to sleep with Bertha, his
distrust of her aside. But he sensed that all of these resorts
would be utterly useless, because he knew that what was there,
waiting to happen, would happen in spite of anything that he
could do to prevent it.

He tried to think about Woolworth's and about all the
jewelry he had seen there. He pictured the prices and carefully
went over, again, his accounts from the bazaar sales of the
afternoon. He thought about the pane of glass from his
mother's window and knew that he must pay for that as well.
He thought about Jo-Jo in Miss Kennedy's lap and about his
father's umbrella.

Above him in the attic Bertha shunted her flat form across
dry sheets, grating it, as she did, to a sitting position on the
edge of her bed. Harper listened to her crossing over to her
bedroom door and heard her open it and descend to the second
floor. She came and stood outside his door and he coughed to
let her know that he was still awake. Then she went down the

hall and stood outside his mother's door listening, he could tell, to some mysterious noises beyond it, because she spoke, very quietly, Mrs Dewey's name.

Apparently, however, she was satisfied that all was reasonably well, because she came back down the hall and went downstairs to the kitchen, probably, Harper decided, to brew herself another of the inevitable cups of coffee.

Harper began a half sleep. He was still aware of his room and of the storm beyond it and of his arms resting against the cold sheets, and yet he slept. He slept and he dreamed.

Again, as in Miss Kennedy's oak tree, he dreamt of his father and of his 'Duty Letter' and of his father's voice. But this time instead of offering Harper the letter his father took it away from him and tore it up so that the pieces blew about in a funnel of wind just between them — obscuring and disfiguring his father's face.

After that he had a dream about 'The War.'

'The War,' to Harper, was a big city where there were men running and also men driving in jeeps and men riding on horses — and all of them, all of these men, made wild shouts into the air and their faces were all puffed out with this shout.

There were men, too, who were silent, but these men were lying on the ground or they were standing against the walls of the city with blood running from their eyes like tears and they moved their lips silently as though they were beggars who had voiced their cry so often that they had no voices left.

'The War' was very noisy though, all about these silent soldiers, and the noise was of running feet, and galloping horses, and of cars being driven so fast that you couldn't see them, and of aeroplanes that flew so low that you could reach up and touch them with your hand. The noise was of a rushing — of everything being rushing onwards and there was no end, neither to the noise nor to the rushing.

Then into the midst of this noise and into the motion of the rushing, came again the picture of his father's face. Harper could see both his father's face and also his father's body — the face close to him and the body far away. Harper was trying to get past his face to the body but the face kept getting in his way. It spoke, over and over again, Harper's own name, but like the silent figures on the ground and the bleeding figures against the city's walls, no voice accompanied the speaking. The lips moved over his name, again and again, but no sound came with the movement.

Soon, beyond the face, he saw his mother and his mother was wearing his own white sun hat with the green eye-shade and she carried the stone jug of 'lemonade' in one hand. She went straight to his father's body and she poured the 'lemonade' into a cup and gave it to the body to drink. Then she hunched down on the ground and began to drink the lemonade herself.

Harper knew that he must stop her — but he couldn't get past his father's face, which continued to blink at him, mouthing the shape of his name.

Harper remembered the Colt revolver in his father's high-boy, which he saw sitting in the corner of his dream. He ran to it and pulled the drawer open. The gun was there and he took it out and ran back towards his father's body and towards his mother hunched on the ground beside him. They were both drinking lemonade and they were laughing.

He was about to reach them, about to throw the gun away, when his father's face suddenly blanked out the entire picture and he shot at it, firing three times straight into the mouth.

The face fell apart as though it had been torn like a piece of paper and the pieces melted into the air and ran, waxlike, down a pane of glass. After that, everything began to fade — the pictures and the noises together — rushing away into final darkness and silence.

Harper lay awake.

He listened, rigid and wet with perspiration. Someone was running down the hall past his door.

He turned his head to listen. For a moment there was no fur- ther sound, until suddenly there was a violent knocking, he guessed at his mother's bedroom door.

Was someone trying to get in or to get out?

He went to his own door, unlocked it and opened it.

Bertha stood near his mother's room, wrapped in a blue dressing gown, barefooted and wild-eyed.

"Harper, get a key," she said.

"What key?"

"Any key. Any key. Just get a key."

Bertha turned back to the closed door and knocked on it again.

"Mrs Dewey!" she said. "Mrs Dewey you gotta let me in. It's your Bertha, Mrs Dewey — you gotta open it up."

Harper, not being able to guess at all what was happening, ran back to his own room and got the key out of his door. He took it to Bertha. She put the key into the lock and turned it from side to side.

"Oh Lord," she said, "you gotta make this work."

The key, however, jammed in the lock and presently broke off in her hand. Instead of becoming angry Bertha turned to calmness. She came to Harper and spoke quietly.

"Honey Harper, we're gonna hafta break it down."

"What's it about?" said Harper. "What's it about, Bertha?"

"I don't know, baby, but something pretty bad's just happened to your mother and we got to get her out. Come on now, what'll we do it with?"

Harper suddenly felt sick to his stomach. He turned away and sat on his little chair beside the door. Sitting there the sick feeling receded and he tried to think.

"We could hit it with a brick," he said.

"That won't do nothing. We gotta ram it right down. I know," she said. "We take away the handle."

"It's the lock that's busted," Harper reminded her. "Handle won't count anyway."

"Dear God please tell me what's to do."

Bertha prayed.

They both fell silent as Bertha waited for guidance.

After a moment she announced mysteriously: "He says we ought to use the phone." She went downstairs, switching on the lights as she did, and took up the receiver in the hall.

"Get me police," she said. "Get me police. Don't wait."

The stunned operator connected Bertha with the police station and the night sergeant answered her thickly.

"Listen," said Bertha. "Get here quick. She's locked the door and you gotta come quick."

While they waited, Bertha telephoned, or at least tried to telephone Dr Hamilton, but she got many wrong numbers and irate answers before she finally reached him. All this while Harper stood, hands behind his back, standing silently by the front door.

The situation having been explained, the first policeman, when he finally appeared on the verandah, carried an axe in his hand.

Bertha was still on the telephone getting Dr Hamilton out of bed, so Harper let them in. "Please now, come quick," she said and banged down the receiver. "The door's upstairs," she said to the policeman. "I guess she locked it first and then I broke another key trying to get it open. But we just got to get inside."

"All right m'am. We'll try and be careful."

Harper followed at a distance behind them and stood at the far end of the hall while they broke the door down with the axe. Actually, all they did was hit it with the blunt edge of the axe-head and the lock and the doorjamb shattered, swinging the door wide on its hinges.

Before they went in they set the axe against the wall beside Harper's chair.

"Is there a light?" one of the policemen asked Bertha.

"Yes sir — over here."

Harper heard the light switch go on and then there was silence.

Outside, the storm had broken and Mrs Jamieson had turned all the lights on in her house. Harper saw them flicker on through the window at the top of the stairs.

Voices drifted from his mother's bedroom and presently one of the policemen came out into the hall. He walked past Harper, patting him on the head as he did so, and went down the stairs at a trot.

Presently Dr Hamilton came up the stairs in his black over-coat and hat, but underneath still dressed in his pajamas. He passed Harper and went straight to Mrs Dewey's bedroom. The door closed.

Harper sat at the top of the stairs. He was numb and cold and he could think of nothing to think about except Mrs Jamieson's lights shining inquiringly forth from next door.

In half an hour his mother's door opened and another policeman came out and stood in the hall.

"Harper?" he said.

"Yes."

"Come here," he said gently, "don't be frightened."

Harper got up and pulled his pajama bottoms up tighter around his waist. He took a final look at Mrs Jamieson's win-dows and went meekly down the hall. The policeman took his hand.

"Your nanny wants to see you," he said.

Harper guessed that he meant Bertha.

When they went in the lights had been turned very low and Harper could only just make out the shapes of the furniture in the room. It still smelt of the spilt perfume.

Bertha was sitting on the far side of his mother's bed and Dr Hamilton was standing on the near side. There were three policemen in the room, huddled over by the highboy. His mother lay on the bed under a blanket.

The policeman took Harper around the foot of the bed to beside Bertha.

Bertha took his hand now and the policeman went back to the bedroom door.

Harper focused on Bertha.

"Honey," she said, "I guess we didn't just pray enough — and now we'll have to pray a whole lot more." She was crying, but she pulled him close to her shoulder and looked right into his eyes and smiled. "God does a lot of funny things — he has a lot of funny ways for us to walk. I'm just awful sorry that I ain't walked closer to your mother and to you these past few months or this might never have happened." She blinked away

some tears and looked down for a moment. She buttoned up
his pajamas coat where it was undone and looked at him again.
"We went and lost her, Harper" she said simply. "We went
and lost your mother to the Lord."

Harper looked shyly at the bed.

His mother was covered to her chin with a blanket, which
was folded back down from her face onto her chest.

She looked confused and her forehead was wrinkled as
though in deep thought and conjecture. Her eyes were closed
and her mouth was slightly open. There was dried blood at the
corner of her lips. She was as pale as that other day, when
Harper had come into the bedroom and had seen her asleep.
He thought secretly — "She's not dead now, but she was the
other day."

Bertha held his hand lightly and looked at Mrs Dewey too.

"I'm sorry," said one of the policemen — "but you'll have
to come downstairs now please and answer some questions. Dr
Hamilton, are you ready sir?"

As they went out Harper saw one of the policemen carrying
his father's Colt revolver in a handkerchief.

Bertha sighed and got up.

Harper reached out and touched his mother's lips with his
finger. They were hard and cold. He stood rigid and still. Bertha waited. Then he put his hand in Bertha's and went down
the stairs and into the living room.

Outside, Mrs Jamieson's windows showed that her lights
were finally going out, one by one, like sighs.

The next day the house was full of people Harper had never
seen before, people who drove up to the boulevard in big,
handsome cars and who came to see his dead mother dressed in
black clothes and carrying fur pieces over their arms or, if they
were men, carrying black hats and umbrellas.

Bertha put on her black uniform and held a Bible in one
hand all day long. She met the people in the hallway and spoke
quietly to them about Mrs Dewey and then led them upstairs to
the spare room where his mother's body had been laid on the
bed dressed in a clean nightgown and one of the pink negligees

of which she had been so fond. Bertha had put makeup on Mrs Dewey's face so that it wouldn't be so pale and she had tried to smooth the wrinkles from her forehead. She had also put a pretty ribbon around her hair. You couldn't see where she had shot herself — that was all covered up.

By afternoon flowers began to arrive, some of them addressed to Harper, some to Bertha and some to 'Rennie' or to 'Darling Rennie' from 'So-and-So.' Harper had some from people he'd never ever heard of.

Also in the afternoon his two aunts, his mother's sisters, arrived and his grandmother, who had been told only that her daughter had 'passed away.' His aunts had thought it best to keep the details of her death from their mother, because of her great age. She came in a wheelchair, his grandmother, and was carried upstairs by her own chauffeur together with Mrs Dewey's chauffeur. No one came from his father's family.

At three o'clock Harper went into the back garden to feed his guinea pig.

He reached under the porch and found the cage swamped in a pool of water caused by the storm. The guinea pig was dead. It had drowned. Harper took the cage in his arms and went and sat under the lilac trees with it. He took the dead pig out and laid it on the ground in front of him.

All around him the birds sang and the insects clamoured for attention. Far away the traffic moved steadily to and fro in the city, humming its monstrous mechanised song.

He tried to think, but nothing happened.

Nothing.

That was all he could grasp. Nothing. Everything was over — everyone went away — and finally you went away yourself.

He got up and went into the house where he got a spoon and returned after that to the garden. He dug a hole with the spoon and put the guinea pig inside and covered it with earth.

Then he stamped it down to a level with his feet.

Bertha came to the sun room door. "Harper, come and say good-bye to your granny, she's going home now."

"No thank you," said Harper.

"She'll be real disappointed," said Bertha, fanning herself

with the Bible. "You come and say good-bye."

"No thanks. You tell it to her."

"All right, Harper, you please yourself," said Bertha. "There's iced tea in the fridge." She went inside.

Harper stood in the garden and listened to the birds.

He looked at the back of the house and counted the rooms by their windows.

Ten minutes later he was standing in the front hallway with Bertha. "I won't be long," he said. "I only have to go and then I'll be right back."

"All right then, if you got to. You didn't disturb nothing up there in that spare room, I hope. There's getting so there ain't no room for flowers almost," she said. "You didn't shunt nothing around I hope."

"No. I just went in and looked," he said.

"All right. You go and come straight back."

He looked at her.

"Bertha," he said. "I take back that I don't like you anymore" and then he opened the door and went down the walk.

Woolworth's was crowded when he got there and he had a hard time making the saleslady pay attention to him because he could only barely see her above the counter and people kept pushing him away. But finally he had all that he wanted and he paid her and made his way home.

In the spare room he closed the door and stood at the foot of the bed.

The perfume from the flowers hung heavily in the air and there was a bee buzzing and banging itself against the screen at the window.

For a moment, Harper was afraid to go further into the room. The silence was terrifying to him and especially the silence that clung like something tangible to his mother's form on the bed.

Harper began to sing and then, less conscious of the stillness, he went up and stood beside his mother.

He looked on her intently, humming the tune in short gasps of sound. When he finished the tune he brought a chair and sat beside her. Then he put the words to it. "Walking in the garden, walking with my Lord —."

He felt as though she lay there listening to him; there was a peaceful expression on her face and she looked as though she only slept and could hear him in a dream. "Walking in the garden, talking with my Lord —." Soon, he stopped singing and just watched her.

He held the Woolworth's package in his hand. He looked at it and then back at his mother. She looked sad. The package was suddenly heavy and awkward in his hand and he stepped back from the bed, blushing.

He felt sorry and confused and ashamed all at once. He went to the door. He opened it, turned for a final look and then ran down the stairs and out into the garden.

Bertha sat in the living room with the Bible open on her knees, reading silently, but aloud, to herself.

"Will you come out?" he said. "I want to show you."

Bertha stood up and put the Bible aside for the first time in the whole day.

"I want to show you," he repeated.

They went out and he led her to the lilac trees. Harper looked up at Bertha and hung on tightly to her hand. "The guinea pig," he said. "Went with her, I guess."

They looked at the grave. Harper had studded it with the Woolworth's jewelry and circled it with coloured beads. Bertha closed her eyes and a look of compassionate sorrow pinched the lines of her face.

"I bought them," said Harper conclusively. "From my bazaar, I bought them. But I thought he ought to have them."

He looked at the grave.

Suddenly he started to cry. It was the first time. Bertha held him in her arms.

"I wish she could see it," he said.

"Yes, honey. Tell me honey."

"Bertha it's not . . . that isn't all, is it Bertha? Is that all? Is it all *really* over?"

"No, honey," said Bertha quietly. "That ain't all. Not nearly. Why it's only just the start here, Harper. There's a whole lot more to come.''

"Will she see, Bertha?"

Bertha crouched down with Harper in her lap. "Sure she will, honey. She'll see. I promise you. She'll see just like you an' me. So long as we are here.''

After that, they sang the song together and it got dark, and they went inside.

War

That's my dad in the middle. We were just kids then, Bud on the right and me on the left. That was taken just before my dad went into the army.

Some day that was.

It was a Saturday, two years ago. August, 1940. I can remember I had to blow my nose just before that and I had to use my dad's hankie because mine had a worm in it that I was saving. I can't remember why; I mean, why I was saving that worm, but I can remember why I had to blow my nose, all right. That was because I'd had a long time crying. Not exactly because my dad was going away or anything — it was mostly because I'd done something.

I'll tell you what in a minute, but I just want to say this first. I was ten years old then and it was sort of the end of summer. When we went back to school I was going into the fifth grade and that was pretty important, especially for me because I'd skipped grade four. Right now I can't even remember grade five except that I didn't like it. I should have gone to grade four. In grade five everyone was a genius and there was a boy called Allan McKenzie.

Anyway, now that you know how old I was and what grade I was into, I can tell you the rest.

It was the summer the war broke out and I went to stay with my friend, Arthur Robertson. Looking back on it, Arthur seems a pretty silly name for Arthur Robertson because he was so small. But he was a nice kid and his dad had the most enormous summer cottage you've ever seen. In Muskoka, too.

It was like those houses they have in the movies in Beverly Hills. Windows a mile long — pine trees outside and then a lake and then a red canoe tied up with a yellow rope. There was an Indian, too, who sold little boxes made of birch-bark and porcupine quills. Arthur Robertson and I used to sit in the red canoe and this Indian would take us for a ride out to the raft and back. Then we'd go and tell Mrs Robertson or the cook or someone how nice he was and he'd stand behind us and smile as though he didn't understand English and then they'd have to buy a box from him. He certainly was smart, that Indian, because it worked about four times. Then one day they caught on and hid the canoe.

Anyway, that's the sort of thing we did. And we swam too, and I remember a book that Arthur Robertson's nurse read to us. It was about dogs.

Then I had to go away because I'd only been invited for two weeks. I went on to this farm where the family took us every summer when we were children. Bud was already there, and his friend, Teddy Hartley.

I didn't like Teddy Hartley. It was because he had a space between his teeth and he used to spit through it. Once I saw him spit two-and-a-half yards. Bud paced it out. And then he used to whistle through it, too, that space, and it was the kind of whistling that nearly made your ears bleed. That was what I didn't like. But it didn't really matter, because he was Bud's friend, not mine.

So I went by train and Mr and Mrs Currie met me in their truck. It was their farm.

Mrs Currie got me into the front with her while Mr Currie put my stuff in the back.

"Your mum and dad aren't here, dear, but they'll be up tomorrow. Buddy is here — and his friend."

Grownups were always calling Bud "Buddy." It was all wrong.

I didn't care too much about my parents not being there, except that I'd brought them each one of those birch-bark boxes. Inside my mother's there was a set of red stones I'd picked out from where we swam. I thought maybe she'd make a necklace out of them. In my dad's there was an old golf ball, because he played golf. I guess you'd have to say I stole it, because I didn't tell anyone I had it — but it was just lying there on a shelf in Mr Robertson's boathouse, and he never played golf. At least I never saw him.

I had these boxes on my lap because I'd thought my mum and dad would be there to meet me, but now that they weren't I put them into the glove compartment of the truck.

We drove to the farm.

Bud and Teddy were riding on the gate, and they waved when we drove past. I couldn't see too well because of the dust but I could hear them shouting. It was something about my dad. I didn't really hear exactly what it was they said, but Mrs Currie went white as a sheet and said: "Be quiet," to Bud.

Then we were there and the truck stopped. We went inside.

And now — this is where it begins.

After supper, the evening I arrived at the Curries' farm, my brother Bud and his friend Teddy Hartley and I all sat on the front porch. In a hammock.

This is the conversation we had.

BUD: (to me) Are you all right? Did you have a good time at Arthur Robertson's place? Did you swim?

ME: (to Bud) Yes.

TEDDY HARTLEY: I've got a feeling I don't like Arthur Robertson. Do I know him?

BUD: Kid at school. Neil's age. (He said that as if it were dirty to be my age.)

TEDDY HARTLEY: Thin kid? Very small?

BUD: Thin and small — brainy type. Hey, Neil, have you seen Ted spit?

ME: Yes — I have.

TEDDY HARTLEY: When did you see me spit? (Indignant as hell) I never spat for you.

ME: Yes, you did. About three months ago. We were still in school. Bud — he did too, and you walked it out, too, didn't you?

BUD: I don't know.

TEDDY HARTLEY: I never spat for you yet! Never!

ME: Two yards and a half.

TEDDY HARTLEY: Can't have been me. I spit four.

ME: Four YARDS!!

TEDDY HARTLEY: Certainly.

BUD: Go ahead and show him. Over the rail.

TEDDY HARTLEY: (Standing up) Okay. Look, Neil . . . Now watch . . . Come on, WATCH!!

ME: All right — I'm watching.
      (Teddy Hartley spat. It was three yards-and-a-half by Bud's feet. I saw Bud mark it myself.)

BUD: Three yards and a half a foot.

TEDDY HARTLEY: Four yards. (Maybe his feet were smaller or something.)

BUD: Three-and-foot. Three and *one* foot. No, no. A *half*-a-one. Of a foot.

TEDDY HARTLEY: Four.

BUD: Three!

TEDDY HARTLEY: Four! Four! Four!

BUD: Three! One-two-three-and-a-half-a-foot!!

TEDDY HARTLEY: My dad showed me. It's four! He showed me, and he knows. My dad knows. He's a mathematical teacher — yes, yes, yes, he showed me how to count a yard. I saw him do it. And he knows, my dad!!

BUD: Your dad's a crazy man. It's three yards and a half a foot.

TEDDY HARTLEY: (All red in the face and screaming) You called my dad a nut! You called my dad a crazy-man-nut-meg! Take it back, you. Bud Cable, you take that back.

BUD: Your dad is a matha-nut-ical nutmeg tree.

TEDDY HARTLEY: Then your dad's a . . . your dad's a . . . your dad's an Insane!

BUD: Our dad's joined the army.

That was how I found out.

They went on talking like that for a long time. I got up and left. I started talking to myself, which is a habit I have.

"Joined the army? Joined the army? Joined the ARMY! Our dad?"

Our dad was a salesman. I used to go to his office and watch him selling things over the phone sometimes. I always used to look for what it was, but I guess they didn't keep it around the office. Maybe they hid it somewhere. Maybe it was too expensive to just leave lying around. But whatever it was, I knew it was important, and so that was one thing that bothered me when Bud said about the army — because I knew that in the army they wouldn't let my dad sit and sell things over any old phone — because in the army you always went in a trench and got hurt or killed. I knew that because my dad had told me himself when my uncle died. My uncle was his brother in the first war, who got hit in his stomach and he died from it a long time afterwards. Long enough, anyway, for me to have known him. He was always in a big white bed, and he gave us candies from a glass jar. That was all I knew — except that it was because of being in the army that he died. His name was Uncle Frank.

So those were the first two things I thought of: my dad not being able to sell anything any more — and then Uncle Frank.

But then it really got bad, because I suddenly remembered that my dad had promised to teach me how to skate that year. He was going to make a rink too; in the back yard. But if he had to go off to some old trench in France, then he'd be too far away. Soldiers always went in trenches — and trenches were always in France. I remember that.

Well, I don't know. Maybe I just couldn't forgive him. He hadn't even told me. He didn't even write it in his letter that he'd sent me at Arthur Robertson's. But he'd told Bud — he'd told Bud, but I was the one he'd promised to show how to skate. And I'd had it all planned how I'd really surprise my dad and turn out to be a skating champion and everything, and now he wouldn't even be there to see.

All because he had to go and sit in some trench.

I don't know how I got there, but I ended up in the barn. I was in the hayloft and I didn't even hear them, I guess. They were looking all over the place for me, because it started to get dark.

I don't know whether you're afraid of the dark, but I'll tell you right now, I am. At least, I am if I have to move around in it. If I can just sit still, then I'm all right. At least, if you sit still you know where you are — but if you move around, then you don't know where you are. And that's awful. You never know what you're going to step on next and I always thought it would be a duck. I don't like ducks — especially in the dark or if you stepped on them.

Anyway, I was in that hayloft in the barn and I heard them calling out — "Neil, Neil" — and "Where are you?" But I made up my mind right then I wasn't going to answer. For one thing, if I did, then I'd have to go down to them in the dark — and maybe I'd step on something. And for another, I didn't really want to see anyone anyway.

It was then that I got this idea about my father. I thought that maybe if I stayed hidden for long enough, then he wouldn't join the army. Don't ask me why — right now I couldn't tell you that — but in those days it made sense. If I hid then he wouldn't go away. Maybe it would be because he'd stay looking for me or something.

The trouble was that my dad wasn't even there that night, and that meant that I either had to wait in the hayloft till he came the next day — or else that I had to go down now, and then hide again tomorrow. I decided to stay where I was because there were some ducks at the bottom of the ladder. I couldn't see them but I could tell they were there.

I stayed there all night. I slept most of the time. Every once in a while they'd wake me up by calling out "Neil! Neil!" — but I never answered.

I never knew a night that was so long, except maybe once when I was in the hospital. When I slept I seemed to sleep for a long time, but it never came to morning. They kept waking me up but it was never time.

Then it was.

I saw that morning through a hole in the roof of the hayloft. The sunlight came in through cracks between the boards and it was all dusty; the sunlight, I mean.

They were up pretty early that morning, even for farmers. There seemed to be a lot more people than I remembered — and there were two or three cars and a truck I'd never seen before, too. And I saw Mrs Currie holding onto Bud with one hand and Teddy Hartley with the other. I remember thinking, "If I was down there, how could she hold onto me if she's only got two hands and Bud and Teddy Hartley to look after?" And I thought that right then she must be pretty glad I wasn't around.

I wondered what they were all doing. Mr Currie was standing in the middle of a lot of men and he kept pointing out the scenery around the farm. I imagined what he was saying. There was a big woods behind the house and a cherry and plum-tree orchard that would be good to point out to his friends. I could tell they were his friends from the way they were listening. What I couldn't figure out was why they were all up so early — and why they had Bud and Teddy Hartley up, too.

Then there was a police car. I suppose it came from Orillia

or somewhere. That was the biggest town near where the farm was. Orillia.

When the policemen got out of their car, they went up to Mr Currie. There were four of them. They all talked for quite a long time and then everyone started going out in all directions. It looked to me as though Bud and Teddy Hartley wanted to go, too, but Mrs Currie made them go in the house. She practically had to drag Bud. It looked as if he was crying and I wondered why he should do that.

Then one of the policemen came into the barn. He was all alone. I stayed very quiet, because I wasn't going to let anything keep me from going through with my plan about my dad. Not even a policeman.

He urinated against the wall inside the door. It was sort of funny, because he kept turning around to make sure no one saw him, and he didn't know I was there. Then he did up his pants and stood in the middle of the floor under the haylofts.

"Hey! Neil!"

That was the policeman.

He said it so suddenly that it scared me. I nearly fell off from where I was, it scared me so much. And I guess maybe he saw me, because he started right up the ladder at me.

"How did you know my name?"

I said that in a whisper.

"They told me."

"Oh."

"Have you been here all night?"

"Yes."

"Don't you realize that *everyone* has been looking for you all over the place? Nobody's even been to sleep."

That sort of frightened me — but it was all right, because he smiled when he said it.

Then he stuck his head out of this window that was there to let the air in (so that the barn wouldn't catch on fire) — and he yelled down, "He's all right — I've found him! He's up here."

And I said: "What did you go and do that for? Now you've ruined everything."

He smiled again and said, "I had to stop them all going off

to look for you. Now,'' — as he sat down beside me — ''do you want to tell me what it is you're doing up here?''

''No.''

I think that sort of set him back a couple of years, because he didn't say anything for a minute — except ''Oh.''

Then I thought maybe I had to have something to tell the others anyway, so I might as well make it up for him right now.

''I fell asleep,'' I said.

''When — last night?''

''Yes.''

I looked at him. I wondered if I could trust a guy who did that against walls, when all you had to do was go in the house.

''Why did you come up here in the first place?'' he said.

I decided I could trust him because I remembered once when I did the same thing. Against the wall.

So I told him.

''I want to hide on my dad,'' I said.

''Why do you want to do that? And besides, Mrs Currie said your parents weren't even here.''

''Yes, but he's coming today.''

''But why hide on him? Don't you like him, or something?''

''Sure I do,'' I said.

I thought about it.

''But he's . . . he's . . . Do you know if it's true, my dad's joined the army?''

''I dunno. Maybe. There's a war on, you know.''

''Well, that's why I hid.''

But he laughed.

''Is that why you hid? Because of the war?''

''Because of my dad.''

''You don't need to hide because of the war — the Germans aren't coming over here, you know.''

''But it's not that. It's my dad.'' I could have told you he wouldn't understand.

I was trying to think of what to say next when Mrs Currie came into the barn. She stood down below.

''Is he up there, officer? Is he all right?''

''Yes, ma'am, I've got him. He's fine.''

"Neil dear, what happened? Why don't you come down and tell us what happened to you?"

Then I decided that I'd really go all out. I had to, because I could tell they weren't going to — it was just *obvious* that these people weren't going to understand me and take my story about my dad and the army and everything.

"Somebody chased me."

The policeman looked sort of shocked and I could hear Mrs Currie take in her breath.

"Somebody chased you, eh?"

"Yes."

"Who?"

I had to think fast.

"Some man. But he's gone now."

I thought I'd better say he was gone, so that they wouldn't start worrying.

"Officer, why don't you bring him down here? Then we can talk."

"All right, ma'am. Come on, Neil, we'll go down and have some breakfast."

They didn't seem to believe me about that man I made up.

We went over to the ladder.

I looked down. A lot of hay stuck out so that I couldn't see the floor.

"Are there any ducks down there?"

"No, dear, you can come down — it's all right."

She was lying, though. There was a great big duck right next to her. I think it's awfully silly to tell a lie like that. I mean, if the duck is standing right there it doesn't even make sense, does it?

But I went down anyway and she made the duck go away.

When we went out, the policeman held my hand. His hand had some sweat on it but it was a nice hand, with hair on the back. I liked that. My dad didn't have that on his hand.

Then we ate breakfast with all those people who'd come to look for me. At least, *they* ate. I just sat.

After breakfast, Mr and Mrs Currie took me upstairs to the sitting room. It was upstairs because the kitchen was in the cellar.

All I remember about that was a vase that had a potted plant in it. This vase was made of putty and into the putty Mrs Currie had stuck all kinds of stones and pennies and old bits of glass and things. You could look at this for hours and never see the same kind of stone or glass twice. I don't remember the plant.

All I remember about what they said was that they told me I should never do it again. That routine.

Then they told me my mother and my dad would be up that day around lunch time.

What they were really sore about was losing their sleep, and then all those people coming. I was sorry about that — but you can't very well go down and make an announcement about it, so I didn't.

At twelve o'clock I went and sat in Mr Currie's truck. It was in the barn. I took out those two boxes I'd put in the glove compartment and looked at them. I tried to figure out what my dad would do with an old box like that in the army. And he'd probably never play another game of golf as long as he lived. Not in the army, anyway. Maybe he'd use the box for his bullets or something.

Then I counted the red stones I was going to give my mother. I kept seeing them around her neck and how pretty they'd be. She had a dress they'd be just perfect with. Blue. The only thing I was worried about was how to get a hole in them so you could put them on a string. There wasn't much sense in having beads without a string — not if you were going to wear them, anyway — or your mother was.

And it was then that they came.

I heard their car drive up outside and I went and looked from behind the barn door. My father wasn't wearing a uniform yet like I'd thought he would be. I began to think maybe he really didn't want me to know about it. I mean, he hadn't written or anything, and now he was just wearing an old blazer and some gray pants. It made me remember.

I went back and sat down in the truck again. I didn't know what to do. I just sat there with those stones in my hand.

Then I heard someone shout, ''Neil!''

I went and looked. Mr and Mrs Currie were standing with my parents by the car — and I saw Bud come running out of the house, and then Teddy Hartley. Teddy Hartley sort of hung back, though. He was the kind of person who's only polite if there are grownups around him. He sure knew how to pull the wool over their eyes, because he'd even combed his hair. Wildroot-cream-oil-Charlie.

Then I noticed that they were talking very seriously and my mother put her hand above her eyes and looked around. I guess she was looking for me. Then my dad started toward the barn.

I went and hid behind the truck. I wasn't quite sure yet what I was going to do, but I certainly wasn't going to go up and throw my arms around his neck or anything.

"Neil. Are you in there, son?"

My dad spoke that very quietly. Then I heard the door being pushed open, and some chicken had to get out of the way, because I heard it making that awful noise chickens make when you surprise them doing something. They sure can get excited over nothing — chickens.

I took a quick look behind me. There was a door there that led into the part of the barn where the haylofts were and where I'd been all night. I decided to make a dash for it. But I had to ward off my father first — and so I threw that stone.

I suppose I'll have to admit that I meant to hit him. It wouldn't be much sense if I tried to fool you about that. I wanted to hit him because when I stood up behind the truck and saw him then I suddenly got mad. I thought about how he hadn't written me, or anything.

It hit him on the hand.

He turned right around because he wasn't sure what it was or where it came from. And before I ran, I just caught a glimpse of his face. He'd seen me and he sured looked peculiar. I guess that now I'll never forget his face and how he looked at me right then. I think it was that he looked as though he might cry or something. But I knew he wouldn't do that, because he never did.

Then I ran.

From the loft I watched them in the yard. My dad was rubbing his hands together and I guess maybe where I'd hit him it was pretty sore. My mother took off her handkerchief that she had round her neck and put it on his hand. Then I guess he'd told them what I'd done, because this time they *all* started toward the barn.

I didn't know what to do then. I counted out the stones I had left and there were about fifteen of them. There was the golf ball, too.

I didn't want to throw stones at all of them. I certainly didn't want to hit my mother — and I hoped that they wouldn't send her in first. I thought then how I'd be all right if they sent in Teddy Hartley first. I didn't mind the thought of throwing at him, I'll tell you that much.

But my dad came first.

I had a good view of where he came from. He came in through the part where the truck was parked, because I guess he thought I was still there. And then he came on into the part where I was now — in the hayloft.

He stood by the door.

"Neil."

I wasn't saying anything. I sat very still.

"Neil."

I could only just see his head and shoulders — the rest of him was hidden by the edge of the loft.

"Neil, aren't you even going to explain what you're angry about?"

I thought for a minute and then I didn't answer him after all. I looked at him, though. He looked worried.

"What do you want us to do?"

I sat still.

"Neil?"

Since I didn't answer, he started back out the door — I guess to talk to my mother or someone.

I hit his back with another stone. I had to make sure he knew I was there.

He turned around at me.

"Neil, what's the matter? I want to know what's the matter."

He almost fooled me, but not quite. I thought that perhaps he really didn't know for a minute — but after taking a look at

him I decided that he did know, all right. I mean, there he was
in that blue blazer and everything — just as if he hadn't joined
the army at all.

So I threw again and this time it really hit him in the face.

He didn't do anything — he just stood there. It really scared
me. Then my mother came in, but he made her go back.

I thought about my rink, and how I wouldn't have it. I
thought about being in the fifth grade that year and how I'd
skipped from grade three. And I thought about the Indian
who'd sold those boxes that I had down in the truck.

"Neil — I'm going to come up."

You could tell he really would, too, from his voice.

I got the golf ball ready.

To get to me he had to disappear for a minute while he
crossed under the loft and then when he climbed the ladder. I
decided to change my place while he was out of sight. I began
to think that was pretty clever and that maybe I'd be pretty
good at that war stuff myself. Field Marshal Cable.

I put myself into a little trench of hay and piled some up in
front of me. When my dad came up over the top of the ladder,
he wouldn't even see me and then I'd have a good chance to
aim at him.

The funny thing was that at that moment I'd forgotten why I
was against him. I got so mixed up in all that Field Marshal
stuff that I really forgot all about my dad and the army and
everything. I was just trying to figure out how I could get him
before he saw me — and that was all.

I got further down in the hay and then he was there.

He was out of breath and his face was all sweaty, and where
I'd hit him there was blood. And then he put his hand with my
mother's hankie up to his face to wipe it. And he sort of bit it
(the handkerchief). It was as if he was confused or something. I
remember thinking he looked then just like I'd felt my face go
when Bud had said our dad had joined the army. You know
how you look around with your eyes from side to side as though
maybe you'll find the answer to it somewhere near you? You
never do find it, but you always look anyway, just in case.

Anyway, that's how he was just then, and it sort of threw me. I had that feeling again that maybe he didn't know what this was all about. But then, he had to know, didn't he? Because he'd done it.

I had the golf ball ready in my right hand and one of those stones in the other. He walked toward me.

I missed with the golf ball and got him with the stone.

And he fell down. He really fell down. He didn't say anything — he didn't even say "ouch," like I would have — he just fell down.

In the hay.

I didn't go out just yet. I sat and looked at him. And I listened.

Nothing.

Do you know, there wasn't a sound in that whole place? It was as if everything had stopped because they knew what had happened.

My dad just lay there and we waited for what would happen next.

It was me.

I mean, I made the first noise.

I said: "Dad?"

But nobody answered — not even my mother.

So I said it louder. "*Dad?*"

It was just as if they'd all gone away and left me with him, all alone.

He sure looked strange lying there — so quiet and everything. I didn't know what to do.

"Dad?"

I went over on my hands and knees.

Then suddenly they all came in. I just did what I thought of first. I guess it was because they scared me — coming like that when it was so quiet.

I got all the stones out of my pockets and threw them, one by one, as they came through the door. I stood up to do it. I saw them all running through the door, and I threw every stone, even at my mother.

And then I fell down. I fell down beside my dad and pushed him over on his back because he'd fallen on his stomach. It was like he was asleep.

They came up then and I don't remember much of that. Somebody picked me up, and there was the smell of perfume and my eyes hurt and I got something in my throat and nearly choked to death and I could hear a lot of talking. And somebody was whispering, too. And then I felt myself being carried down and there was the smell of oil and gasoline and some chickens had to be got out of the way again and then there was sunlight.

Then my mother just sat with me, and I guess I cried for a long time. In the cherry and plum-tree orchard — and she seemed to understand because she said that he would tell me all about it and that he hadn't written me because he didn't want to scare me when I was all alone at Arthur Robertson's.

And then Bud came.

My mother said that he should go away for a while. But he said: "I brought something" and she said: "What is it, then?" and now I remember where I got that worm in my handkerchief that I told you about.

It was from Bud.

He said to me that if I wanted to, he'd take me fishing on the lake just before the sun went down. He said that was a good time. And he gave me that worm because he'd found it.

So my mother took it and put it in my hankie and Bud looked at me for a minute and then went away.

The worst part was when I saw my dad again.

My mother took me to the place where he was sitting in the sun and we just watched each other for a long time.

Then he said: "Neil, your mother wants to take our picture because I'm going away tomorrow to Ottawa for a couple of weeks, and she thought I'd like a picture to take with me."

He lit a cigarette and then he said: "I would, too, you know, like that picture."

And I sort of said: "All right."

So they called to Bud, and my mother went to get her camera.

But before Bud came and before my mother got back, we were alone for about ten hours. It was awful.

I couldn't think of anything and I guess he couldn't, either. I had a good look at him, though.

He looked just like he does right there in that picture. You can see where the stone hit him on his right cheek — and the one that knocked him out is the one over the eye.

Right then the thing never got settled. Not in words, anyway. I was still thinking about that rink and everything — and my dad hadn't said anything about the army yet.

I wish I hadn't done it. Thrown those stones and everything. It wasn't his fault he had to go.

For another thing, I was sorry about the stones because I knew I wouldn't find any more like them — but I did throw them, and that's that.

They both got those little boxes, though — I made sure of that. And in one there was a string of red beads from Orillia and in the other there was a photograph.

There still is.

About Effie

I don't know how to begin about Effie, but I've got to because I think you ought to know about her. Maybe you'll meet her one day, and then you'll be glad I told you all this. If I didn't, then maybe you wouldn't know what to do.

I don't remember her last name, but that isn't important. The main thing is to watch out for her. Not many people have the name Effie, so if you meet one, take a good look, because it might be her. She hasn't got red hair or anything, or a spot on her face or a bent nose or any of those things, but the way you'll know her is this: she'll look at you as if she thought you were someone she was waiting for, and it will probably scare you. It did me. And then if she lets on that her name is Effie, it's her.

The first time I saw her, she saw me first. I'll tell you.

I came home from school one day, and it was springtime, so I had to put my coat in the cellar stairway because it was all wet. There was a terrific thunderstorm going on and I was on my way upstairs to look at it. But after I put my coat away I thought I'd go into the kitchen, which was right there, and get a glass of milk and a piece of bread. Then I could have them while I was watching.

I went in, and there was a shout.

Maybe it was a scream, I don't know. But somebody sure made a noise and it scared the daylights out of me.

Right then I didn't know what it was. It looked like a ghost, you know, and then it looked like a great big gray overcoat, and it sort of fell at me.

But it was Effie.

Of course, I didn't know her name then, or who she was or anything, but I figured out that she must be the new maid that my mother told me to watch out for because she was coming that day. And it was.

It was then that she gave me that look I told you about — the look that said 'Are you the one I'm waiting for' — and then she sat down and started to cry.

It wasn't very flattering to have someone look at you and then burst into tears, exactly. I mean it doesn't make you want to go up and ask them what's the matter with them or anything. But I thought right then that I had to anyway, because I felt as though maybe I'd really let her down by turning out to just be me and everything. You know, I thought maybe she thought it was Lochinvar or someone. I'd seen maids break up like that before, when they didn't like Toronto and wanted to go home. They just sat around just waiting all the time for some guy on a horse.

I soon found out that I was wrong, though.

Effie was waiting all right, but not the way most women do. She knew all about him, this man she wanted — just when he'd come and what it would be like, all that stuff. But the man she was waiting for certainly didn't sound like any man I'd ever heard of.

She just called him 'him,' and sometimes it was even 'they,' as if there were a thousand of them or something.

That first afternoon, for instance, when I went up to her and asked her what was wrong, she sort of blew her nose and said: "I'm sorry, I thought you were him." Then she looked out of the window beside her and shook her head. "But you weren't. I'm sorry."

I couldn't figure out whether she meant 'I'm sorry I scared

you' or 'I'm sorry you weren't this man I was expecting.' But I guess it didn't matter because she really meant it, whichever way it was. I liked that. I didn't know anybody who went around saying they were sorry as though they meant it, and it made a big change. So I got my glass of milk and my piece of bread and sat down with her.

"Would you like some tea? I'll make some," she said.

"I'm not allowed to drink tea, but I could have some in my milk. I'm allowed that. My mother calls it Cambridge tea."

"Cambric—" She stood up.

"I thought it was Cambridge. I thought my mother said Cambridge tea."

"No, cambric. Cambridge is a school," she said.

Then she smiled. Boy, that was certainly some smile. And it was then she told me her name and where she came from. Howardstown.

I'd seen it once — it was all rocks and chimney stacks and smoke. I saw it from the train and it didn't exactly make you want to go out and live there. Howardstown had that sort of feeling that seems to say 'I wish everyone would go away and leave me alone for a change.' So you can see what I mean. And that's where Effie came from. So knowing that, you could tell why she preferred to come to Toronto to wait for this man she was expecting.

About that. I had to ask her but I didn't know how. I mean when somebody flings themself at you like that, how do you go about asking them why? You can't say 'Gee, you sure did behave sort of peculiar just then.' You can see what I mean. It would just be rude.

So I sat there drinking my milk; and while she waited for the kettle to boil, she came over and sat down beside me at the table.

"Do you like the rain?" she asked me.

"Sometimes."

"Like today? Like now?"

"Sometimes."

She gave up on that and said: "When does your brother come in?" instead.

"Bud? Oh, he doesn't come in till it's time to eat. He plays football."

"In the rain?"

"No, I guess not. I don't know, then. Maybe he's over at Teddy Hartley's. He goes over there sometimes."

"Oh." She didn't know about Teddy Hartley and Bud being such great friends.

I began to wonder if when Bud came in she'd leap at him too. I had a picture of Bud's face when she scared him. The trouble was that he'd probably start right out with his fists. He was like that. If you surprised him or anything, he just started swinging. With his eyes closed — he didn't care who you were. Sometimes you can really get hurt that way. Surprising Bud.

When I thought of that, I thought maybe I should warn her. But I couldn't figure out how to say that, either. It was the same sort of thing. I thought of saying 'By the way, if my brother comes in, don't go leaping out at *him* — or *else*!' But before I could, the kettle boiled.

Effie got up and put some of the hot water into the teapot.

"Always warm the pot," she said, "first. Then pour it out and put in the tea leaves. Like this. Then you pour the boiling water over them — see? Or else you don't get any flavour. Remember that."

I do. My first lesson in how to make tea.

She came back and sat down.

"Now it has to steep." I remember that, too.

She folded her hands.

Her hair was black and it was tied in a big knot at the back. She had brown eyes that sort of squinted and she had a smell like marmalade. Orange marmalade. And she looked out of the window.

Then she said that the tea had steeped itself for long enough and was ready. She filled my glass because I'd drunk all my milk. I hoped my mother wouldn't come in and see me.

Effie said: "Your mother told me I could have a cup of tea every afternoon at four o'clock. It's four-fifteen now." And she poured her own cup.

I got back to what I wanted to know.

"That sure is some thunderstorm out there," I said.

"Yes." She went very dreamy. "That's why I thought you were him."

"Who?" I certainly would have made a terrific spy. Why, you wouldn't have known I really cared at all, the way I asked that.

"Him."

"Who's that?"

"There has to be thunder, or he won't come."

"Why is that? Is he afraid you'll hear him or something?" I let myself get sarcastic like that because I thought it was time I got to the bottom of things.

"On a cloud," she whispered. "A big black cloud. That's a rule."

All those other men always come on horses — white horses. Not Effie's. A big black cloud. I felt pretty strange when she came out with that one. It sort of scared me.

"Will he take you away?"

"Of course he will. That's why he's coming. That's why I'm waiting."

"Do you wait for him all the time?"

"Oh no. Not always. Only when it rains. Then I get prepared."

I looked around, but there weren't any suitcases or anything. I wondered what she meant by 'prepared.'

"That's why I thought you were him. There had just been a pretty big thunder and there was lightning and then you were there. I even thought I heard music."

"Maybe my mother has the radio on."

I listened, but she didn't.

"Did you hear anything?" she asked.

"You mean like music?"

"Yes."

"No, I didn't think so. I can't remember, maybe I did —"

"You *did*!" She leapt up. I got scared again. "Did you, did you? Tell me if you did. Tell me. Did you hear it? The music? Did you hear it?"

"I don't know."

"Oh, but you said . . ."

Then she sat down and it looked like she might cry again.

"Do you want Howardstown?" I asked. I had to say something.

But she said: "No, thank you."

"Wouldn't you like to go back?"

"No, thank you."

"I was there once. It was pretty."

I lied again, but I thought maybe I had to for her sake. Then I lied again.

"I was there in the summertime. We spent our whole summer holiday there because we liked it so much. Don't you want to go back?"

"No ——— thank you."

That long line there is where she blew her nose.

"Don't you want to see those nice rocks and everything? I liked those."

Then I thought of something. I thought I had it.

"Effie?"

"Yes?"

"Doesn't it rain there?"

"In Howardstown?"

"Yes."

"Of course it does."

"But does it thunder?"

"Of course it does."

"And lightning?"

"Certainly."

"Oh."

I guess it wasn't such a brilliant idea after all. So I thought again.

"Did he say he'd meet you here — I mean in Toronto?"

That at least made her laugh, which was something. It was nice when she laughed.

"Of course not. Don't be silly. Why, if I went to Timbuctoo he'd just as soon find me there. Or in Madagascar even. I don't have to wait around in any old Toronto."

"Oh."

I was trying to think where that was. Madagascar.

"Besides, it's not just me he's after."

That really got me. I thought he *was* after Effie.

Then she looked at me and all of a sudden I felt it. That it wasn't just some knight in shining armour she had in mind. Or some crazy man on a black cloud, either. No, sir. Whoever he was, he surely was coming. You could tell that just from the way she looked.

Then she said: "Some day when I know you better, I'll tell you. Right now it's four-thirty."

And she put her cup into the sink and washed it. And my glass and the plate from my bread and butter. She ran the water over them and she sang a song.

And it rained and it rained and it rained.

But there was no more thunder.

That was over.

The next time it was the middle of the night. About two weeks later.

There was another of those storms. I didn't wake up at first, but then there was a crash of thunder that really did shake my bed. I mean it. I nearly fell out, even.

I called out in a whisper to Bud, but he was asleep. I forgot to tell you we sleep in the same room. Anyway, I knew I didn't *have* to be afraid, so it didn't matter that he didn't wake up. Thunder doesn't scare me when you can look at it — I even like watching it — but when it's night-time and everyone is asleep but you, then you begin to wonder if it really is just thunder. And sometimes you begin to think that maybe somebody will come and grab you when you can't hear them because of the noise. I wondered if that was what Effie meant.

"Thunder and lightning and music," she'd said. It was like that. If there was ever thunder and lightning and music, then he'd come.

I began to get scared. There was thunder all right, and there was lightning, but there wasn't any music.

Then there was.

I didn't exactly think I'd sit around to make sure. I thought

I'd better tell my mother.

Thunder and lightning and music. Yes, there certainly was music all right. It was faint, but it was there. Maybe I'd better warn Effie too, I thought. Mother first, and then Effie.

I went into the hallway. My mother's door was open, and she was lying there only covered with the sheet because it was so hot. She was asleep, though. The street lamp shone through the window and I can remember the metal smell of the screens. They smelt sort of electric.

"Mother."

She sort of moved.

"Hey, Mother."

I was very quiet, but I had to wake her up. I could hear that music even more now.

"Neil?"

She rolled over towards me and took my hand. I could tell she really didn't want to wake up. Maybe she'd been dreaming. Our dad was away.

"I'm sorry, but I had to."

"Are you sick?"

"No."

"Then what is it?"

"Can I get in with you?"

"All right. Pull the cover up. That's right."

We lay there and heard the rain.

"Now tell me about it. Can't you sleep?"

"No." I didn't know where to begin. "Mother, has Effie ever talked to you?"

"What about?"

"I don't know. But she said to me that if there was rain, and if there was thunder, and if there was lightning, then maybe something would happen."

"The end of the world?" Mother laughed very quietly.

"No, I don't mean that. Some man."

"A man? What do you mean?"

"Well, she said if there was thunder and lightning and everything, to watch out for music. Because if there was music too, then he'd come."

"*Who'd* come, dear?"

"This *man*. This man she's waiting for."

"Well, if she's waiting for him, then it's all right."

I guess she didn't take it very seriously.

"Besides," she said, "there isn't any music."

"Yes there is."

"There *is*?"

She sounded serious *now* all right.

"Yes, I heard it. That's why I woke you up. I thought maybe we'd better tell her so she could be ready."

"Ready? Does she . . . does she really know who he is?"

"Well, she seemed to. She never said his name or anything. She just said that —"

"And you heard it? The music, you really heard it?"

"Yes."

"Now don't joke with me, Neil. This may be very serious."

"Spit. Honestly, I really heard it."

"Where from?"

"I don't know. I just heard it."

My mother got out of bed.

All this time the thunder was getting louder and the lightning was like daylight.

"Well, we'll wake her up and ask her what it's all about. Is Bud awake?"

"No."

"Leave him, then."

She tried to turn on the lights, but they didn't work. (That always happened two or three times a year in those big storms. Toronto never worked when you needed it to.) So we went into the hall in the dark.

Effie's room was at the top of the stairs. Very small, but it was the only one we had for her. It used to be mine. It had a sloping ceiling.

We knocked on her door.

No answer.

It was pitch black. Effie always pulled the blinds. My mother went over and opened them and a bit of light came in. And then we saw that she wasn't there. Her bed was all slept in and everything, but she wasn't there.

My mother let out a yell. Very quiet, but it was certainly a yell.

We didn't know what to do.

We went out into the hall again.

"Shall I get Bud?" I said.

"No. No, not yet." She was trying to get calm. Very calm. And then she was all right.

"Maybe we'd better go and look downstairs. We can get some candles from the dining room."

We started down the staircase. Half-way down we heard the music again.

Very low it was. No words or anything, just the tune. It didn't seem to come from anywhere in particular — it was just there.

We stood still and listened. If we hadn't been so scared, it would have been pretty. I mean it was a good tune. One that you could hum.

My mother caught my hand and we started down again.

"Dining room," she whispered.

The dining room was down the hall, and beyond it there was a sun room, all glass windows, and in the summertime, screens.

We got into the dining room all right, and from there the music was louder.

Then we saw her.

She was in the sun room, watching from the windows. All her black hair fell down her back. When there was lightning she stood up, and when there wasn't she sat down. All the time she sort of rocked to and fro to the sound of the music.

She was crying — but she had that wonderful smile.

Just once, when the music stopped, she said something. I don't know what it was because she said it too quietly for me to hear. And the reason she said it when the music stopped was because *she* was the music. *She* was. It was Effie singing.

My mother and I didn't bother her, though. She looked so happy there — even with the tears down her face — and as my mother said "It doesn't hurt people to sing once in a while.

Even at night.''

So we went back to bed and my mother said would I like to sleep with her, and I said yes. We got in and we thought about Effie downstairs.

"Do you know?''

"No. Do you?''

"No.''

Then, later on — I think it was about three months later — Effie came to my mother and said she'd been called away.

"Where to, dear?'' my mother asked her.

"Just away,'' said Effie, like a princess. "And so I've got to go.''

My mother didn't ask her because Effie had been such a good person in the house, and Mother knew that if she had to go away then she had to, and it was honest. You never had to think about that with Effie — she always told the truth and everything had a reason. Even if you didn't get to know what it was.

We certainly hated to see her leave us. Even Bud was sad about it, and he was never much good with maids. He used to be too shy with them.

Before she left, she gave me a set of toy animals, little ones — a pig and a cow and a horse and four sheep — all in a box. She knew that I had this toy farm.

And for Bud she had a box of toy soldiers. Only they were very peaceful soldiers, just standing at ease, and there was a little sentrybox too, for them to go into when it rained.

She gave my mother a hankie with an M on it because my mother's name is Margaret. It was real linen and she still has it.

The day she left, she was having a cup of tea just before she went to get on the streetcar and I found her in the kitchen just like the first time. I had some flowers for her. Little ones, that she could carry without them getting in the way.

And she looked at them and said: "That's his favourite colour.'' (They were purple.) And she thanked me.

So I asked her right then and there.

"Tell me who he is."

She smiled and winked at me.

"That's a secret."

"But is he real? Will he really come for you some time? Please tell me."

Then she did this wonderful thing. She got down on her knees and put her arms around me and her head against me. I remember looking down at her hair underneath her hat.

And she said: "Don't worry about me." Then she got up. "Now it's time to go. Thank you for the flowers."

She picked up her suitcase and went in to say good-bye to my mother.

"Do you want Neil to take you to the streetcar?"

"No, thank you, Mrs Cable. I'll be all right. It's such a lovely day."

I think we both knew what she meant.

I didn't watch her go. Not at first. But then I ran out to see her before she turned the corner. Then she did — and was gone.

Effie.

So you can see what I mean. It still worries me. And that's why I want you to be sure — to be *sure* to recognize her when you see her. She'll look at you, just like she did at me that first day in the kitchen, as though you were someone she was looking for. But if she does, don't be scared. This man, I don't know who he is, but if it's Effie he wants, then he's all right.

Sometime — Later —
Not Now

1950

We're over thirty now, Diana and I, but in 1950 we were
twelve. It seems such a long time ago that I can't quite connect
it up to the world we live in today. Certainly, there seem to be
no straight lines back to that time, only the crooked, wavering
lines of spliced memory. We were peaceful children, then.

No.

We were placated children.

Our world had been secured for us by a World War that
closed in a parable of Silence. And so I think we were placated
children — doped — by horror. And I only say it here because
I think there was a crazy serenity to our childhood which you
might not understand if you were not alive then. The adults we
lived with walked around our lives very often on tip-toe, with
plugs in their ears and with shaded eyes. So much of holocaust
had happened that people acquiesced to reality without daring to
look at it, because it could only turn out to be another nightmare.

And so we grew up protected from all subtlety. We were quiet and with good reason. We knew the big things — life and death, period — but none of the small things. The best we knew was how to be still and quiet, which meant that we learned, excessively, not to know ourselves.

My name is Davis Hart and I grew up loving Diana Galbraith.

Her parents and my parents had been in the War together — which is to say that our fathers had served in the same regiment and that our mothers had spent the War wandering from army camp to army camp, sometimes taking us with them, but more often leaving us behind with a woman called Maria Tungess, whose grasp of discipline was still back in the "Child-in-the-Locked-Cupboard" era.

When the War ended our fathers returned to civilian life, which was a life of absolute comfort supported by absolute money — got by absolute panic. People didn't just want to be rich in the 1940s. They *had* to be.

The Galbraiths owned a summer island and we would spend our vacations there like one family — my brother Eugene, my sister Maudie and me and Diana.

I remember a day of the summer in question, 1950, when Maudie, Diana and I sat high up on a rock we called, for obvious reasons, the "Elephant's Back." Eugene, being older, was allowed to own a gun and he was elsewhere on the island trying to kill something. He was fourteen, then, and Maudie was eight — almost nine.

My memory of this conversation starts with Diana flinging a stone into the water far below us and I look back on the whole scene as if I were that stone — looking upward — plunging down. I see us, high on our rock, through the shimmer of a surface I shall never be able to break open. And our conversation is as stilted and formal as something heard without inflection.

"Mother thinks we're going to get married," said Diana, and Maudie laughed. "It isn't at all funny. She really thinks so."

"Maybe we will," I said. I was lying down with my hand over my eyes.

"No. I don't think so," said Diana, and I sat up. I was hurt by the matter-of-factness with which she dismissed me from her future, and not at all by just the marriage question — which, naturally, had never entered into my thinking at that age. "In fact, I'm quite certain," she went on, "I'm not going to get married at all."

"How do you know your mother thinks we'll get married?" I said.

"I heard her say to your mother. She said 'when Diana and Davis are married . . .' — just like that. And Aunt Peggy didn't argue about it, either. They both think it's going to happen."

"What'll happen to your children," said Maudie, "if you don't get married?"

"What children?" said Diana.

"Your *children*," said Maudie. "Aren't you going to have them?"

"You don't just *have* children, stupid. Doesn't she know anything, Davis?"

"I don't think so," I said, and lay down again.

"I know everything," said Maudie — and immediately refuted that by saying, "You're not allowed to have your babies until you're married. And if you don't get married your babies die inside of you."

"Who told you that?"

"Miss Tungess. She didn't get married yet and she's had seventeen babies die right inside of her. So far."

"You can't walk around with something dead inside of you," I said. "If you did — you'd die yourself."

"She flushes them down the toilet."

There was some kind of pause after that while we all thought about what might be floating around in the sewage system and then Diana said, "Anyway, the important thing is, I don't want to know who I'm to marry at all — 'til I decide to get married. And so far, I've decided not to get married, so I don't need to know anyone."

(She stands like a boy in my memory, wearing khaki shorts. Feet wide apart. Canvas running shoes. A pale yellow polo shirt with a hole over the point of one shoulder blade, and she pulls her braid over this shoulder and starts to undo it and then to do it up again: weaving, unweaving her hair. She is always preoccupied with some nervous gesture of this kind.)

"If you don't get married, what will you do, then?"

"I'm going to play the piano. You know that. Go to Europe and go to France. I'm going to become a very, very famous person."

She wet the end of her braid in her mouth and looked at it closely.

"As famous as Rubinstein," she said after a moment, drawing the braid through her fingers. "As Rubinstein. As Malcuzinski — as Moiseiwitsch." These names were magic to her. Incantation.

"They're all men," said Maudie.

"They're the three greatest pianists in the world. That's what they are. And I'll be one of them."

I watched her carefully. As I've said, I was "in love" with her. I had loved her from the moment I realized she could be taken away from me, which first happened for about six months when we were seven years old. I didn't want her to grow up to be Rubinstein, because I realized that being Rubinstein meant belonging to another world and to a lot of other people.

Later on it was clear to me that Diana herself knew this about love — that she always had. But she never mentioned it because, as a child, (which I take to mean the period up until she was fourteen or fifteen) as a child, she was aloof from it. She was aloof not just from loving, but from being loved. I think that probably, out of her dark eyes, she stared at times at those of us who loved her and said to herself, "they love me" and knew it and was grateful — but she never would mention it to us — or to anyone. She was an only child — the only child of parents who were close to their money in the way that they might have been close to a preferred firstborn son. They loved Diana, but she came second.

Diana had a very strict, very demanding father (we called him Uncle Ross) and all her life she was nervous with the ambition to please him. The piano was her mother's idea, for Mrs Galbraith had once had concert ambitions of her own. She started Diana early, and as it turned out, it was highly probable that a prodigy (or at any rate, a greatly gifted — even brilliant pianist) had been discovered. But she was not allowed to concertize, only to study. The concerts and the fame would come later, when they should, and in the meantime there was the promise of that — and the work.

In many ways, like many people of talent, Diana only had power over one part of her mind — the driving part. Over the rest she exercised no power at all. Moments of incident came into and went out of her life, strewing about them the careless, thoughtless wreckage of all uncontrolled events. And there were times (this was equally true of her as a child as it was true of her as an adult) — there were times when it seemed that she simply did not care about events — while at other times, as you will see, it was as though the events, or happenings, within the emotional territory of her life were a complete mystery to her — guided, as they were inevitably guided, by outside forces — her mother, her father, her friends.

But the "piano thing" — as we referred to it then — was of the driving part of her. It *was* the driving part. It was her ambition. Through it Diana became an unchildlike child. She had the features of a child, but not the mien. She had the voice, but not the words. She dressed like a boy, but there was no tomboyishness about her at all. She was really more like an adult dressed up as a child — forced, for a while, to play the part of a child. But as a child she had no childhood. None that I witnessed. None that Maudie did, as her friend, and certainly none that her parents saw.

And so on that day, on the Elephant's Back, I heard about the future from Diana herself.

You could tell — absolutely, once and for all — that it was her real ambition — the piano thing. You could tell that she really did mean it. She wasn't dreaming about it, or just hoping about it. It was something that was going to come true. It was there, in her face, that day. It was in the way she held her hands out and in the way her feet were set right down into the rock. Diana was going to be famous and I knew it — and I knew, right there, that that meant I would not go on being a part of her life.

"So I don't want to know anyone now I may have to marry later," she said. "I only want to know myself. And that's all."

And Maudie had said, "But what about your babies?"

And Diana said, "They'll never happen, that's all. Because I'm not going to marry."

And that seemed to be that.

"They'll all die," said Maudie with a requiem tone that was rapt with thoughts of Miss Tungess and her flushing toilet.

"No. They won't die," said Diana. "They just won't happen."

It was her own epitaph.

1958

When I was twenty, Diana introduced me to a girl whose name was Tanya. Naturally, I fell in love with her. I fell in love with everyone Diana introduced me to. If they were close to Diana, then loving them would make me a little closer to her, myself.

Tanya was a poetess. Not a poet, a "poetess." She had straight blonde hair and a round, incredibly beautiful face. Her eyes were green and her only drawback was that she bit her fingernails. At parties — and in fact the first time I met her — she wore gloves in order that people shouldn't know. But she had a good figure — round — and she had that face and her voice was marvellous, too. It was the sort of voice one imagines the French courtesans must have had — hoarse from too many pleasures.

Tanya wore black stockings long before they were adopted by fashion, and her shoes had the highest heels I have ever seen. Aside from that, her style of dress could be described as "Mexican-Russian" — a lot of white with basted-on colours and eccentric things like shawls and capes. On some occasions she dressed as a man, but she was never without her stiletto shoes.

I adored her. Leave it at that.

She was at the University and she shared the same lectures

as Diana, who by now was a student of languages as well as of
the piano. I was not a student, myself. At that time I was an
actor — the thwarted competition (I took the thwart to be my
age, in those days) of Guinness, Olivier and Redgrave. Tanya,
Diana and I were inseparable — and there was one other.

His name was Brett Slatten and he belonged to Diana.

Brett Slatten had a big head. I mean it quite literally,
however much it could be said in the other sense. It was
immense. It was the head of David, with hair like that — curly
(black) and worn naturally — shorn ad hoc, never barbered.
("We're going to a party . . ." snip, snip.) He had bad teeth,
but that didn't matter. He had a crooked smile. (I practised
this smile for several weeks but it always came on straight.)

Brett Slatten was the son of a Mennonite farmer, and his
ambition in life, somehow, was to write the definitive
biography of Hart Crane. I don't think that I could sum him
up with a better description than that.

And so, as I say, we did everything together. Brett and I
hardly ever spoke. Diana and Tanya did all the talking. We
just stood there with them, smoking cigars, Brett looking
incredibly Byronic, and me wishing that I did — thinking that
I did — and probably looking more like Shelley after he'd
drowned. (I had started to let my hair grow long just two days
after I first laid eyes on Brett, but my hair is straight and the
effect was somehow different. I was also the colour of paste.)

In those days you could still buy beer in quart bottles. They
were green, and Brett and I both wore dark corduroy jackets
most of the time with great, wide pockets. At parties we would
walk about with a quart of beer in each pocket and another in
hand. It was the best time of my life. Drinking didn't hurt you
then. You never had a hangover. You could smoke until you
couldn't breathe and it didn't matter. Sex was still something
you expected to perfect, and it involved a lot of fun and a lot of
excitement. Your bodies were clean and they were like walking
laboratories in which you experimented with everything at
length. The mind stretched wide, like elastic, as you encountered all knowledge, and it was all let in and it was all let out.
You weren't obliged to hold onto it. Your eyes never tired of
looking and they were never shut.

Until we met Jean-Paul.

Jean-Paul was a French millionaire who wore carnations in the lapels of exquisite suits and who carried a cane and gloves and wore hats. He had great, sleepy eyes and he had been in an automobile accident.

He was the first person we had met to whom anything of great physical consequence had happened. Part of his skull was missing and had been replaced with a metal plate. He drank pernod. We had never drunk pernod. We met at a party.

Within half an hour of meeting, Jean-Paul had captured us and was whisking us away.

"Steal a little something thoughtlessly on the way to drink," he said, organizing our escape in typical French phraseology.

Brett stole a bottle of wine and I stole five bottles of beer.

We threw on our overcoats (it was winter) and we left.

Jean-Paul led us to a Citroën parked haphazardly partly on and mostly off the street. It was the old kind of Citroën. Ugly and black.

"My dear," said Tanya, "he really *is* French."

"You refer to the way I park?"

"No," said Tanya. "I mean the Citroën."

"Ah!" said Jean-Paul. "I am more French even than that." And he winced, as though in pain, and made a very Gallic gesture which suggested he was resigned to a burden of immorality too heavy to bear.

This delighted everyone, naturally, and once he had passed around his cigarette case filled with Gauloises, we were absolutely his.

For the rest of the evening we rode around in the car and went to several bars, some of which we'd never visited before. The waiters everywhere seemed to recognize Jean-Paul and we were given immediate and excellent service everywhere.

Eventually, after we had made a mysterious stop at the request of Jean-Paul — at the bus depot so that he could use the washroom (he must have been ill, because he was gone for almost half an hour) we drove off, singing gaily, to another party.

At that party we all got drunk and I can only remember Tanya dancing a Russian dance and some serious-faced old man insisting that she was one of the Romanovs in exile. Asleep, we were driven by Jean-Paul to his house where we all awoke in various bedrooms the next morning.

Sometimes, there is a day whose atmosphere you spend the rest of your life trying to recapture. Such a day was that next day in Jean-Paul's house.

First of all, perhaps it should be explained how it was that Jean-Paul lived alone in such a large, expensive house, in a city where he was ostensibly only a visitor. He let us know very little about himself, but he did say that he was here attending to some business for his father. His father was an outrageously wealthy man, Jean-Paul told Brett, and the wealth was in some sort of exotic, possibly intriguing business. Jean-Paul was often abroad, and this time he was to be here for two years. And so, he had rented this house from an interior decorator who had gone to Europe. Fair exchange.

As houses go, it was the epitome of purchased taste. Most of the furniture was Empire and there was a lot of plum carpeting and velvet drapery everywhere. Rococo mirrors, Olympian paintings and Regency gew-gaws completed the picture. It had the charm of money and it had authentic atmosphere, but the latter, I am certain, was attributable to the presence of Jean-Paul and not to the ownership of the interior decorator. For Jean-Paul brought with him a collection of recordings, prints and books that were not entirely suited to the house and which became, for us, its predominant atmosphere.

The music was the music of Bartok, Satie and Poulenc. The prints were of works by Klee and Munch. The poetry was the poetry of Rilke and the books were the novels and other writings of Hermann Hesse, Gertrude Stein and Guillaume Apollinaire. There were prints, too, from Marie Laurencin, drawings by Pavel Tchelitchew and photographs of Nijinsky, Lincoln Kirsten and Josephine Baker. It was all, as you can see, the cult of Paris in the twenties and early thirties, and from that moment we made it our own.

On the morning of that day when we awoke in that house, we drank black coffee, listened to the Poulenc recordings and smoked Jean-Paul's cigarettes.

We drove out in the Citroën and we bought bread, smoked oysters, Dutch gin and escargots in tin cans. We all bought flowers that day and we all wore them. We became a parade. It was the only time that it ever happened without calculation or without the wish of repetition. I remember it all without recalling a single important detail. It was that innocent — that betrayable.

So.

At two o'clock we went to an art gallery somewhere and booed the paintings. At two-thirty we were put out on the street. By three we were back in Jean-Paul's house, where we drank the gin and ate the snails with melted butter, lemons and garlic, and where we lay on the floor and listened to the Poulenc records again and again and again.

And Diana.

Diana let down her hair and she laughed and laughed and laughed.

Later on we all danced and Diana tried, very successfully, to play one of the Poulenc pieces on the piano from memory. After that there was a terrible argument about Kafka — about the Metamorphosis story — and it was loud and operatic with everyone taking part.

All I can remember is that Jean-Paul proposed that the metamorphosis had been self-induced — that it was wished for and that it was profoundly sexual — that it represented more than man-into-bug-like-incapacitation. It represented a sexual change as well, the change from aggressive to passive participation in sex. The man lying under the bed when the woman wanted to come in . . . the hugeness of the woman. The way she fed him. He saw a great deal of significance in the writing around all the entries into the room. Shoving things under the door . . . the fact that it was a *man's* room. He went on about it for a long time, with a smile — until Brett exploded.

When the argument was over we all pretended that we were bugs and we crawled about, flapping imaginary legs at the ceiling and passing gin in saucers across the floor at each other. Finally, this induced Brett to laugh and Jean-Paul said, "Yes. There is only one here — one — who would be capable of that, of really changing from one to the other. Only one."

We all cried, "Who?" each hoping to be the one — the one who might be so dramatically doomed. "Who?" we said. "Me?"

"No," said Jean-Paul, "not you. Brett."

Immediately we all looked under the piano where Brett had crawled to drink his gin.

"I'm a bug," he said. "Don't bother me. See me! The bug! I'm the beetle under Diana's piano. I will never change!!"

We all roared. Even Diana, whose one abhorrence was beetles.

I forget the rest, except that later on that evening we went to yet another party — given, I think, by an artist, (at least it was in a studio-like place) and Diana drew an enormous beetle on the wall and labelled it "BRETT." Underneath it Jean-Paul wrote "do not look under the bed" and he added, smiling at Diana, "Any bed, my dear. He might be there."

This period of our lives lasted for about a month. Of course we all returned to our own homes once a day and most of the nights. Diana and Tanya went on attending lectures at the University and I did some acting on radio. Jean-Paul had his business to attend to nearly every day. The only immediate change was in Brett.

He decided to leave the University. He was going to commence his book. Studying didn't matter. There was only one thing to study, anyway — the work of Hart Crane. It was decided that he might as well live in Jean-Paul's house, because it would be quiet there, and Jean-Paul had seized on the opportunity of playing philanthropist and patron to a budding genius.

Jean-Paul bought a great many books for Brett and every day he went off to his place of business, leaving Brett alone with paper and ink and bottles of beer so that he might create his masterpiece.

All of this happened about two weeks after we had met Jean-Paul.

And now it was, when they had a house in which they could meet — a place for privacy — that it became clear to me how

much in love Diana was with Brett. She would go there
between lectures every day and make things for him. She
would even go if she had only five minutes. She would stand
beside him and pour his beer for him, empty his ashtray, put
her fingers inside his shirt, kiss him and go away. She would
not even speak.

I asked her if she was studying piano every day as she should
be and she said, "Of course. Of course I am. One has to — one
must — if you want to be Rubinstein." And then she would
look back through the door at Brett and put her collar up and
ask me if I wanted her to drive me anywhere. "No," I would
say. "I'm not going anywhere, Diana. Bring Tanya as soon as
the lectures are over . . ." and then she would drive away.

When I wasn't rehearsing or actually doing a radio show I
would sit in Jean-Paul's living room and look at books. That
was when I read Scott Fitzgerald first and Gertrude Stein and
Thornton Wilder. But I have not gone back to Fitzgerald or to
Gertrude Stein. Someday, perhaps I will, but Melanctha made
me incalculably sad and Nicole Diver disturbed me to such a
degree that I remember reading about her just a page at a time,
and then pacing up and down that lovely room and playing a
Bartok piano concerto on the gramophone, until Brett nearly
went mad and would yell at me, every day, to find a new, sen-
sible heroine — like Anna Karenina or Emma Bovary. Of
course, I never found either. I was stuck with Nicole. She was
part of the scenery.

Tanya and I had a fight, I remember, one evening — and
she left. I asked Jean-Paul if I could spend the night. He said,
"Yes."

Diana had to leave early that evening, and so Brett, Jean-
Paul and I were left alone. We drank. I got wildly drunk and I
passed out. In the morning I awoke in the living room.

I remember the waking up very clearly.

It was a beautiful, snowy morning — white and secret and
enclosed. The house was comfortable and warm and it smelled
of furniture-wax and cigarettes and of Diana's perfume. Yes.
She had even given in so far as to wear perfume. I forget what
it was called but I would know it in an instant if I should ever

smell it again. It had the odour of a ballet — of flowers and of
wine and of air that was stirred by the movement of dancers.
You smell it sometimes at the theatre when the curtain rises. It
was a sad smell — old-fashioned and nostalgic and lovely, like
the remembrance of a person whose mementoes are found
between the pages of an antique book.

I lay on the sofa and lit a cigarette. I even drank some pernod, I remember, lying there like that. And I thought for the
first time in years of our conversation on the Elephant's Back. I
thought, "It doesn't matter, because Diana is in love, and even
if it isn't me she loves, and even if it never will be, the fear of
being without her is gone. And the fear, forever, that she will
never love. It's good," I thought, "it's good that Brett is good
— that he loves her and that he's a genius," (we really all did
think so) "and she will be safe. One day she will play the piano
for her children and be glad that pianists *can* have babies and
her fame will be that she is Brett's wife."

I gave her up so easily, lying there that morning, because I
couldn't bear to be unhappy.

And so I lay there, almost as happy as I might have been if I
had been Brett himself, with Brett's future, and with Brett's
assurance of Diana and with Brett's unbounded genius. It did
not matter that it was not true. I, after all, was me. I, too, had
a future, and if I did not marry Tanya then I would marry
someone else and the someone else would love me or I wouldn't
marry them. I tried to remember why Tanya and I had fought.
I laughed. I could not remember. So I decided to telephone
her. I would wake her up and apologize and tell her that I loved
her and that I wanted her to come right over and drink a
pernod breakfast with me.

I got up, then, and went into the hall. The phone was in
Brett's study. But he'd locked the door — or someone had.
Wasn't there another telephone? One upstairs in Jean-Paul's
bedroom? Yes. There was.

And so I went up and I must have gone up quietly and for
some thoughtless reason I have always ever since regretted, I
forgot to knock on the door to Jean-Paul's room. Instead I
simply opened the door and stood there.

Writing that down — re-reading it — I feel as if I had stood there ever since because what I saw opened a vista for me of enduring despair and of unhappiness, forever, for Diana.

They were naked. I guess they were doing something. I didn't see. All I could see was who they were and what they'd betrayed.

It wasn't that it was two men. That didn't even cross my mind. It was just the infidelity. The lie.

And the structure of everything came apart.

SPRING: 1960

Miss Galbraith played with such cold command that I wondered at her given age. She sits as though her real desire was to hypnotize the keyboard. In the whole recital there was not one hint of warmth. It was as though she might be taking vengeance on the music. I received the very distinct impression that Miss Galbraith was one of those electrical machines that immobilizes things at the touch. Her playing is faultless — even brilliant — but there is the definite feeling after each successive interpretation that Miss Galbraith has carved something for you out of rock. This works, exquisitely, with the Scarlatti and Bach pieces which she chose. It has its moments, even, in the Beethoven, but it certainly did not suit the Debussy. Furthermore, Miss Galbraith is too young to have chosen to play the Poulenc pieces with which she concluded. She was either too young or, oddly enough, too old. At any rate, she does not understand them. They are witty, humorous and light — not pieces of ice. Perhaps when she is a little further along, life will serve to melt a little of this damaging overlay of complete withdrawal from her performance, and I am sure that we will then have the right to lay claim to a superb new artist — of the first mark.

1964

When I was twenty-six, which means that Diana was twenty-six as well, I had been acting in New York for three years, and I got a phone call at the theatre one evening.

"It's Diana."

"Diana!"

"I've been here for months. But I just couldn't phone or get in touch. I wanted to be sure I was staying. You know me — I hate to make announcements before I'm sure of them."

"But I'm so glad you phoned," I said. "Will you meet me tonight after the play?"

"No," she said, "but I will tomorrow. I want you to come to Columbus Circle. I'll meet you there. I have something to show you, Davis. But I don't want to say what until you get here."

"All right," I said. "I'd be delighted. What time?"

"Come at two o'clock, Davis. Two o'clock."

I said that I would and we hung up.

Diana.

She sounded different. She sounded old. She sounded muted. It was like the sound of the trumpet with its mute applied — the same, but distant; the attack all gone.

The next day I went up on the subway to Columbus Circle and came out into the traffic by the Park. I looked everywhere. It was two o'clock on the nose but I could not see her. And then I did.

She wore the braid of hair still; it was bound in a circle on top of her head. She wore no make-up — and a blue overcoat. Her hands were in her pockets.

Her eyes looked tired. The braid of hair had been sloppily coiled and it was not clean. When I came close to her, all I could smell was her coat. It smelled of camphor and I could tell that it was second hand.

She did not smile. She took my arm.

"We can walk, Davis," she said.

She called me by name nearly every time she opened her mouth. Her speech was entirely formal and her voice never achieved anything beyond one tone.

"Are you married, Davis?"

"No."

"How is Maudie?"

"She's fine. She's still in Canada."

"And Eugene, Davis, how is he?"

"He's fine, I guess. He's coming here, you know. With Mavis Bailey. You remember her."

"Oh, yes. Did they marry?"

"No."

I smiled.

"But one day . . . I suppose they will."

We walked up on the Park side into the Seventies until we came to a corner with a light. There we crossed and saw a street of houses — old, red-faced, probably boarding houses — or perhaps houses where dentists had offices. They were lit with a long arm of sunlight from the Jersey shore. I had friends up in the area and I remember someone saying that Marc Connelly had once lived in an apartment on the corner.

"What is this," I asked.

"The street, Davis."

"Is this what you want to show me, love? The street?"

"Part of it, Davis. Look. That one there. It's mine."

She pointed out a tall rust-coloured house on the north side. In front there was an iron railing and there was a sign.

"PIANO LESSONS — ACADEMY TO GRADE 7"

"Inside," said Diana, "there are five pianos."

For the first time, she smiled.

Then we went in.

All the rooms and the hall, downstairs, were empty — except that in each there was a piano, a chair and a bench.

"Upstairs is just old bedrooms, Davis. Don't look. Come now into the kitchen. We'll have a drink together."

I followed her and in the kitchen we took our overcoats off and she poured us each a glass of scotch. I noted that she poured herself more than a double and that she drank it neat.

"Well, what is all this?" I said.

"I'm going to teach," said Diana. "I will love it."

The tone — the pitch — the gaze remained the same. Fixed.

"I will love it," she said.

"And how did you manage it?" I asked.

"Daddy died."

"Oh, Diana. I'm sorry."

"He left mother the house in Toronto and the island and some securities they'd held in tandem. Since I'm his only child and of age, he left all the money — all the actual money — to

me. Mother has her own inheritance from her family and so
Daddy left me *his* money. It was kind of him, Davis. It was
very thoughtful.''

"And so you bought yourself a houseful of pianos?''

"Yes.''

"But why New York?''

Her expression altered very slightly.

She poured herself another drink. I noticed now that she had
developed a nervous habit that involved her hair. She would
wet her fingers, absently, as part of any other gesture she happened to be making, and in the course of the gesture she would
then wet the tip of the braid with her fingertips. It was a
graceful thing, the way she did it, but once you had cottoned to
it, it became annoying because you saw, then, that it was con-
tinually happening.

She did it while she poured her drink and while she answered
my question.

"I went to Mexico,'' she said.

I looked away. I did not really want to hear the rest, but I
was curious enough to have to listen.

"Yes. I followed them. But I had other reasons. I went to
study with di Luca. In Mexico City. But after I'd been there a
month he told me that I should not expect to concertize . . .''

"Why, in heaven's name? You were brilliant.''

She held up her hands.

"Too small,'' she said. "I do not have the 'ultimate extension'.''

She said that in quotes herself, and laughed ruefully. It made
me angry.

"Who the Christ-all is di Luca, anyway? He's only one
man. One lousy retired pianist.''

"He's the best, Davis. He is the best. He does know.''

"I've heard you play,'' I said. "I've seen you. I've seen you
play Liszt — I've seen you play Ravel. Where in the name of
God do you need more extension than that?''

"Flexible — growing extension, Davis. The ultimate. No —
don't . . .'' I had started to speak again. "It's all right. It's
over. It never began. And so I will teach. And I *will* love it.''

"Stop saying that, for God's sake."

"I'm sorry, Davis," she said. "But it's the truth. I will."

She paused. She sat back in her chair, holding her drink. She lit a cigarette, touching her hair in the process, and then she said, "Anyway, after Mexico City I went to Acapulco."

"I wish you hadn't," I said in a whisper. I don't think she heard me, for she went right on talking.

"Of course, it was pointless. I didn't see them. I don't think I wanted to, but I did want to know. I saw Jean-Paul's father. He winters there, you know. Straight out of a movie. He had a moustache and he was terribly, terribly French. I explained, more or less, who I was and he invited me to lunch. The long and the short of it is Jean-Paul is dead. After you came here — I don't know when, exactly, we discovered Jean-Paul was taking dope. He needed it because of the pain. That metal plate — you remember."

"Yes."

"Well, it began to press on his brain and it gave him great pain. And so he began to have morphine — or heroin — or something. God knows where he got it from, but he got it — probably through his father's connections in Mexico. You know that his father is mysteriously rich. Well, it's all in drugs. He's not a criminal, but of course, in that world, I suppose there are criminal connections. And Jean took advantage of this."

"Yes. Well. Now we know. I wondered about his colour, sometimes."

"Well, that's what it was. Anyway. Jean-Paul was taking these things and . . . well . . ."

Here she paused. I could tell that it was because she could not quite bring herself to mention Brett as casually as she would like to. Her face twisted and the nervous gesture happened twice, very precisely, before she continued.

". . . and so, I believe, was Brett."

Inwardly I sighed. It was hard to listen.

"He looked awful. Of course, after what you found them up to, Brett made no pretence at all. He looked it, he dressed it — he even began to talk like that. I don't know — I don't know,

Davis. I don't mind. He was beautiful. He *was* perfect. In every way. Oh, need I say more? I could understand. I could understand. I *could* understand. I . . . But he . . . he wouldn't let me.''

"That was his pride."

She changed, instantly. She stood up. She yelled.

"It was *not* his pride."

She turned away.

"His pride was that he would do anything — be anything — for or to anyone — to get what he wanted. That was the genius in him. It had never been *me* to begin with. Just money. I didn't know it. I didn't know that. But it was. It was the money I had and the fact — the fact that we lived — could live — the way we did. And Jean-Paul's money. When there was Jean-Paul, then there was Jean-Paul's house. And the books. And ultimately, of course, Jean-Paul would bring him to Mexico. To Hart Crane's old doorstep. They even went on a boat, for God's sake, and threw roses into the water where Crane jumped."

"I think that's rather nice," I said.

"Do you really!" she flashed. "Well, you would think that was nice, wouldn't you!"

"I'm sorry."

"Oh. Yes. I'm sorry too. I didn't mean that."

"Go on."

"Well, they never arrived anywhere. Because Brett gave Jean-Paul an overdose — by mistake — by *mistake* and Jean-Paul died on a train and Brett — Brett, the Beetle — do you remember, Davis? Hah! Brett went down to some crazy Puerto where the film people go and now he plays his metamorphosis under the beds down there. He sells his ability — you remember — his talent for change — to *them.''*

At the end I wanted to tell her not to talk like that — that she mustn't talk like that because it would lead to the dangerous thought that she had not just been *used* by Brett, but that *she* had used him. That she had bought him for herself. And I knew that wasn't true.

"And so you came here."

"It was away. It wasn't home. I had the money — oh, not so much as all that, once I've paid for all this — but enough. And so I'll end up with children after all."

She turned then. We smiled.

She poured another drink. I could tell that there was something else, but she did not know how to say it.

"Davis?"

"Diana?"

She looked into the glass.

I was glad to see that she was crying. It was better than the monotone — the stare — the twitch — the hardness.

"Davis," she said.

"Yes, Diana."

"Now tell me the truth, Davis. The honest to God truth."

"I will try, love."

I watched, then, and as she began to speak, I didn't watch, because at the first movement of words across her face I knew what it would be and I thought, "What an awful world it turned out to be, Diana, the world we thought was such fun." And I loved her so, right then, from so far back — so long ago — that I could not look at her for fear of seeing the disappointed face, at last, of a child.

She said, "That night, Davis. That night. The three of you — all alone. Tell me . . . did *you*?" she said, looking at me, I thought, really unafraid of the answer. There was even the try for a smile. "After all — I mean . . . I was a good girl, Davis. And so . . . if you . . ."

The hair again.

Pause.

". . . what was it like? To belong to Brett?"

1969

About a year ago I saw her mother, Mrs Galbraith. It was at the theatre in Toronto. I was not in the play — I was a member of the audience, for a change. (I was home for Eugene's wedding to Mavis.)

She stood away, perhaps thirty feet away from where I was standing, with friends, in the lobby. It was intermission.

As I say, it was Mrs Galbraith I saw first, but then I saw that there was another figure beside her. It was the figure of a child who was dressed in drab brown — a coat cut straight with a little fur collar, and she wore brown cotton gloves. Her hair was cut very short, even for a child, and she wore a beret — one of the kind with the little tail of string on the top. She wore lisle stockings and flat-heeled, patent leather shoes with straps across the instep. I wondered whose child it could be. Perhaps it was a niece. This child was at least eleven or at the very least, ten.

I looked at her, wondering who it was — whose figure that could possibly be, so bent over (she bent in towards her middle, from the small of her back) and I was thinking that perhaps she was ill, or perhaps retarded, when all of a sudden one of the gloved hands strayed up to the string on the top of the beret. And I knew.

And I knew.

And I knew and excused myself from my friends and I crossed the foyer.

I said "hello" to Mrs Galbraith.

"Davis," she said. "Oh, my dear boy. I'm so glad you're here. In a letter four or five years ago, Diana said that she had seen you."

I looked at Mrs Galbraith. I looked her straight in the eye, all the way back to my childhood. And she looked at me but her expression wavered on the verge of tears. She nodded.

I looked at Diana. It was almost impossible for her to look back. Her eyes were only able to open if she looked straight ahead, from a set position.

She said, from a seeming distance, "Is it you, Davis?"

And I said, "Yes. It's me."

She said, "Let me see you, then."

I looked at Mrs Galbraith. Mrs Galbraith said, "Put her hands on your shoulders, Davis."

I did so, and as I did the action lifted Diana's head.

"That's quite an extension," I said.

She smiled.

"Hello."

Nothing will ever be as hard again as that. Looking back. Right into her eyes.

It mattered so.

I said, "Hello, Diana."

And she let down her arms.

Her head fell, till all I saw was the top of her beret.

I made a hopeless gesture at Mrs Galbraith and simply walked off. I think I went to the washroom. I don't know. I certainly didn't go back to the play.

I haven't been able to say it till now, but now I will and that's the end of it.

"Good-bye, Diana."

Good-bye.

What Mrs Felton Knew

On October the sixteenth a car pulled onto the shoulder of the road at about 10:45 a.m.

The driver was a man called Green, and beside him sat his wife and two-year-old daughter. In the back seat of the car, his mother, his father, and his aunt lay asleep, and his four-year-old son was stretched out across their knees.

The car could be described as beige, the colour of dust. The license plates were black, and the chrome of the fenders had worn away. It was the sort of motorcar you would call "serviceable" — but little else.

Neither of the children stirred or showed any sign of life, but Mrs Green was partially awake and she said, without opening her eyes, "Where are we now?"

Mr Green said, "This road is called the eleventh concession road of Horace Township, but I can't tell you what county we're in."

And she said, "Oh. But I had a dream and I thought we were climbing." It was at this point that she opened her eyes. "We're not alone," she said. "There's a house right there."

"Yes," said Mr Green. "I've been looking at it. Wondering."

"Wondering what, Harry? What?"

"It looks lived in."

"Yes, it does," said his wife, "and there are flowers in the garden, too."

"Those are Scarlet Runners," said Mr Green. "Not flowers. Beans."

"Do you think . . .?" said Mrs Green.

"I am thinking," he said. "I am. Be quiet."

Mrs Green watched him as he thought. Her eyes were a dusty colour and for some reason she had no eyelashes and no eyebrows. She was thirty. There was a sore on her hand. She was afraid to comb her hair. Her nostrils and the roof of her mouth were in constant pain. And she touched her daughter but her daughter did not wake.

"The children are hungry," she whispered automatically.

"Be quiet, Verna," said Mr Green. "Just be quiet."

"But Harry. A house. Red Runners. A rocking chair, for Christ's sake!"

"I know it. I know. I'm thinking."

They both sat quiet and listened.

A dog barked and Verna Green caught her breath.

"A dog, Harry. Oh, God — a dog . . ."

"I know," said Mr Green. "I heard."

Mrs Green gave a frantic look through the windows. They did not want a dog to find them. A dog could be very dangerous. Two weeks ago they had found a car by the side of a road with its doors standing open and three dogs . . .

"Get that out of your head," said Mr Green. "Right now. This instant. Quit it."

"I'm sorry."

"Roll up the windows. Forget it. That isn't going to happen. To us."

"Yes, Harry. I know it. All right. I'm fine."

She watched him carefully. His eyes, like her own, looked terrible. His hands shook involuntarily. She wanted to touch him, to calm him, to calm herself — to let him know, irrevocably, that she was right there with him, but she knew that they mustn't touch. That much she remembered. That much she knew.

Outside, the weather was calm and warm and brilliant. The sunshine hurt them, but it was beautiful if you squinted to see it. The road they had pulled onto rose and fell before them in a straight line, passing over hills and valleys with farms down either side.

"It's a little like our own road was," said Verna. "And our own farm. Eh?"

He didn't answer.

Instead he tried to glance at his parents, aunt, and son in the back of the car. He had to use the rear-view mirror to see them because he could not turn around. They were gray-coloured and he was not certain this was because of fatigue. He thought of trying to force his way into some town.

And then there was an old man all of a sudden standing with a dog on the lawn across the road.

"We'll have to move on now," said Harry.

"No," said Verna. "He has the dog on a rope. Wait and see what he does."

The old man, whose name was Turvey, stared at the Greens and the Greens stared back.

"Shouldn't we speak to him?" Verna asked. "Please? He looks so nice and quiet over there."

"Don't open the window," said Harry. "The dog might smell us."

"But I'm not afraid any more," she said. "The dog is on a rope."

"That man might let go of the rope. Do as you're told and leave the window alone."

"But Harry — the *children*. Move on? Jesus! Move? There are *beans* over there . . ."

"Look at the children," said Harry. "Look at them."

She did. "But Harry — please — move on is crazy anyway."

"Look out the window. At that man."

"He's a nice old man is all . . ."

"*Look* at him. He knows what we are."

Verna stared and knew that her husband was right. The old

man had bitten off the look of compassion in his eyes and his lips were set with that awful resignation everyone knew about now. It was second nature to read this look and never to have to hear the words "get out — I can't help you — I want to but I can't." You just considered all that *said* and moved on.

"Should we wave at him to say we understand?" said Verna.

"No. He knows we understand. See? He's trying to find the right things to say . . . so — we'll just go. Are you with me? *Shall* we leave?"

"Yes, Harry. All right. Yes. We'll leave. I love you." She looked down at the pale head in her lap. "If I was still a mother — but I'm not. So we can go . . ."

Harry Green looked at his wife. He broke the rule and touched her. "You mustn't cry," he said. "You'll hurt yourself so bad."

"I can't help it," said Verna. "After all, my God, I'm still human — whatever they say."

She held their child and Harry started the car and they began to leave.

The old man across the road raised his hand and Harry nodded.

"The old man saluted us," he said to Verna.

"Yes," said Verna, "I saw him. He was a nice man. He understood."

"Yes," said Harry and they were driving now, back on the highway, with their eyes out for the tanker trucks or any other signs of danger.

"Did you notice," said Verna, "the church at that corner? Across from where the old man lived?"

"No," said Harry. "I didn't."

"Well, yes. There was a church. There really was. Isn't that just crazy?"

Driving faster, Harry said yes, that it was crazy, and Verna held on tighter to the body in her lap.

"I wonder," she said, "If it's going to happen to *them*. There, on that road."

"Of course it will," said Harry. "It only takes time."

Better they should kill themselves now, she thought. But I

mustn't say that. And I won't.

They just drove.

And the next day was Sunday.

The first sign that it was happening to them, that it was their turn, came late on that Sunday evening.

An airplane flew over.

But not everyone was quick enough to leave.

Only Arthur King arose before first light on that Monday morning to set his remaining animals free in the valley. By four-thirty, rigid with silence, he had completed loading their truck with supplies and necessities and his wife had roused the children from the last ignorance of sleep.

At sunrise there was the putt of a motor. No one had spoken yet. Not even a child. Arthur and his wife gazed with stoic regret upon all that they left behind them — house and happiness, land and animals, and then, with their children beside them, they clambered into the cab of the truck and went away.

They did not say good-bye to their neighbours, knowing that whoever was left behind would understand their leaving and, hopefully, do likewise. At once.

The eleventh concession was exactly two-and-a-half miles long, corner to corner, and the Kings' farm was located more or less centrally. All told, there were six farms and up west, near the highway, the abandoned church. Right by the highway you could not really say there was a *farm*, but there was a small house and two acres and old man Turvey.

Perhaps Turvey was a Mennonite, because his house was unpainted shingle and on a day of winter sunshine it shone silver with age like a gray mirror in the snow. Turvey had only the dog — no wife, no children, and very little identity. No one ever saw him except on summer mornings when he would sit on his small green lawn, scratching the head of his dog. By late autumn, man and dog had retired into the house and did not emerge till spring. Like everyone else, Turvey had been dispossessed of radio, television, and telephone, but unlike everyone else, he did not fall back on gossip for news. People said that of all those allowed to live along the road, only Turvey had found the Secret of Life — which was silence. For all speech had become synonymous with Fear.

Moving east, then, from the old man and the church, you came to the Jewell place, Kings', and Feltons'. Past Feltons' there was a breach of wilderness which was cut by the river. On the west bank of the river were the Cormans, and beyond them, on the other side of the road, was Barney Lambert. By Lambert's the road turned and was gone. It disappeared townward into the trees.

Monday at noon, the childless Jewells got into their station wagon and went away, leaving their farm to the whisper of mice — and there remained then only the Feltons, Cormans (by the river), and Barney Lambert — plus old Turvey.

At 2:00 p.m., Monday, the second airplane flew over. It cut a few high white lines into the sky and departed without making its presence more than obliquely obvious. It was there; it was gone. Its meaning remained a question.

Harvey Felton phoned Joe Corman and said, "Well, are you staying?" and Joe Corman said, "Yes, until we're absolutely certain."

But Felton was feeling more than mere apprehension now because his neighbours, the Kings, had already left. Through binoculars there was something very unnerving about their barn door standing wide open like that, and the horses gone and the cows gone and only the cat wandering lost and sitting silently magnified at the back door of the King house, which did not and would never again open for it.

So, at four o'clock, Harvey Felton, his wife and two sons got into their truck and drove down the road to the Cormans'. One boy sat between them and Mrs Felton held the other on her lap. As they went along, Kate Felton stared quietly at the annual tragedy of the falling leaves and thought: this is so natural. It's natural. Why can't they just leave us alone with what's natural like this?

Joe Corman's house was particularly small, so the two families, replete with babies and dogs, held their meeting on the bridge, while the children threw stones into the water.

Felton had long, rustic bones and gray skin — except on his face, where the bones were feminine small and the skin remarkably pink. He had great thick fingers whose dried, cracked skin had not been flesh-coloured since he'd ceased, at twelve, to be a schoolchild — and standing on the bridge, he kept trying to jam these fingers down the closed collar of his denim shirt, or into the belt loops of his pants, or, fisted together, into his armpits. To no avail.

It couldn't ever be right to leave, Felton's erratic posture seemed to say. It was wrong. No matter what the Government said, or how many licences they issued or denied, these people had always been here — always — all of them — for genera-tions impossible to tell — and it didn't matter that they *should* leave or that they *must*, according to law — it was just wrong, and he simply could not get over that. He could not reason any more and his wife became afraid.

Mrs Corman, so large that she was semi-invalid, was not afraid but she was curious. She stacked her bulk against the stone abutment of the bridge and watched the laconic anima-tion of the men and the stilled, waiting face of the only other woman — Kate Felton. Mrs Corman cleaned her fingernails with an old guitar pick of her son's, but Mrs Felton was pale and catatonic, with a blanket thrown over her emotions.

Mrs Corman felt so sorry for Kate Felton that it was difficult to watch her and to stand so close to her. Stay or go. She herself was relatively relaxed in the knowledge that her own husband could make up his mind to act on a set decision. But poor Kate was caught in a terrific panic of wanting to go *now* — of having to get out clean without the delay of debate — even without the delay of thought — but her husband, Harvey, just stared with a reminiscent eye into the sliding water, not knowing what to do. Afraid to stay, fearful of going, Harvey Felton was beyond being able to save his wife and children — and Mrs Corman knew it. She wanted to say so, but it was not her place to speak. A family was a family; you simply didn't interfere.

She could not quite hear the voices of the men and she could no longer bear to look at Kate, so she turned away and looked back at her own beloved house — semi-lost among the trees by the river. We've lived here all our lives, she thought. Joe laid that shingle only last May, and I planted the bulbs on Thurs-day. Why, they renewed our licence in July! So why won't they let us stay here now? And what'll we do with the dog?

At five, the E.R.A. Forestry Siren began to wail on the outskirts of town and the meeting on the bridge broke up. If another plane came that night, it was decided, or if there was even a hint of tanker trucks on the highway, then the Cormans would leave. But if there were no plane and no activity on the road, then they would be satisfied that it was not happening yet and they would stay. For a while. Until it did.

Still, Harvey Felton went home from their meeting not knowing.

And it happened.

At 3:10 a.m. a helicopter stuttered through the night and was above the road for at least fifteen minutes before it finally departed. The Cormans had lain awake and now they began to rise and dress, knowing exactly what to do. They started in to fill the back of their truck and both the men, father and son, went down to set the livestock loose.

Up at the Feltons', Harvey heard the helicopter and sighed and got out of bed and went into the bathroom and locked the door. He was thinking that if he could be alone, with just the lightbulb and the mirrors and the mesmeric glitter of being bathed and warmed and steamed in memory — if he could just sink into this roomful of pleasures, womb-like, with the comfort of water — if he could only stay there a moment — an hour — he would be safe. Perhaps he could even gain admission to his courage, if he could be alone with the sanity of the past.

But Kate got up and hadn't slept either and went down the hall to the door and stood there scratching at it lightly so as not to wake the children. And she wanted to get in, through to him, but he would not let her and so she stood there (leaning, really), whispering through the door but thinking that she was shouting, until at last she lost her voice. And when all she got was a stammered protraction of Harvey's indecision of the afternoon (in fact, she thought, of all his life), she wandered from the door so quietly that he was not aware she'd left.

The Arthur Kings being gone, there were no immediate neighbours to hear her when she fired a gun, point-blank, into the temples of each of her sleeping sons. Or when she prayed and turned the thing into her own mouth without amen because she didn't want time to think about conclusions or how you came to them. She simply pulled the trigger and the whole thing was over.

For her.

So, at about five o'clock, when Harvey Felton rode away on the back of Joe Corman's pick-up truck, his feet dangled bare from his long-boned legs, and one hand was over his face. He hadn't even dressed, and as if to fortify his reason, he'd gone over to Kings' in just his pajamas, and had brought along the abandoned cat when he'd walked down the road to the bridge.

Neither Joe nor Joe Junior, spoke of the blood that covered him, and because of it, no one asked after his wife and his sons. In her mind, little Nella Corman was certain that Harvey had committed murder, but Mrs Corman, having taken her private look at Kate on the bridge the previous afternoon, merely sighed and tried to remember whether they had brought with them their own guns. And saw that yes, they had.

Barney Lambert's wife was many years dead and his daughter had some time ago been accepted for Government-approved marriage in the City. So he lived alone.

Barney had set the expression on his face the day his wife died and no one had seen it alter since. It was not a dour expression, or even sad. It was just set and there was never animation.

But he was liked. His eyes showed you his whole life and sometimes yours, too, as you stood talking to him. Through his silence he could make the wisdom or the foolishness of what you said apparent. For a man who did so much listening, he had remarkably small ears, and when he was in his twenties and thirties, people had regarded him as the best-looking, the most athletic, and the kindest young man in the district. He had married Ethel Felton, a cousin of Harvey's. But that was all a long time ago, before you had to have a licence to live, and Barney was fifty-two years old now, living on remembrance.

When his daughter met and married her man and was given her clearance to live in the City and was gone, Barney closed the gates down by the road and without ill will of any kind, just removed himself from the people around him and became inaccessible. But he remained all that he had been — kindly, intelligent, friendly if met — and silent. He took to cultivating cabbages (a difficult crop) and to raising a menagerie of animals culled from their world without any apparent thought for their usefulness to him. Only of his usefulness to them. He had three burros, a mule, two goats, a cow, three Canada geese, and a dog. In the house he kept a cat and another dog who was too old to get around.

He lived a plain life within a certain discipline that was neither rigid nor lax. He was aware of Time but never ran to do anything. He was not a paragon of tidiness, but he never threw a paper or a pillow on the floor.

Barney had heard all that was going on — the aircraft, the various leave-takings, and the E.R.A. Forestry Siren. When the Cormans drove by from the river on the Tuesday morning, Barney was watching from the upstairs windows of his house, moving from room to room to see them out of sight. He noted the posture of Harvey Felton as he slumped there, holding the cat and his own face, and he remembered his own grief and he knew, more or less, what had happened to Kate Felton, and maybe to the boys, too. Barney had ceased at about the same time as everyone else to be aware that there was a God, and so he did not pray, even mentally, for these would-be survivors. A few women could tolerate prayers, but men could not, and children were alarmed by the ridiculous posture of prayer and by the closed eyes and the silent, moving lips. Still, Barney had respect and awe for something and that something was Nature and so, when he saw his neighbours depart and one of them was in grief, he slapped his thighs with the palms of his hands and gave the Universal sigh.

Then he went down to the kitchen where the old dog was asleep under the stove, and he lit the fire to make coffee.

Five-thirty, and a pale, high light beyond the windows.

Barney went outside and remembered where the wheelbarrow was and brought it round to the back door. It was a sizeable barrow of the kind used for carrying manure — not one of those small, neat, garden types, but large and serviceable. He piled blankets and two pillows into it and then went back.

He got out a cardboard carton and a can opener and filled the carton with tinned and bottled food and put the can opener in his pocket. He filled two five-gallon tins with water. Then he stuck toilet paper and a First Aid Kit under his elbows and lifted the carton and carried it outside. He came back for the water and out again, and then back again.

At last, about 6:00 a.m., he sat down to smoke a cigarette and to drink coffee and he tried most of all not to look around the room he was in, and not to want to get up and go through the house, memory by memory. He wanted everything to be as it was now in his mind, even if he remembered it wrong, without the pain of refreshment. So he sat still and squinted at the cup and at his hands and at the cigarette. He did not even look at the table top. He just thought about right now and he saw only what was right there.

There was, however, one very bad moment when the sun made it absolutely all the way over the horizon and had ceased being red or orange or any other colour and was just light — and Barney felt a terrific urge to put his head down and hide. He did then, for one faltered second, give his glance to the rifle in the corner and his mind to the box of bullets in the drawer. But he got out of it by standing up. His pride reminded him that his child had been accepted into Civic Society, that one of them at least had made it and that he could make it, too, if he tried.

He took a spoonful of honey and ate it and another spoonful which he carried over carefully to the old dog.

"Come on," he said, "it's time to wake up now. And go."

And he got to his knees and the old dog, still lying down, licked the spoon clean, and then Barney put the spoon down on the floor and left it there forever — and pulled the dog's box out from under the stove and soothed the old dog with a litany of hums and haws and lifted him up so that the old dog's head could rest against his neck and he walked out of the house and laid the old dog very carefully in the barrow on the blankets and pillows and surrounded him with the tinned water and the boxed food and the toilet paper and the First Aid Kit and, at the very last, the cat — and they set off toward the barn.

And all the while the E.R.A. Siren screamed at the edge of the town: This is the End. This is the End. This is the End.

In some instances there were spectators, but this depended on the season and on the direction of the wind. It also depended upon the availability of masks and on whether the event took place on a weekday or on a weekend.

Civic people, rich in safety, could afford to watch from the privacy of the air, and there were usually a few groups of trainees who went up, too, in University helicopters, but as with all such things, Time creates tolerance and even boredom and on this particular day the only people who were by were there to work.

You may wonder what the townspeople made of all this, and probably question the morality of their silence, because they were so close to these events and even neighbours of the victims. But they were neighbours only in the tactical sense. In fact, they formed a bulwark — a wall of protective innocence — between the City-dwellers and the Rural Expendables. The townspeople smiled among themselves and nodded at the sounding of the E.R.A. Forestry Siren and said things like "Goodness, another fire" or "When will it ever end?" and they went inside on these days and closed and locked their doors and pretended through the following weeks that they did not smell or see or hear what patently they did — what certainly they had to. They were particularly adept at going blind.

Barney went down the lane unnoticed and got to the barn and opened the doors.

He had known all along that when the time came he would not leave his animals, as most people had, so there was an air of well-rehearsed ritual to all that he did. His plan was to get as deep into the swamp in the valley as possible, and thereby to try for temporary survival, at least. If he could save himself or even one of his animals, then his protest would register with Nature, which was all that mattered to him.

Barney hitched the mule to the wagon and transferred the contents of the barrow onto the wide, long planks, together with several bales of hay, three bags of feed, and the cage with the three geese. The old dog lay trustful and quiet on the nest of blankets and the stable dog got up on the seat beside where

Barney would sit. The cat dug a hole in the barnyard and relieved itself and afterwards leapt up beside the old dog and lay down to stare at the geese.

It was at this point that Barney remembered his sheepskin coat and knowing that without it he might perish in the cold of the swamp he went all the way back to the house to get it.

When he got into the house the echo of the opening door leaked into distant emptiness upstairs like a prowling animal and Barney closed his eyes and waited for the silence to return.

But it didn't.

A new sound shied in behind him and beyond him and it came from so far away that he could at first only imagine that he heard it.

Trucks.

Tankers.

The highway.

Barney gained his composure by remembering anger.

They were coming now and he was to be the next victim of the new E.R.A.

And so he went very calmly into the back hall and got down his sheepskin coat from its peg and put it on — for all that it seemed to be a summer's day — and he took his binoculars and went out onto the road to see what he could see.

In his mind he practised the moment when he must leave the road and run to the barn in order to save the animals and then he sat down on a large rock near the gate and watched, through the binoculars, the distant end of the road where there was a hill beyond which you could not see the deadly highway.

He wondered if Turvey and *his* old dog had got away. And he thought not. He wondered if he could get the beautiful old church into his mind, but, along with God, he couldn't. He thought of Myrna Jewell's chickens and what might have become of them and of Arthur King as a boy when they were both boys and he tried to get by the Feltons' house in his mind, without going inside, but he kept thinking that he knew Harvey too well and too long not to guess at what had happened and for the first time since she'd died, he blessed his own wife's death as a prize of good fortune that she should not have had to face this moment now because she might have had to do what he instinctively sensed poor Kate had done.

And then he was able to take a real look through the glasses at the Cormans' new roof and to go along by the lenses into their barnyard and to see there some stupid cow who'd come back from the swamp in the valley and he wavered on the brink of going over with the gun to drive her off or to kill her but there wasn't time.

The E.R.A. Forestry Siren gave another earnest wail at the moment, rising into a steady blast — a wail that would continue into the night and perhaps even into the next day, depending on whether it rained or not and on whether a wind rose or not and on whether anyone was seen along the road.

It was not until rehearsing that sequence in his mind, as he sat there waiting and listening to the siren, that Barney knew he was going to let himself be seen.

He was going to do what perhaps no one else had done till now. He was going to force a pair of eyes to look into his own. Someone had to *see* someone.

The incongruous sun blazed down and Barney loosened the sheepskin coat around him, lit another cigarette, and gave a look through the glasses at his own barnyard.

All was quiet. The dogs and the cat and even the geese seemed to sleep and the other animals just waited as if they must know, and had trusted that he would do this. He smiled. He would do it. He would start a conscience. Somehow. In someone. Right here. On this road.

There was no wind at all — not even a breeze — and it was so clear that when the first sign that the tankers were in operation came to him, it was in the thought that the sky was filling with beautiful great clouds and that he might be saved by rain.

But the sweeping hiss of the distant hoses cut that hope short before it was real.

They were spraying.

Barney tried not to, but could not avoid rising to his feet. Instinctively he threw down his cigarette, stood up, and began to breathe great gulps of the last pure air. He felt dizzy, both from fear and from too much sudden oxygen. He fought back the temptation of paralysis which wanted to conquer him. The end of the road was alive.

Great swaying flowers of spray arched into the blue, topped with a rolling flood of cloud.

This was what they called E.R.A. — or, to give the solvent its soothing Administration name: "Environmental Redevelopment Agent." Sprayed from hoses, its crystal drops burned the oxygen from the air, killing every single living thing within the circumference of their fall. It wasn't rain it formed — it was beautiful snowy mist. And when a thing died, it died in a flameless acid fire so intense that only ashes remained.

The E.R.A. tanker trucks were yellow and they were manned by suited E.R.A. Foresters in orange and green, who wore oxygen tanks on their backs and asbestos gloves and shoes, and who could only be faced through the treated plastic visors of their helmets, and who had no voices except amongst themselves, inside the safety of their suits.

They came along the road in mechanical procession, stepping out in unison to the spurting rhythm of their hoses.

The siren had mounted to its ultimate wail now — continuous.

All Barney wanted was one face — just one pair of eyes before he ran. He knew that he could only hope to see them through his binoculars, that he could let them get no closer than the Cormans' by the river, but he knew, too, that from that distance he could see the moment of recognition and that was all he wanted: a look to mark his own existence in another man's eyes, before he fled.

They were approaching the river now — three tankers, each leashed by hoses to six men, and behind the tankers a travesty of hope so insidious that Barney could not believe his eyes — an ambulance, marked by huge red crosses. How could it ever stop to take in survivors when of course, by the very nature of the solvent, there could be no survivors? It was there only to satisfy the grotesque conscience of the Government and of all the World Bodies that were dedicated to Cities and that supported this scheme for the control of rural populations.

He had risen now and was standing, poised on his toes, so

completely flooded inside with adrenalin that he was virtually ill and retching. But he jammed the binoculars against the bones of his face and waited.

It was unfortunate that he did not run instead. But it was too late. The meeting of eyes was adhesive when it happened and once he found them and was staring and being stared at, everything but panic stopped.

He heard himself saying, "Child — child — child — they're only children" and he felt his stomach heave over and the sickly sweet taste of curdled honey rise into his mouth. For he had seen the eyes of a boy no more than sixteen years old. And they had not been what he'd thought he'd see. For there was no fear in them and not an ounce of human recognition and he had not known that that could be — that such eyes existed as he saw there beyond the glass and the plastic — blind, but cognizant. Signalling sight, but reflecting nothing more than the reaction of a meter when it registers the presence of electrical force. The boy's eyes looked and let him go, without a flicker of human response.

Barney threw down the glasses and ran.

And all this while, old Turvey and his dog had been ashes for almost half an hour.

When he got to the barn, Barney threw open all the remaining doors, letting free the cow, the goats, and the burros, and he began to shout at the mule in such a peculiar way that he himself did not recognize the language. Perhaps there were no words any more. Perhaps there never had been and certainly there never would be again. He could not even gather the sentence of a thought. He was noise and movement and something that seemed furious, but was only afraid.

The wagon slugged off toward the top of the hill and as it went it rolled so slowly, drawn by the mule and pushed by Barney, that all the animals, Barney included, had the time and misfortune to catch the smell of E.R.A., which is to say, the time and misfortune to begin to burn.

There came screams, utterly unlinked to any pain that can be described — because as they pushed and pulled and dragged themselves forward, parts of them were already turning to ash.

The clouds of E.R.A. mounted back along the road in the terrible beauty of their purity and they were rolling up like walls around them, hissing with the massive immolation of trees and grass and flowers and insects — birds, mice, and anything that lived that comes to mind.

Barney only knew to push and the rest was all pain.

Until he got to the top of the hill.

And was saved. With his three geese, the old dog, the cow, three burros, two goats, and the mule.

By the dying thought of green.

But he had tried.

There is no ending to this story. There is only what is and was and will be. How can I possibly say that any one of the survivors survived? For how am I to *know*? But you must have seen as many abandoned cars and trucks and trailers as I have. And heard as many packs of wild dogs. And come to as many "Detour: Road Closed" signs as I have.

I, too, live in a house by a road.

So, perhaps, do you.

But I'm not fooled, as I fear many are, by the current propaganda.

For instance, they recently moved the yellow tankers up to a station near us. Now they're telling us (and certainly many have believed it) that these trucks are only oil tankers. Some new delivery system for a factory that hasn't been built yet. How gullible we are. The other day I saw two men in green and orange suits and I actually heard some fool describe these costumes as a new snowsuit to wear skiing. And they've blown the Forestry signal constantly this last week and there hasn't been a single fire — so why is that, I ask you? And last night there was a helicopter . . .

But my neighbours are believing. They trust. Why, a government man was around here just last week selling bug killer. D.D.T. they call it.

And my neighbour bought it.

Now *why*, do you think, in the present scheme of things, would he do that?

The People on the Shore

In the summer of 1960, on a Friday, Mrs Lewis was brought down onto the sand by her daughter Elvira and by her Nurse, Miss Cunningham. She caught my image in the corner of her eye; turned to see me head-on; gave me a look of recognition and farewell; chose *me* to say good-bye to with her final glance — and died.

The place I speak of — write of — where Mrs Lewis died, is an old hotel that sits above the sand in Maine. Every summer, since the summer I was born, we have gone down to this hotel from Toronto, just as all the summers since the summer *he* was born, my father went down before us. That is the sort of hotel — of place — it is.

In front of the hotel, between the hotel and the sea, there is a stretch of sand precisely one-and-one-eighth miles long, on which the children play and the athletes run all summer. This sand is also walked by a variety of older people; some, like my father, life-time summer residents: and there is one old man who, every summer, stops each person in turn, to remark that, if he had the eyes of several hundred eagles and was facing out to sea, nothing should hinder his view of South America. But, of course, the distance does and there is nothing to be seen but the endless curve of the horizon. And there are the ships: an occasional tanker, or steamer, or Boston-bound freighter puffs away, always losing its balance and disappearing over the edge and there are sailboats on the weekends and lobster-boats whenever the traps are ripe or need resetting.

At either end of the beach there is a promontory, each with descending stretches of sea-rocks that are prone to the tides. In the olden days, these were the scene of much shipwreck and disaster. Now, there is still the occasional fool, trapped out walking on the rocks, who will be drowned at high tide: but this is rare and there has been no death by drowning for the last three years.

The hotel itself was built in 1855, though I have always thought it was older than that: as old as the trees themselves that were cut and planed and painted to make its clapboard sides.

Like myself, Loretta Lewis had come to the hotel as a child, but we were not of the same generation: when she died, Mrs Lewis was fifty and I was twenty-five years her junior. "In her day," as my mother was wont to say, "she was a great beauty" with dark hair and a flawless complexion; the marks, in those days, of incomparable good looks. However, as she aged and married, aged and had her children, Mrs Lewis grew larger until, in her latter years, she was one of those round women you cannot quite bring yourself to call "fat" because their beauty is somehow enhanced by the extra pounds. She shone with good health and exuded the sort of warmth that in the theatre would be described as "star-quality."

She was far from being a paragon. When she called her children, for instance, the whole beach turned and wondered what was wrong. And I once overheard her, myself, telling the venerable and much kow-towed to Mrs Hogan to "go to hell." And then there was the terrible argument she had with the Ottawa Jacksons, (not to be confused with the Cincinnati Jacksons), which took place in the lobby of the hotel one evening before supper. Everyone overheard her, this time, and the

Ottawa Jacksons were so mortified by the fury of Mrs Lewis' anger that they didn't eat in the dining room for the next two days, but had all their meals sent up on trays to their rooms. I forget what the argument was about, and I doubt that anyone — (with the exception of the Jacksons) — remembers that, except that we all remember Loretta's terrific anger and the way she dominated the dining room that night, with her enormous back set against the whole room; and the tone of her voice, as she spoke to Mr Lewis and to the Lewis children, sharp and clear and precisely enunciated through ritual requests for "a little more salt" and "a little less fidgeting" from Elizabeth, Elvira and Angus, all of whom had somehow lost their appetite. But not Mrs Lewis. She ate all their dinners that night, as if in defiance of the room at large — knowing, I suppose, that everyone was watching her. She even ate part of her husband's dinner and when, at long last their meal was over, Mrs Lewis led her family with ringing steps across the floor and out onto the South porch, visible to all, where she immediately broke through one of the older rocking-chairs, by sitting on it too suddenly.

There was a quick and deathly hush, which seemed to pervade the entire hotel. It appeared even to invade the lawns, for not a single bird gave sound. The sea-flow could be imagined ceasing, while we waited. Knives, forks, spoons and napkins were poised between plates and open mouths. Mrs Hogan had been in the midst of pouring her laxative-salts, and even the fall and effervescence of these were dried up.

And then it came.

Loretta's laughter: ringing out over the porches and in through the windows: pouring down over the lawns and through the dunes to the beach, where, for all we knew, it might even have reached South America.

We could all look out and see Loretta being lifted by her family onto her feet, with the cane seat of the broken rocking-chair sticking out like a grotesquely mangled straw-hat or wicker halo round her behind and, at that, *we* all began to laugh. Us, the Lewises, even Mrs Hogan — everyone was laughing: everyone except the Ottawa Jacksons, who were

ensconced far away from laughter, up in their rooms with
supper-trays balanced on their knees.

No, she was not a paragon, but she had extraordinary vir-
tues. One of these was an understanding of children that was
beyond the normal everyday understanding you could expect
from a parent. Loretta had some way of remembering what it
was, precisely, to be a child.

I was ten. Would that make her thirty-five or so? Approximately, yes — and she already had Elvira, who toddled, and
Elizabeth in arms, though Angus was another three-four years
away from life. Angus was born when it was said Loretta was
getting too old for children — but, that isn't part of this story.

On the day I'm trying to remember, I could see my brother
far off down the sands, in a white sun-hat and a black bathing
suit. He was wading far out after some other child's model sail
boat that had got marooned in one of the tidal pools. Michael is
older than me, and — at this time — he was on the verge of his
adolescence. He was a worldly child, who read a great deal and
he made a great fuss about being 'shy.' But, the fact was, he
had a great many friends and, amongst them, he was always
accorded the rank of leader. In fact, he was leading now,
followed by a lot of children, out towards the model shipwreck.
To me — his back was his most familiar feature. I just wasn't a
part of the world he was trying to create: neither was he, with
the exception of his back, a part of mine. My world was a place
devoid of other children, pretty well. I intended it to be so:
something in me — possibly perverse — didn't like other
children: particularly of my own age. They seemed always to
be something I was not — and to know something that was
beyond my understanding.

Along came Mrs Lewis, with spade and pail.

I was sitting on the sand, with my feet and ankles covered
with a towel and I believe there was a rise where I sat, a sort of
hummock, perhaps created by an old, deflated castle. Mrs
Lewis had lost Elvira.

To have lost Elvira — even by the sea — was not so alarming
as it might seem. There was always a life-guard, who kept his

eye on the children: Elvira was probably with Miss Cunningham, anyway — or with her father and so, when Mrs Lewis
spoke, she was merely curious:

"Tiffy — have you seen Elvira?"

"No ma'am."

She stood there, casting down shade over my shoulders and
out-stretched legs.

"Oh well. If she wants her pail and shovel, she'll scream for
them — " (Mrs Lewis smiled) — "and that's always the
easiest way of finding out where she is. Mmm?"

She laughed.

I looked away.

There was a pause, behind my back, and I could sense that
she was making up her mind about whether to stay or go away
and leave me alone.

She stayed.

"My ankles sunburn, too," she said. "Do you mind if I sit
down — or, do you want to be alone?"

"I don't mind," I said.

She began to scoop out an indentation in which to sit.
Nobody ever sat directly onto the top layer of sand. That was
the sure sign of a novice on the beach — and 'lifers' knew
better.

Finally, Mrs Lewis sat down and placed Elvira's pail and
spade between us.

"I had the most extraordinary dream last night," she said,
at once. "Would you like me to tell you?"

"Yes, please."

"Well — we were all lined up, right here, on the sand, looking out to sea. There was something going on out there and we
were all very carefully watching, trying to see what it was. It
wasn't a storm and it wasn't a sinking ship. It wasn't someone
drowning — or any of the things you might think it was."

"Was it a submarine?" I asked.

"No. It wasn't a submarine. And it wasn't an airplane
crash, either: nothing at all like that."

Mrs Lewis lighted a cigarette from a package she carried in

Elvira's pail and, as she was waving the match out, and taking the first, deep puffs of smoke, old Mrs Hogan went by — (old even then — old always, I suspect) — down by the water, with her parasol tipped at the sun, a relic of her mother's and another age.

"There goes Mrs Hogan," said Mrs Lewis: "all alone, as ever. But, not in the dream. Do you know, Tiffy, in the dream, Mrs Hogan stood right up here on the sand with all the rest of us — and, I guess you don't remember him, but I do, from a long, long while ago: Mr Hogan was standing here with her. Oh! There were lots of people here. People you *would* remember — people you might not. Have you ever looked in the photograph albums in the library?"

"Yes."

There were books dating way back to the 1800s and the earliest guests at the hotel.

"Well, all of those people were here, too, dressed exactly as they are in the pictures: up here on the sand, in their photograph-clothes. And we still didn't know what it was we were looking for. All we knew was — there it was out there, somewhere above, or on the water. . . ."

"Why not *in* it?" I asked.

"Well, now: that's a good question," she smiled. "We didn't even think of that one."

"I still think it might have been a submarine."

"No. It definitely was not a submarine."

She smoked for a moment and, when she saw that I was looking off towards Michael, who, by now had reached the marooned toy ship, she looked off towards him, too, and then she said:

"I had a sister who was always saving things. And I always used to think — oh, dear — I'll never, never be able to save anything — because she'll always get there and save it first. . . ." Mrs Lewis looked at me, very frankly, through the smoke from her cigarette. She met my gaze, as serious as any friend, without that autocratic-adult smile that children dislike so much: just looking at me — and then:

"It's just as good to want to be brave — just as good to get there second, you know, as it is to *be* brave and get there first."

I was so shocked by her understanding that I looked away, and I can remember thinking that if I looked at her, the meaning of what she had said would alter and that we wouldn't understand one another any more.

Mrs Lewis must have sensed this, because she watched, for quite a long time, a sea-gull, floating above us on the off-shore draught: and then she sighed and buried her cigarette in the sand and said: "the most curious thing of all, about this dream, was that here we all were on the beach — every single person you can think of, as I say, and *more* — Mrs Hogan, Mr Hogan, me . . . Elvira . . . Mr Lewis — the Jacksons — you — and your mom and your dad, Michael, Miss Cunningham, Joe — Frances — Joellen — Harry . . . Mrs Clarke: everyone you can think of, ever . . . ."

"Janet and Aunt Kay?"

"Yes, yes: *everyone*. Bill and everyone. There we were — all of us, over and over again in all our different ages. Oh — I don't mean one of us for every year of our lives — but, well . . . I was there as a baby, being carried and I was there as a little girl and — hah! — there in those terrible pigtails my mother made me wear when I was fifteen. And, there I was older, too — and married to Mr Lewis and then with Elvira and then with Elizabeth and then . . . ."

I waited.

There was a very long pause.

I looked at her.

Her expression was curiosity itself: as if she truly couldn't comprehend the numbers of herself there had been. Or that were possible. As if there might have been too many Mrs Lewises — too many Mrs Hogans — too many Elviras — too many of each and every one of us, so that she could not fit us all together onto the beach — so that the beach had become different, larger, wavering in size.

"Were you there as old as Mrs Hogan?" I wanted to know. . .

"No, I wasn't," she said, too quickly. And after that, she shook her head and looked at me and laughed out loud. "But, *you* were," she said. "You were — and you were very, *very* old!"

We both laughed at that and finally, I asked her what it was we were watching in the dream. But, she didn't answer me all at once.

I think the answer came in two parts, with something in between, so that I thought one thing was the answer and that the other was inconsequential. Only now, do I see that they were both the answer.

"I had on a red dress," she said, evidently thinking of one of her 'selves' in the dream. "A red, *red* dress. And I hate red. I mean —" she looked at me: "I never wear it — *do* I." And then, she looked away and then she said: "Oh — look!" and she was looking out at the ocean and then, not making it clear whether this was what she had just seen, or what we had all seen in the dream, she pointed and said: "a seal. A seal. More than anything I can think of — what I've always wanted to be: and I would swim way out — a way, way out — and I could turn and look back at the people on the shore . . . ."

Her mouth was open, still open, as though there might still be more to be said: some concrete explanation — but, then Elvira was screaming: "Mummy! Mummy!" and Mrs Lewis was opening her arms to her own child, who was running across the sand and I was forgotten.

Or — so I thought for fifteen years.

It was cancer and she had asked specifically that she be allowed to come to the sea to die.

Some of the guests had thought this request was grotesque, and they shunned her altogether. Some others (a very few) were so distressed, they cancelled their accommodations and left, taking up residence at another hotel, further down the beach. But, most of us stayed: a fact that I think stands best without any explanation.

Still: there were moments when it was worse than difficult to watch her and to be there. She came down twice every day, either with Elizabeth or Elvira, and always with Miss Cunningham beside her and, until she had been seated, most people on the beach found some reason or other to look away. But, once she was down, with towels spread under and over her legs, and this great umbrella tilted to give her all its shade — and, once her back-rest was in place and her sun-hat re-adjusted — then, there would be a gradual return to the normal activities.

Games of tag sprang up from the sand like pop-up tableaux from a children's book and the swimmers ran yelling back into the waves, and all the old ladies with dogs let all their dogs off the leash and, instantly, there was dispersal, abandonment and chaos. Oh yes — one or two people would amiably pass her by, from a distance of about ten feet, making certain not to look away as they crossed her sight-path, and for a while, it was awful. It took Mr Lewis, coming up, from some other place on the beach, to bring one or two of his friends — or one or two of hers and, more and more spontaneously, as the days went on, the selected guests would be put at their ease by Loretta, and they would sit and chat with her, crossing their legs and leaning back in their chairs with every semblance of normal people. She was always so genuinely glad to see them, that, after a while, you knew you could count on the laughter. And, it always came. There was more genuine *laughter* from the Lewis enclave that summer, than from any other enclave on the beach: real laughter, never merely reassuring.

Elvira and Elizabeth each had a boy-friend that summer. Perhaps Elvira had two, although I think she was only 'serious' about the one. But, each of the girls would make a point of sitting with her — one all through the morning session — the other through the afternoon. Angus brought dogs and sea-shells to meet her.

But, curious things did take place.

The Ottawa Jacksons, for instance, who had long since reconciled their differences with Loretta, took up drinking on the beach. That is to say, they set up a bar and began their drinking at ten o'clock in the morning. Great show was made of this — the bar being decorated with a grass skirt from Hawaii and a cocktail shaker shaped like a flamingo. Music was added. A gramophone was brought down from the attic of the hotel and records entirely from another age — pre-War, distressing and confusing.

With the music, there was often 'dancing' and the dancing, one day, led to a piece of crude, unlikely exhibitionism: Mrs Jackson let the straps fall from her tailored Jantzen and exposed her breasts. No one knew what to do: after all, what could one do? She was a friend — she was a guest at the hotel. For a moment, Mrs Jackson stood there, defiantly refusing to cover herself and, when she turned, as if on purpose to show Loretta, she also smiled and there was just the flash of triumphant teeth — as if she had made an obscene gesture at Death.

Loretta looked away and someone, (I forget who it was), handed Mrs Jackson a towel and she covered herself and walked across to the bar, where she turned the record up and poured herself another drink. Later, that same day, *Mr* Jackson made a "speech to the seals" — which was meant to honour and glorify Loretta's "undying beauty." Loretta herself applauded when it was over. Nobody else did, not even Mrs Jackson: and for awhile, they retired once more to their rooms, as they had on the earlier occasion when Loretta had been so angry.

One other afternoon, very hot and lazy, the children were building moats with which to trap the incoming tide down near the shore. There was a single runner, sprinting the length of the beach, and I remember the red bandanna tied round his hair and the tireless beating of his heels on the sand and I was watching him as if he were a runner through a dream, when all of a sudden Loretta screamed.

It was not like any other sound I have ever heard, having nothing to do with fear, or alarm or even, so it seemed, with pain. It was more a shout, perhaps, than a scream and she gave it as one might shout at a distant sail on an otherwise vacant sea. It was a cry of such terrible loneliness, that it made the crowded sand seem empty.

Nobody looked around toward her: except the runner — who stopped and scanned the figures lying on the beach or sitting in their chairs. And he took off his red bandanna; made up his mind that nothing had happened and continued on his way.

She worsened. She had to. There was nothing to be done. Loretta knew this, but it was we who would not accept it.

She grew very thin; so thin that it was a marvel to see that she could walk. "How long it takes to die," she said one day to Elvira, and I have often thought of her saying that. It really only took three weeks for her to die — but she thought it was eternity.

Well.

I remember Elvira kneeling at her side, with tears streaming down her face. That was once — once only. And I remember Angus burying himself in the sand before her eyes and calmly announcing that he had "dug his own grave." I remember Elizabeth, too, kneeling there, carefully holding her mother's chin — telling her not to move — putting on lipstick for her, powdering her nose. I remember Mr Lewis standing apart with the Chairman of the Ottawa Trust, each of them digging his toes into the sand — bellies in and arms across the old men's chests, when some of the college girls, who served as waitresses, raced down to the sea in their bikinis. I remember Elizabeth's boy-friend finding an old blue bottle, which Loretta said she would "keep forever." And, I remember one last thing — and then the death of Loretta Lewis.

That August, they had put up some new kind of satellite and, since those were the young-years of space, the event of its passage through the sky was treated with the same excitement as the fall of a comet or the full eclipse of the moon.

It was planned that a "lookout" should be posted, and that when the satellite broke our horizon, the lookout would call us and we would all come running. It was expected that, if we were quick, we might have a view of the thing for just under a minute.

No one, of course, knew exactly what to expect, or what precisely to look for. Many envisioned a great, golden globe; while others expected a silver rocket, spouting stars. The children had all been allowed to stay up, and the lobby was filled with a large number of "space captains" that night —

and with a great many rocketry-experts and a multitude of miniature Flash Gordons. Some of these were the children — and others were the old men who had been in the War.

Mrs Hogan and the rest of the Delphic old were arranged, as usual, by order of ascendancy in the dowagers' corner. There, they were safely out of drafts and out of the path of running children. Each one wore a crown of blue hair and a cashmere stole, although one or two favoured a fur besides, because the nights on that particular arm of the seaboard can be as chilly as a night on the Sahara.

Out in the middle of the floor, stood the men: their backsides favouring the fire.

Everyone was present, except Loretta Lewis, Miss Cunningham and Angus.

I was standing over by the reception desk, with a view of the stairs. My companion was 'Baby' Frasier, a woman not many years my senior, whom I had known all my life. We were smoking, I remember, and drinking ginger-ale out of pale green bottles, and Baby had just said something about a movie we might go in to town to see, when Angus appeared on the staircase.

He was walking backwards, step-by-step, descending with his arms held out and up towards his mother, who was clutching his hands with her own — making her way down not *one* step at a time, but a quarter-step — an eighth-of-a-step at a time. She was talking to him all the way, telling him where to place his feet, smiling and laughing at him, while Miss Cunningham came down after them, holding Loretta upright by the back of her dress.

Baby, who had seen them too, went on in a sort of dead-voiced way about the film we might see, and I remember thinking "I wish she'd shut up about the god damn movie" and then Loretta made the last two steps to the floor of the lobby and Baby smiled at Loretta and said: "That should have been set to music: one of the nicest bits of dancing I've ever seen."

Now, while we laughed at what Baby had said, this final thing happened and it happened all at once, with a great, chaotic rush of sound and movement, so that again, it remains as a picture, for me — or perhaps as a sequence of rapidly fluttering photographs that tell a story in a few, quick seconds.

The "lookout" rushed in from the porches and gave the alarm that the satellite had been sighted. And I guess my eye swept the lobby from group to group, because it seems, in retrospect, that I can see them all. The dowagers' corner rose like a wave, with a flurry of cashmere and fur, and was joined at one end by children and at the other by what I can only describe as a "pack of mothers and fathers." A whole flotilla of nannies, dressed in evening-blue, appeared from god-knows-what far recess and crowded after, waving and calling for their wards, who were far off in the forefront of the whole stampede.

A Major-General from Boston had the good military sense to perceive at once that the pass being blocked, he and his regiment of elder statesmen and businessmen would do better to circle round through the dining room and achieve the objective with a flanking movement.

All this in seconds, as I say, and then I was aware of the girl behind the reception desk muttering "Will you please excuse me?" and then I could feel, but not see her pass me — and then Angus was standing tip-toe, trying desperately to see past the general melee by the doors to the porches: and then Loretta was saying to Miss Cunningham, "quick — quick — take Angus and follow the General through the dining room! That way, I'm sure you won't be too late to see it."

Miss Cunningham mumbled some small excuse — was forgiven — and Angus was rushed away at the run. All of a sudden the lobby was empty.

That is: there was Loretta, standing at the very centre, and Baby and I, still standing near the desk.

Loretta, I think, had forgotten even the possibility that we were there. So far as she was concerned — everyone had gone off to see the satellite.

It can't have been for long — but, it seemed a very long time that Loretta stood there, feeling herself alone. She sighed and reached out for the backs of some chairs — nearly tripped, but didn't fall down: collected herself: stared at the ceiling: raised one hand to her lips: touched them very gently with her fingers:

turned — half-turned — and almost was already looking at the floor, when she saw us.

That lobby was so high and vast, while she had stood there 'alone' — but as soon as she saw us, it shrank back down around her, and she smiled.

"You'll miss it," she said, and I thought she was going to faint, her voice was such a whisper and her colour so completely drained.

"Miss it?" said Baby: "Like bloody-God damn we will!"

And Loretta gave over completely to laughter.

"Your mother would *kill* you!" she said, and Baby said: "Let her! I don't care. Come on!"

And "come on" we did. We seemed to float — I don't know how we did it — but, all at once, we were across the lobby, Baby and me carrying Loretta all the way to the doors.

Outside, by the railings, we all three looked up with one glance and there it was: shining, floating as we had, silver in the sky, like a moon — the satellite.

Its pace was perfect: like something of glass — a small, glass hollow bulb, filled with an incandescent gas — tossed up, it seemed, or held through its perfect arc at the end of a string. We watched it in absolute silence — rising and sailing and passing over us — from the south-west, heading north-east — and, as we watched, we turned our heads and then our bodies round, to see it fall away into the dark of the horizon. But, when it was gone, we were met with the concerted gaze of the whole packed arena at the far end of the porches.

"What *are* you watching?" someone said, with faint amusement and chagrin.

"Why — the satellite," said Baby, "of course."

"But, my dear Baby," said Mrs Trent, whose voice was all catarrh and eminence: "the satellite is over *there*." And she pointed — and we stared — and she said: "Or it *was*. We have just all seen it pass."

"Then, what have we seen?" said Loretta, staring back up at the sky.

"Oh —" said Mrs Trent, fumbling with her purple scarves and silver lamé purse: "probably just another falling star —"

and she hurried away out of the dark, before she could be caught by the August chill.

There was a pause, and then Loretta said: "I think you people are remarkable" — addressing the rest of the guests, still assembled on the porches: "I mean, imagine! Mistaking a falling star for a satellite. How can you have? Why —" — and she made a gesture at the sky, as best she could — "— there it was, right there! And I guess we three are the only ones that saw it." She paused and then looked them all in the eye.

"Isn't that a pity," she said.

The following day, Loretta did not come down to the sand. Her doctor had arrived from Montreal and, in fact, the only member of her family we saw that day was Elizabeth, who sat for about two hours at the sea-tip of the eastern promontory. No one bothered her, but I did notice that she remained seated even while the tide was turning and that it seemed a long time before she decided to quit the rocks and make her way back through the pools to the beach. Also, I saw, as she made her way past the Garrison enclave, that she did not stop, as she usually did, to speak.

It was the Garrison boy who had given Loretta the blue bottle.

Then the day came, and there is nothing much I can think of to add to what I've already written at the beginning, in the middle, at the end.

"I was sitting on the sand, with my feet and ankles covered with a towel and I believe there was a rise where I sat, a sort of hummock, created, perhaps, by some old, deflated castle. My brother, Michael, was saving someone's sailboat, which had lost its balance and was slowly disappearing over the edge of our horizon. Down by the water, old Mrs Hogan went by, with her parasol tipped against the sun — relic of another age — and a tableaux of a children's game and dogs popped up out of the sand. Someone was calling someone and the life-guard had his eye on the shore.

I looked up. I looked over.

It was so casual.

Baby Frasier was dropping a pale-green bottle from her lips and, once her elbow had descended far enough towards her waist, Loretta, who stood behind her, beyond her, was able to catch my image in the corner of her eye. One instant sooner — later — and our eyes might not have met. But they did, and she gave me the look of recognition and farewell: chose me to say good-bye to with her final glance and then Elvira was screaming: "mommy! mommy!" and Loretta was opening her arms to her own child, who suddenly was falling with her towards the ground and then — then only it was, that I saw:

She had on a red dress.

And all the people were on the shore.

Hello Cheeverland, Goodbye

Damn the bright lights by which no one reads, damn the continuous music which no one hears, damn the grand pianos which no one can play, damn the white houses mortgaged up to their rain gutters, damn them for plundering the ocean for fish to feed the mink whose skins they wear and damn their shelves on which there rests a single book — a copy of the telephone directory, bound in pink brocade. Damn their hypocrisy, damn their cant, damn their credit cards, damn their discounting the wilderness of the human spirit, damn their immaculateness, damn their lechery and damn them above all for having leeched from life that strength, malodorousness, colour and zeal that give it meaning. Howl, howl, howl.
JOHN CHEEVER, Bullet Park

I guess Thornton Wilder and John Cheever are the greatest living American writers: that is, if you're talking about literature. With Cheever, though, there's an odd and rather sinister problem. People have begun to live — to actually take up residence inside his books — forsaking New York, Connecticut, New Jersey, they've foundered in this place called Cheeverland.
NICHOLAS FAGAN, Essays and Conversations

At the end of the street there are stone steps leading down to a beach with a wide view of Long Island Sound. On the far shore, barely visible, is the home of William F. Buckley, Jr.

Everyone looks over there with envy — liberals spitting on the sand, conservatives quietly narrow-eyed and muttering the Platitudes. It is a large place, the lawns of which are encroached upon by rocks, some casual — deposited by the whim of Nature — others cast by the art of man. No one goes there: apparently not even a Buckley.

The street itself is not very long, with only about ten houses on either side. It has a 'dead-end' because of the steps and, once in the morning, once again in the afternoon, the maids trundle down to the beach with all the little children and sit on the sand drinking Pepsi-Cola. And the maids smoke hand-rolled cigarettes, lifted with chocolate fingers out of pilfered gold and silver Benson-and-Hedges packets; the ones with the cardboard sides that look like little whorehouses stuck in the sand beside the matchbox billboards advertising the tin-can restaurants next door.

Back in the proper houses, the real ones on the street, the wives are on the telephone, ordering this and that, looking out of their windows, wondering what time it is. And, if you could look down from the roofs or down from the sky, most likely you would see some others of the wives, drifting out into the sun with highball glasses in one hand and suntan lotion in the other. And there in the gardens these wives begin their daily disappearance-act: their bodies fading away behind the Coppertone and the Bain du Soleil; their minds fading away behind the gin, the vodka, and the scotch. And the sounds of the street are of music drifting from many open windows; of distant traffic and of the children chattering down on the beach — blissfully out of mind and sight. And this is the morning and the afternoon of any day but Saturday and Sunday.

Facing the Sound, at the end of the street, looking down at the beach, is a large white clapboard house with shade trees all around it and an adjoining smaller house that was once a garage or stables. In the large house can be found the Bakers and in the small house their estranged son Dennie, seventeen years of age.

Mrs Baker spends her days in New York, although she never uses the trains. The Bakers have lived in Cheeverland, on this

street, since the late nineteen-fifties and the fact that Mrs Baker
has never used the trains is quite remarkable. Everyone else in
Cheeverland has been on the trains and it is thought that Mrs
Baker has placed herself above the mass by refusing to do so.
She and her sister (who *has* been on the trains) instead take
turns driving one another into the City in a rented limousine.
There is also a rented limousine chauffeur, and this man is
thought to be Mrs Baker's sister's lover, and neither Mrs
Baker's sister nor the rented chauffeur has a name: they are
simply known (and widely) as ''Mrs Baker's sister, dear, and
her lover, the chauffeur.'' As for Mr Baker, he has never
appeared, although someone once claimed to have identified
him, seen high up at a window on a rainy, wintry afternoon.
Mr Baker has six million dollars — of his own, not his wife's;
for Mrs Baker only has two million — of her father's, not her
own.

Late every afternoon, when the older children come home
from school, the Bakers' other son, whose name is Neddy,
looks down over the beaches and out over the Sound towards
the Buckley Place and, for an hour or so at a stretch, he will
lace the air with unbridled obscenities. No one has ever found a
way to stop him. Not even Dennie, his brother, whom he loves
— for Neddy is twenty-three years old, with a mental age of
five. He has a nurse, but the nurse sits up, under earphones,
on the terrace, reading books and listening to ''white sound''
— unattentive, remote, and therefore highly regarded by her
ward.

Neddy weighs two-hundred-and-thirty pounds and he often
has to be lifted to his feet if he falls down, or if someone pushes
him, or if he sits down on purpose. His co-ordination is not the
best and the obscenities he screams are often bawled through
the tears of frustration and a flail of fists that once broke
Dennie's jaw. So far as he is able, Neddy runs from one side of
the lawn to the other, pointing and shouting, shouting and
pointing out to sea like a man who cannot make others believe
he has seen a sinking ship or a hand that has waved and disappeared.

On the other side, at the end of the street, way in behind a
screen of trees and a veil of shrubbery, lives Professor Orin
Dinstitch, late of Harvard, late of Princeton, later still of M.I.T.,
and a onetime resident of Chicago. Professor Dinstitch was
"one of the originals" at Los Alamos, and as if to remind his
neighbours of that fact, the trees with which he has screened his
house are poplars and cottonwoods, which every spring give off
the smell of heaven. He lives thus in aromatic seclusion with
his sister — not at all like Mrs Baker's sister, but the epitome of
all that being the sister of an older man implies: meticulous to
the point of madness, lifting every fallen leaf from the sidewalk
with delicate bridge-player's fingers, scrutinizing every visitor
on the street for signs of decadence and dirt through watery,
failing eyes. The Dinstitch couple are poor — a description admittedly relative; for anyone living across the road from a man
worth six million dollars is bound to be thought of as 'poor'.
And someone once said, "That poor old gent. I wonder how he
gets along now. Living there all alone with his sister . . . having
given his all to his country, and now no visible means of support." To which some wit had replied: "*except his cane.*" They
were frugal and they refused to own a car. Miss Dinstitch is
very proud of this latter fact. "The automobile pollutes, you
know," she will say, turning to her brother with a smile, lifting
the dust from his lapels with a fingernail. The old are so
strangely cruel to one another, with the things they say and the
trees they plant and the dust they turn and the doors they close.
And, as Orin Dinstitch once found himself thinking against his
will: "With the way they will not die."

Of the rest of these houses, only one other has the importance
of personality, and up to it one afternoon in May (observed
beyond the poplars by Miss Dinstitch across the road) there
drives a taxi.

Out of this taxi gets a young man of about thirty-eight years,
whose right to be called "young" lies in the extraordinary
mask of his face — innocent of all experience save imagination.
Nothing has ever happened to this young man that did not take
place in his mind.

Call him Ishmael.

He carries a suitcase, a briefcase, and a paper-wrapped bouquet of flowers. He wears a fawn-coloured suit and a pair of highly polished boots. He is five-foot, ten-and-a-half inches tall. His eyes are pallid blue and the shape of his mouth betrays the fact that his mother fed him at her breast long after her milk had dried. He has come a long way to Cheeverland, from Toronto.

Having paid the taxi-driver, Ishmael stands, unaware of Miss Dinstitch's stare, watching the house before him as though to make himself believe that it is there. Books have been his life and he has only read of Cheeverland. He has never been. So now he is nervous, for here he is: he is here at last.

The house is expensive, with an effective façade: pseudo-revolutionary, guaranteed rust-resistant, with antiqued pre-weathered wrought-iron fixtures such as carriage-lamps and railings and little ornamental spears sticking out of the ground around the cherry trees that line the rubbermaid walk. The cherry trees are real and he touches them one by one as he makes his way to the door, holding all his belongings and the paper flowers to one side.

The people who live in this house are on their way up in the world of television: hoping to make it all the way up to the world of films. Their name is Anderson: Arthur and Alicia. Alicia writes; Arthur produces. Alicia says "A-lee-secya" and has a very large collection of *hats*. Arthur is a shoe-and-boot man, being the owner of twenty-two pairs. Ishmael also writes — but novels and stories: a writer of books. He is here because Arthur is trying to raise the money to produce a "Film of the Week" (not the same thing as a FILM) based on Ishmael's only successful book, a novel called *Blackwater Falls*. Alicia has written, or rather 'concocted,' the screenplay, and the author has come down to read it.

Now Ishmael walks to the house with his things and he rings the bell. The door is opened. He steps inside and Miss Dinstitch loses sight of him. The door closes and the street is empty, too soon for the children's return from school, too late for the taxi-cab to come back and take the young man away.

Miss Dinstitch herself goes inside through the porch and closes
all the doors, one by one, in order, all the way to her bedroom,
where she lies down on the bed and stares at the ceiling. She is
wondering what will happen and will not close her eyes for an
hour.

Mr and Mrs Anderson are both very large people; tall, with
almost identical faces and oversized, beautiful heads. Long-
armed and long-legged, they move with a good deal of care,
very slowly through their low-ceilinged home. Their rooms are
filled with books and paintings and musical instruments. Mrs
Anderson is as highly strung as a violin, but she plays the cello.
Arthur is more phlegmatic, drinking a great deal of gin, laughing a little more than Alicia does, making his way to the top of
the television heap with chinless tenacity and the best pair of
rubber-soled shoes that money will buy.
    The Anderson's maid is black and her name is Rosetta Filli-
more, and the day she came to apply for the job Alicia opened
the door and said: "But . . . you're a *darky*!" And Rosetta just
sat right down on the step and almost wet her pants with
laughing, and ever since then she has been enslaved to Alicia's
charms. However, in 1968 all the coloured servants working
the street, even Rosetta Fillimore, left off living in these houses
and went downtown to live in *the district*. Now they come in
only by the day. After the events in Memphis, a meeting was
held and the decision was made to move out. It was one thing
to work there and to eat there, but quite another to sleep there,
and so their bedrooms on the top floors and in the basements
were abandoned and their sheets and towels were given away
to the Salvation Army. Rosetta's lover, Clyde, was a leader of
this movement and he has since convinced her to carry a Smith
and Wesson .32 snub-nosed revolver. And why not? Doesn't
Alicia Anderson?

In the present absence of both the Andersons, Ishmael is shown
upstairs by Rosetta Fillimore to her own old room.
    (Miss Dinstitch's eyes still seek the possibilities of this scene
in the cracks and the corners of her ceiling.)

"You want a drink? Perhaps some tea?" says Rosetta.

"Some tea," says Ishmael.

"Okay," says Rosetta and goes on down to the kitchen, where she puts on the singing kettle and pours herself the scotch refused by the man upstairs. " 'Rob 'em blind,' Clyde says," she says out loud and lifts the glass into the sunlight before she drinks. "But Sweet Jesus, how I hates this crap . . ." and throws it down her throat. "H - agh!" and is nearly sick in the sink. Then she looks up towards the attic: So that's the booby who wrote that book that Mrs A. adapted, hunh? Well, I guess Clyde says another drink on *that* . . ." and she pours a jigger and lifts it to the windows and thinks: I can't do this — and pours it down the drain again and caps the bottle.

Rosetta has read *Blackwater Falls* and has not been able to grasp it, quite; though somehow she liked it, 'kind of.' It had seemed to be a true book, filled with real feelings — but the people were unknown to her, living in another time, and a place so far away it was not on her Map of America. Ontario. In Canada. And the lives described were lived before the war, before the war that was known as '*the* war' and was the war that she herself remembered from her childhood — the one that ended with Dinstitch's bomb. But anyway the hero in the book was a man whom no one had ever met before — a stranger who came to Blackwater Falls where certain things happened to him in 1910 and where he did things not understandable — and when he left the town the book was over. He was a saint, she guessed, but she wondered what on earth kind of movie it would make with its saint and its sombre darkness and its utter lack of people Rosetta could put her finger on (except a woman called Glorianna, who did not get killed). Oh well, the Andersons were both very clever, so Rosetta decided not to commit herself, but only to wait and see what happened, at which point she could properly say "I tol' you so" no matter what the outcome was.

Up in the attic Ishmael unpacks his suitcase; hangs a few things in the empty closet; sets out some underwear on the bed; pours himself a tumbler of vodka — taking both tumbler and bottle from the suitcase — and then sits down, without his shirt, to open the briefcase. There is just a moment, just a second, before he lifts the lid, and when he does, inside there are twenty, maybe thirty magazines. Ishmael closes his eyes. He wants and does not want to see. But must, and so he opens his eyes and lets his fingers down from his lips and he caresses the cellophane wrappers and these in themselves have such a sensuous quality that, after a moment, he rises quickly, selects a magazine at random, and walks across the hall, where he locks the vodka, himself, and the magazine into the bathroom.

Downstairs, the kettle boils and sings.

Rosetta watches it slowly boiling dry. And she listens to that boy at the end of the street — to that Neddy Baker kid shouting his afternoon obscenities at the sailboats on the Sound. It's four o'clock and with a sigh she rises and once more crosses to the sink where she fills the kettle and puts it back on the stove. She leans against her forearm, resting her weight on the counter. This man has arrived. And he has asked her for some tea. Right? And he is still upstairs in the bathroom. And his hosts, the Andersons, have not come home to greet him as they said they would, and here she is, Rosetta, leaning in the kitchen, waiting for god knows what — for nothing — to happen. And he is alone and she is alone and they are alone and the kid down the street is alone and — great Jesus — what is it that makes these people so undependable, discourteous and . . . (looking from the window) . . . sad?

Alicia Anderson, returning at long last from wherever it is she has been, stands, crouching slightly in the living room. She wears a plain cloth coat and gloves and she carries an attaché case. Her *hat* is but a veil, pulled tightly to the chin, and her shoes must be called 'eccentric' because of their heels, at least three inches high, lifting Alicia, already attenuated, even further towards the ceiling.

"Well . . . he's here," says Rosetta, standing askew in the doorway: "but, hc's locked hisself in the bathroom."

"In the bathroom?" Then, gazing off at the mail piled up on the desk: "Isn't that strange?" Turning back: "And you invited him down?"

"Sure did."

"Well. How very odd. . . ."

"Maybe he's afraid of darkies," says Rosetta.

"Pah!" And they both laugh.

"Anyways, I made'm a pot o' tea, which he asked for and never come down for and so I drank it mysel' an' threw the tealeafs onto the roses like you tol' me. Okay?" She began to depart the room.

"Okay." Distracted.

"You people in or out for dinner?"

Alicia uncrouches. "If we're 'in,' I'll make a salad. That should be all right. Shouldn't it?"

"Sure."

"What is there? Is there any lobster? Crab? Any squid? Anything like that?"

"*Like* that, yeah. There's shrimps in tins, I think."

"Then open the shrimps and put them in a bowl of ice and make sure you pour off all that liquidy stuff before you do. . . ."

"On the roses . . .?"

"It's poison, Rosetta. *Poison*. Okay?"

"Okay. Don't panic. Don't panic. An' oh . . . speakin' o' *panic*. . . ."

"Yes?"

"I di'n't say nothin' about your sister comin' t'morrow. Was that right?"

"That's right." (How dare she?) "That's right." (How *dare* she?) "Don't say anything just yet." (You black bitch!)

Rosetta, smiling earnestly, begins to go away. "Rosetta?" She turns, impertinent, but silent to the voice. "I want you to put a bottle," says Alicia, "of Mr Anderson's gin in the fridge. And . . . I want you. . . ."

"Yeah?"

Rosetta squints her gaze and sets her mouth. Alicia sees this and thinks: my god, I'll kill her, but only says: "I want four fingers of scotch. In a chilled glass. With a single piece of mint."

Rosetta fishes around in her pockets for her false eyelashes, kept in a small enamelled box that she is always losing. It is nearly time to walk to the corner, catch the bus, and go home to Clyde. She makes a rosette of her mouth.

"*Now*," says Alicia.

"Yes, ma'am," says Rosetta — and gets away with it and goes.

Alicia straightens, meaning to continue on into the den and the desk where the mail waits, but she strikes her head, almost impaling it on the iron chandelier that mars the entranceway and she spouts: "Great bleeding Jesus!"

She looks at the cello in the corner, wanting very much to kick it into the hallway, but she knows (having done it before) that afterwards she would regret that. Instead she throws a convenient paperback in its direction and misses it by a mile. She sits down, wanting to scream, perhaps, and the telephone rings. Alicia throws it across the room.

Arthur Anderson is escorting Ishmael to the top of the steps above the beach. Each man carries a glass — the one of gin, the other of vodka.

"That blue ketch there belongs to the Kileys," says Arthur. "They'll see we have a guest and insist on taking you out tomorrow, if you can bear it."

"Yes."

"I can't. I get sick. But maybe Alicia would go with you."

"They don't actually go to *sea*, do they?"

"Oh, no . . ." and a laugh. "They never leave the Sound. But the Sound's quite big enough for a proper sail. Do you know this place at all?"

"No. No. I've never been. . ."

"That place over there belongs to William F. Buckley, Jr."

Ishmael spits.

Arthur puts one arm behind his back and they begin to descend.

Several children play on the beach, including a token black boy with an Afro.

"That's our 'token black boy', " says Arthur with a smile. "We get quite a laugh out of calling him that." Stepping downwards. "He thinks it's funny, too, you know. We like his hair."

Ishmael nods: "Unh-hunh. What's his name?"

"I don't know. He's the son of one of the maids."

"Oh."

"But she doesn't work this street anymore, so it works out fine. Nobody's embarrassed that way. And boy, can that kid ride a bike! Fantastic!"

"That person there,' says Arthur, indicating the woman with a wave of his gin, "is Lydia Harmon. She's a lesbian and she wants us to pay attention. That's why she wears an open shirt."

They get off the bottom step and make for the tide.

"*That*," says Arthur, stepping from one stone to the next, as if he had them all by heart, "is a certain Mr Crosley. *Beware*."

He does not elaborate.

Ishmael says: "I will."

They stop and stare across the water. Arthur sighs.

"We call it 'Buckley-ham Palace,' " he says, "and it's really supposed to be rather dreary." He lets the vision sink. "Not at all like Hyannis Port," he sighs again and then walks on. "Do you know who I met the other night?"

"No idea," says Ishmael.

"Truman Capote," says Arthur and is disappointed when Ishmael only says: "Oh."

Now it is Ishmael's turn to walk on the stones.

"Oh, yes," says Arthur: "and Johnny Carson and Linda Lovelace too. All the same night. It was a riot. Just a riot! Everyone got stoned and lay on the floor and played Monopoly. Linda Lovelace kept winning. . . ."

They cross on over the slimy greening stones that once made up retaining walls but now are fallen to the sand. Arthur gets some distance ahead of Ishmael here and then turns round and says, with a certain grave contempt: "Truman Capote wears a *bracelet*."

Ishmael stops. Then Arthur turns away again.

"It was a private party, of course."

"Of course."

"But . . . we all had a pretty good time. It was fun."

". . . I wish I'd been there."

Arthur now finds a dead fish and must avoid it by walking out into the Sound.

"These shoes cost me forty dollars," he says — apparently delighted by what he is doing. "Isn't that a scream?"

Over the shrimp, Alicia asks: "Did you get to the script at all?"

"Not really," says Ishmael. "I've read the first sixteen pages, that's all. I'm sorry."

"Oh! Don't be sorry, dear. I'm glad that's all you've read, because," she looks at Arthur, "I wanted to forewarn you."

"Forewarn me?" says Ishmael.

"Yes." Alicia waves her fork above the plates like a wand, but the food remains what it is — just shrimp salad, lettuce, hard-boiled eggs, and radishes. "You know in the book, where what's-his-name is lying in the barn and Glorianna is getting undressed beyond the windows . . .?"

"Yes."

"And he's lying there, thinking what a pity it would be to go ahead and kill such a lovely woman after all . . .?"

"Yes."

"And in his mind he forgives her for what she's done and he decides, right then, not to kill her, but to leave her alone?"

"Oh yes."

"Well . . . on page 122 I have him get up and go in and kill her."

"Oh."

Supper is over. They stand on the lawn.

"Who's that?" Ishmael asks.

A figure is wandering along the street, the epitome of another age: Edwardian and elegant and carrying a walking-stick.

"That's Professor Dinstitch," says Arthur. "He invented the atomic bomb."

The allure of violence hangs in the air for a moment and then is gone, replaced by the faint and lovely odour of the lilac trees next door.

"I think I will go to bed," says Ishmael.

"Sleep well," says Alicia.

"Yes. Goodnight."

"Goodnight."

After Ishmael has gone, Alicia takes Arthur by the arm and they hang there, two cadavers in the twilight.

"Addie will be here, tomorrow," says Alica.

"Oh dear," says Arthur.

And it gets dark.

By morning spring has well and truly come. Rosetta comes up to the house without her coat — not even carrying it over her arm. She is full of news. There has been a fire in the night, downtown, and even now the soldiers and the firemen are sifting through the ashes for the victims.

"Soldiers?" Alicia asks, hung-over.

"Well, I said the same thing to Clyde," says Rosetta. "But it seems they's legit. Th' army's usin' it as some kinda trainin' program. Or something. You know? Like them games they play — only this one's real."

"What's it like out?" Alicia asks.

"Warm," says Rosetta. "Like lemonade weather."

When Ishmael awakes, he hears this distant narrative of fire and lemonade and he thinks it must be floating up to his windows from the garden. But when he looks, the garden is empty below him and nobody there but the cat, asleep in Alicia's canvas deck chair.

He can see the Sound, or part of it, beyond the roofs and the tree-tops, and already there is someone sailing: two white sails smack out in the breeze and he imagines he can hear them. Will he have to sail today? He hopes not.

Suddenly a power-mower shatters the pristinity of the atmosphere. The usual unseen person is ruining Saturday.

Ishmael leans on the bar of heaven and watches the world as he lights a cigarette. In the Baker House he perceives a figure in one of the windows staring out directly at him through a pair of binoculars. Hastily he remembers his robe is only loosely tied and he snatches it shut and kneels on the floor so that only his head and shoulders, together with his folded arms, can be seen. He slides his eyes back carefully, to see if he is still being watched and something in him, perverse, is sorry to discover he is not. The figure with the glasses is staring *down*, now, into a yard that Ishmael can only barely discern through the trees and the froth of flowering shrubs. The lawnmower shrieks and complains that it has hit a rock. The fingers holding the binoculars seem only to be bones, barely fleshed, with great knuckular rings of heavy silver and opals. Now Ishmael sees what the glasses are watching and watches it too: the naked thighs, the naked breasts, the naked buttocks of Lydia Harmon exercising in her garden.

Ishmael bites his lip. He has been unnerved and now he forces his head forward, leaning further out, remembering that Arthur has said "She wants us to pay attention" and now sees a knotty little man in a sweat-shirt and walking-shorts working in a flower-bed. He is pulling up fistfulls of weeds, presumably; all the while he works he is apparently whistling, for the shape of his lips betray him. Then all at once the power-mower dies and Ishmael hears the tune: it is Beethoven's 'Seventh Symphony,' the Apotheosis, and he turns away, already wondering how many victims have been sifted from Rosetta's fire.

In the bathroom, Ishmael stands before the mirror and regards his whole self. The vision is brief; having dropped the robe to the floor, he now reaches round and takes the largest towel and wraps himself out of sight from the waist down. Then he puts his finger to his lips and studies the contents of the shelves: colognes, blades, razor, brushes, combs, and that new, untried, but intriguing man's deodorant: "Lash." Then he commences, as always, with the tumbler of vodka and the running of the bath.

In the kitchen the table is covered with tabloids, oily rags, and Q-Tips. Rosetta is seated, already at work, Alicia is standing by the counter, emptying the contents of her handbag over the arborite. Being terrified of any combination of drugs and alcohol, she has refused all offers of aspirin and Anacin and suffers the effects of her hangover like a pro: bad-tempered, mean, and nervous. Rosetta refrains from humming and from turning on the radio. There is only the sound of their mutual clanking, clinking, and cluttering — and then their conversation.

"You got that oil-can there? That all-purpose oil?"

"Three-in-One, Rosetta. It's called 'Three-in-One.' "

"Don't throw it! My floor . . .! Jesus!"

Pause. Alicia shuffles in blue slippers to the table and sits.

"Do we have to do this every damn week?"

"Clyde says if we don't, the barrels gets musty and then they explodes in your hands. . . ."

"Well. I don't want *that* to happen."

Another pause and the chambers thrown open, inspected, poked at with Q-Tips. Bullets laid in two neat rows over the headlines: "PULLING WIRES BEHIND THE SCENES" and "MAN'S WORST ENEMY: THE DOG." Rosetta is nonchalant about her work, but Alicia gets right down to it with her glasses falling from the end of her nose.

"This fire, do you think it was *started*?"

"I think there isn't a fire in this world, M's Anderson, that isn't *started* somehow. . . ." Rosetta holds her .32 up and stares through the empty chambers at the pots of winter savoury on the sill. "Clyde says he's sick o' niggers startin' these fires in the District. Clyde says to us: 'Why not move up-town?' "

Alicia's glasses fall at last. Rosetta flips her chambers closed with a snap.

"But there's nowhere for you to live up here," says Alicia, whose policy is always reality. Her coffee is cold, but she drinks it. Rosetta grunts.

"Oh, *we* ain't gonna move," she says. "It's the gasoline that's comin' up."

This receives silence, so Rosetta says, changing the subject: "You want me to put them flowered sheets on your sister's bed?"

At about eleven o'clock from the Anderson household there is a short expedition to the shopping plaza, where the sun is reflected in over a mile of plate glass windows, causing Alicia to mutter the words: "Bloody sadist," not making it clear whether her reference is to the designer of the shopping plaza or the sun itself. Here Arthur departs to purchase four bottles of gin and two of Alicia's favourite scotch. Later he will have to pretend, as always, that he has bought the scotch by mistake — forgetting "Alicia's problem." This *forgetfulness*, which some might have called a tolerance, is not a tolerance at all, but only a symptom of exhaustion. The will to fight Alicia's battles has been submerged in the need to forget his own.

Meanwhile Alicia and Ishmael have visited the A and P where they have bought such items as half-a-dozen large bottles of Canada Dry ginger ale ("in honour of your lovely country, dear") and a bottle of pickles and two dozen cans of Schlitz. Alicia has also bought some nippy English humbugs and when they all get home again they all dine standing up, from plates of gritty lettuce, cherry tomatoes, celery sticks, and a bowl of pretzels. At two o'clock there is target practice.

Bang!

"Alicia?"

Bang!

"*Ali*-cia!"

Bang!

Alicia: "What?"

"Ishmael and I are going to the beach."

"All right, dear. When I'm through with this —"

Bang!

"— I'm going to have a rest."

And so, Arthur thinks, no doubt, are the neighbours.

Bang!

"Goodbye, dear."

Bang!

"Goodbye."

Rosetta would like to see Miss Addie before she leaves and so she hangs around, sucking humbugs and looking up the movies in the papers. Nothing is playing she likes and at three o'clock a cab arrives.

Miss Dinstitch watches Addie's arrival from between the bushes across the road.

She sees the taxi-cab is not a local one, but a Yellow Cab from New York City, and this gives her curiosity just enough adrenalin to propel her forward under the trees.

The girl who emerges is slim, but of ordinary height, with short blond hair only slightly longer than Lydia Harmon's. She wears a dress so thin that it must be unlined, and its material is patterned, not unlike Miss Dinstitch's view of the street, with pale, translucent leaves. Addie is barefoot and carries a shoulder-bag, and while she is paying the taxi-driver the bag slips all the way down her arm to the ground, causing her to laugh. Miss Dinstitch does not like this laughter: it cannot be heard and it must be caught in the girl's throat, somehow — the way actresses laugh, and singers — or worse. And now the girl is saying good-bye to the driver, who has a strangely satiated smile. There are words and waves and then he is gone, leaving the stink of his exhaust behind him. Miss Dinstitch draws back, for the girl has done something inexplicably moving. All at once she has clasped her hands before her chin and closed her eyes and let her whole demeanour of ebullience escape through parted lips. Then she breathes it back in and picks up her bag and squares her shoulders and *marches* to the door.

The stairwell is cool: a good place to stand and wait.

Alicia is on the lawn, asleep in her hat, the very image of Virginia Woolf. Addie has seen her there through the mullioned windows of the den and has left her there, unspoken to, ungreeted. Rosetta has left, but has told her that Arthur and the house-guest are down on the beach and that, perhaps, the young man has gone sailing. And Addie smiles at the thought of this, for once when she was here a long, long while ago she too went sailing and Mr Kiley made a pass at her and she wondered if Mrs Kiley would make a pass at the young man whose name was . . . *Ishmael?*

She listens to the house. Her sister will not be glad to see her here and, as always, Arthur's smile will be cool and patronizing: "Nice." Her fingers touch the banister. It doesn't matter. Here she is: *away.* That's all that counts — that matters: to be safely away somewhere else. The rest of anything is possible to deal with. Anything and anyone.

She looks up the stairs. She closes her eyes. The house smells of safety and cut-flowers, of lemon-wax and musty-rugs, of her childhood. And Addie sits down, neither part-way up nor part-way down but exactly in the middle of the stairs. A vantage point from which she can see through the doors who will come to be with her first.

Arthur is watching the ketch through his telescope. There sits Edward Kiley and Emmaline, his gorgeous wife. So far so good. They have not ascertained that the Andersons have a guest. For a change they are sailing alone. Edward Kiley has a strange expression on his face. Arthur adjusts the lens. Yes, fascinating. *Fascinating.* Is Edward Kiley . . . amazed? Or . . . desperate? Or . . . angry? Or *afraid*?

He's afraid.

Arthur, in his own amazement, claps the telescope shut and then at once re-opens it to see what Emmaline is up to. Below him, on the beach, Ishmael is reading Alicia's screenplay, piling it page by page under the stones as he reads. He is a good deal over half-way through, and it passes through Arthur's mind: *I wonder if he'll forgive her?* And then, at once, he is searching for Emmaline Kiley.

There. In a shirt, with her hair tied back and her dark, southern skin deeply oiled, almost black with her passion for the sun. Her face is flat and broad and her features wide: Ava Gardner's chin. Her breasts have always been the cause of turbulence, of a wincing disquiet in Arthur's soul. Her figure can truly be described as being made up of handfuls of flesh. Even now, as he sees her, his fingers sink round the phallus of his telescope, twisting it out of focus. Dear Jesus — that woman. . . . But what is she doing? Here, now — something is very wrong. She too is angry and alarmed and she sits unnaturally forward (damn her breasts), with her hands full of halliard and her movie-star's chin unsheathed and knife-like pointed at her husband — *screaming*. She is screaming invective — god! — the worst that a taxi-driver could think of — flailing at him with the words until the words are not enough and the forces behind them suddenly possess her hands and she leaps at him, driving him backward over the rear of the boat and the tiller snaps free and all the lines are let out and the ketch begins to make a crazy drunken course across the Sound that is so irrelevant to all the rules of sailing that everyone else on the shore begins to watch it, wondering what can be the trouble. And then, it must be, beyond the curtain of the sails, that Edward has regained his balance and has somehow fought her off, for on the next turn beachwards he is sitting there calmly, fitting the tiller back into place. And Emmaline has resumed her seat to one side of him, not screaming now, but adjusting her shirt and rubbing her arms.

"Who's winning?" says a voice behind Arthur's right shoulder. He turns like a child caught stealing loose change from the bureau and sees that his fellow eavesdropper is Lydia Harmon. Not liking her makes Arthur's predicament worse. He cannot share her smile, with its twist of lemon. He hates the way she stands, which is like a disturbingly seductive boy, hipless and smooth and wet. She is lightly beating time to the music of someone's transistor, blathering rock from nearby.

"Uhm . . . winning *what*?" says Arthur like a fool.

Lydia makes a face and touches Arthur's cheek with a deprecating pat. "Never mind, Sweetie," she says. "I'll find out later for myself." Arthur grits his teeth at her touch. And then she says: "You and Ali going to the Powells' tonight?"

Arthur would be delighted to say no, they are not going. But the fact is they *are* going, and have to go, because Alicia would bring the house down if they didn't. So he says: "Maybe."

Lydia smiles. "Chapter two, baby." And she looks out towards the ketch. "And you wouldn't want to miss chapter two, now, would you?" Her big toe caresses the leather instep of Arthur's boot.

"I don't even know what you're talking about," says Arthur. "And will you please take your God damn toe off my boot?"

Lydia pouts and Arthur is not quite sure the pout is not genuine. Maybe she *needs* to seduce someone, he thinks. After all, there isn't much game for a Lydia here on the beach. It must be difficult, not to have an outlet for all that . . . (looking away from her) whatever it is. And worst of all, he is disturbed. She has moved him, for no one has placed her toe on the instep of his boot for a very long time.

He gathers up the telescope and makes to move away. But Lydia beats him to it. She has suddenly stripped off her jeans and gone running out to the water, which is shallow and will not hide her.

"Does she call that thing a *bathing* suit?" Arthur says aloud, and turns at once to see if Ishmael is nearby. But he is not, and only the screenplay under its pile of stones remains to show where his guest has been seated. This afternoon, that should have been so lovely, has been ruined by the fact of everyone's unfinished business.

That argument, for instance, Arthur thinks as he picks his way through the slime revealed by the ebbing tide. *Is the Kileys' argument ever over?* All they do — or certainly all they do in public — is rage at one another; batter one another with words and fists. Now, it seems that Edward and Emmaline want to kill one another. What, then, keeps them together? Edward's money, bulging in Emmaline's pocket book? Emmaline's beauty, sagging from Edward's arm? They're the perfect age for divorce, Arthur thinks — and smiles. As I am. And Alicia. The Kileys will and *we* won't, that's what everyone thinks. The perfect age. Like the perfect age for marriage and the perfect age for giving birth and the perfect age for heart attacks and cancer. . . .

Arthur — one foot lifted to begin his ascent — is confronted by the open mouth, the merry eyes and the filthy paws of Kileys' dog. It has just come bounding down the steps to say hello to everyone: to *anyone*. Kileys' dog is always looking for its owner; and its name. It is large and brown with one black patch on its back near its tail: a kind of square, curly dog — close cropped. Almost an Airedale. It has no name and is simply known as "Kileys' Dog." This does not suit the dog at all, who wants a proper name like any other dog. No one has ever been witness to how the Kileys summon it for meals or for guard duty. Probably they cry; "here, Dog!" or "here, You!" or some such thing. Its lack of a name can be seen in the dog's expression. It seems to be waiting — always — for someone to say; "your name is Spot." Or George. Or whatever. Anything can satisfy the dog. It is friendly to the point of wretchedness. The expression in its eyes, the tilt of its head, the incessant movement of its tail are downright melancholy.

Arthur moves toward one side and decides he will sit with the dog on the sea wall. "Poor old dog," he says and lays his hand along the side of the dog's head. "Poor old everyone," he adds, surveying the crowded stones and all the people known to him by the numbers on their houses, by their license plates and the names of their phobias and manias and not much else. "Poor old us."

Slowly, the dog begins to fawn on Arthur's hand and Arthur wonders how often any other hand, especially a Kiley hand (Edward's with its dreadful rings — Emmaline's with its sun spots) is ever laid this way, receptive of an ear to scratch and received so gently into the wet of that eager mouth to have its fingers chewed. Probably never.

The first one through the door is Ishmael.

Addie watches him. His hair looks wet, as though he's been swimming. His hands are full of stones and paper, some of the paper enfolding the stones. He does not see her, lost as she is in the dimness of the stairwell.

Her eyes are yellow-green.

The stones are very hard to manage and Ishmael wants to put them all down and rearrange them into one hand, to make a package of them in the paper, but the table tops are all covered in the hallway with Alicia's bric-a-brac. So he bends and kneels and places them, smelling of the dead sea-Sound, on the lower steps.

Outside there is going to be a storm and the sky is turning green with distant electricity and the smell of copper is lifted from the screens like dust and there is a long, long pause.

Ishmael smooths out the page of screenplay, and the words "CUT TO: INT: NIGHT: GLORIANNA'S ROOM" lean up at him, seemingly three-dimensional, off the paper. He begins to arrange the stones in the centre, leaving the corners foldable. One-two-three — twenty stones. Each different, but all a memento of Cheeverland.

Ishmael makes his package and rises.

A woman is seated on the stairs — someone he had not known was in the house.

"I beg your pardon," he says and turns towards the doors. Crazily it goes through his head that somehow he is in the wrong hall, has wandered somehow into the house of a stranger. But then he recognizes the walk beyond the screens and turns again to Addie.

She smiles.

"Hello."

"Hello . . . uhm . . . do you live here?"

"No. I visit. You visit, too, I take it."

"Yes."

Their eyes are locked so tight that Ishmael has to turn away.

"Don't drop your stones," Addie warns him.

"No."

She rises.

Her feet are still bare, but she has changed her dress and now she wears something white and Mexican, with silver chains and rings.

"I have been sitting here, almost for an hour. My sister is asleep on the lawn. Alicia. Yes, I'm her sister. Addie — or Adele, if you prefer. I don't prefer, I'm afraid. I think it kind of sounds stuck-up — or *French* — or something: I don't know — I just don't like it." She is coming down the stairs and there is only the living room to go to. Or, the walk outside. "I suppose Alicia neglected to tell you I was coming." Ishmael nods. She is backing him into the living room. "Well . . ." and a dazzling, broken laugh: "I forgive her. *I forgive her.*" More laughter. "I phoned her up once and I said: 'This is Addie. This is *Addie,*' and she said: 'Addie who?' Do you believe it? *Believe it!* You probably know that she *writes*. Well, people who write are a pain!" (Does she know what she's saying? Ishmael blushes. But Addie knows what she has said and she turns to him and wins him over completely.) "Unless, of course, they write *well*!" Rosetta had told her who Ishmael was. "Do you drink?" He nods. "Then let's. Here it is after five and I haven't even started. . . ."

They enter the living room and Addie attends to the record player while Ishmael attends to the bar. The stones, still folded in their paper, are laid on a sofa, where bit by bit the tension eases and the paper opens.

Page one hundred and twenty-two.

INT: NIGHT: (etc.)

The STRANGER enters GLORIANNA'S ROOM with his KNIFE. . . .

"Do you dance?" Addie asks.

"Oh yes. But . . . not well."

"With me it couldn't matter less."

Johnny Mathis: "For the Good Times."

On the lawn Alicia is sitting up, more Woolf-like than ever, one hand on the back of her hat, holding it down under the rising wind. Her expression is pained. Perhaps she has had a dream, or several, and she is longing to talk and she is talking to Arthur, but Arthur is not really listening. Arthur is wondering if the Kileys will be at the Powells' tonight, but Alicia is saying something: "And yesterday, sitting there with Doctor Toffler — sitting there after so many sessions where nothing has happened, nothing has *emerged at all* — I suddenly realized, all at once, that for the longest time, I have had this . . . *thing* inside me: a desire — a wish — a need — a longing, Arthur, to forgive someone."

Alicia looks at her husband and blinks and after a second it sinks in, apparently, exactly what she has said to him, for he turns and gives her a stare of grateful amazement.

"No, no, dear," she says. "Not *you*. Not you. I don't know why, but somehow this need is a desire to forgive some . . . *stranger*. Do you see? I have this desire: this need to *forgive* someone. And Dr Toffler says it doesn't matter who I forgive as long as the 'forgiveness' emerges. It's the *feeling* that matters. The feeling. Of having done something . . ." (searching for the word) ". . . magnanimous, gratuitous, and . . . *lovely*, for another human being."

She was through. That was it. What Alicia had to say.

Arthur stares into the sky. He takes a deep breath.

"That's terrific, dear. Terrific. Good for you," his voice

absolutely toneless. "I think you're going to make it."

"So do I," says Alicia, fishing for, finding a piece of Facelle and blowing her nose. "And so does Dr Toffler."

"Good."

Twenty-six miles away, there is thunder. Arthur knows it is exactly twenty-six miles because he has counted the seconds between the sound and the previous strobe of lightning.

The doors burst open and the dancers are interrupted.

"Will you, for god's sake, come and help? Alicia's hat has blown itself across the lawn and into the trees in front of the Professor's house. . . ."

Alicia stands in the kitchen and pours herself a glass of milk.

"I find if I line my stomach before a party," she says to Ishmael, who sits in a handsome sweater at the table, "then the results aren't nearly so devastating."

"The results of what?" he asks.

Alicia blinks and smiles, ingratiating, not believing for a moment he can be serious. She crosses to the sink and rinses out the glass. Still letting the water flow, she turns and looks at Ishmael.

"I know you're upset because of what I've done to your story," she says and turns the tap off, flicks her fingers and reaches for the towel across the table. Then she sits down opposite him and removes her many rings with a sense of ceremony, staring at each one, laying them all in a row on the cloth, and one by one she dries her fingers, so many pieces of silver, knives and forks and spoons, laying them out like the rings for inspection — silver fingers and pewter nails. "I've only added the murder to the script because people insist on that. It's an element of fiction they won't forgive you for leaving out. In the movies, Ishmael, there has to be violent death — or people won't go. Surely you must *see* that?" On with the rings. "It's not that your book isn't good. It's just. . . ."

"That it isn't good *enough*."

"No. No. You don't under*stand*. It's different in the movies. . . ." Arthur comes into the room and she corrects herself: "In *films*. It's different. Isn't it, Arthur?''

"What, dear?"

"The needs. The *needs* are different."

"In what way?"

"In the movies . . . in the *films* . . . people have to be different. They have to . . ." She waggles her hands expressively.

"Kill one another." (Ishmael)

"Yes."

"I think it's time to go to the party," says Arthur.

Alicia rises.

"And is Addie coming?" she asks, with her back to the room.

"I had thought so. Don't you want her to come?"

Alicia shrugs. "It's immaterial." She lifts her handbag from the counter and turns to Ishmael.

"What do *you* think of her? Do you like her?"

"I don't . . . know her."

"You were dancing with her, for heaven's sake."

"Come on, Alicia." (Arthur) "We're late."

"And you aren't coming?" says Alicia to Ishmael.

"I'm afraid I'd feel out of place." Arthur looks at him and Ishmael adds: "But I may come over later."

Arthur smiles. "Through the back gate and across the alley. The *Powells*. I'm sure you'll hear us."

"All right. Have a good time."

They go. Ishmael sits and listens to the crickets in the yard beyond the screens. The storm is over; the air is wet and fresh. It is nine o'clock: Saturday night. It is May and the whole of Cheeverland is poised on its toes: on the toes of its dancing shoes — waiting, as Alicia might have said — or as Ishmael might have written in one of his fictions — to be killed, or to be forgiven. It will depend whether, in Cheeverland as in the movies, the people have to be different.

Just after eleven o'clock that night, Miss Dinstitch comes out onto her porch to say "Goodbye . . . goodnight" to her departing guests and the guests are come for by a large silver-brown Rolls Royce. The driver is a uniformed person of either sex and

indeterminate colour who declines to get out of the car or even
to reach around and open the doors for the ladies on the walk,
who comprise a haggle of silver shoes and lamé bags and
shouldered furs. They cannot decide whether Maude will sit
over here on this side with Grace, or over on that side with
Theresa. The answer is, disappointingly, that she will sit up
front with the driver, where Grace had been forced to sit on
their arrival. Theresa, it seems, must be the owner of the Rolls.
Miss Dinstitch watches all the shuffling and listens to the argument and dismisses it, along with the ladies, the moment they
are gone. She wavers on the porch before going in.

"Who's that?"

There is someone hanging about the steps leading down to
the beach, unsavoury pale and thin, in a tank-top shirt and a
pair of white jeans. His hands are in his pockets — one hand
out, now picking at something dark on his cheek, and she
recognizes him. The profile gives him away. *Dennie* — that boy
from across the street. That Baker boy with the broken jaw:
waiting. Waiting. Always waiting for someone. Always hanging around in the shade, either of the trees or of the night. By
day he hid away in his rooms, in his little house or out at the
fringes of his mother's lawns, where the trees swept down to
the sidewalks. He was sad, she had always thought, but unsavoury, and then: oh well, she thinks — he's young, resilient,
pliable, and *someone* must love him. When you're young, someone *always* loves you: a friend . . . or a . . . friend: or a friend.
And then she turns away in the other direction. And then she
thinks: *oh — everyone*, and, standing there in the amber lights,
Miss Dinstitch is the very image of a giant Cecropia, trapped
and pinned to the trellis with her Chantilly wings waving in the
breeze and the dust of her Yardley's powder scenting the air
with despair.

Oh, everyone.

And she hangs there for a moment more, wondering,
wondering what to do. It is such a *fine* night and all the houses
have now the faint odour of music about them.

Yes: it is not to be disputed through her tears.

To be young and to be able to seek adventures is everything.

It should be stated here that Edward Kiley has a mistress whose name is Carol Careless and that, presently, Arthur is trapped in a dingy corner at the Powells' party with this woman. She wears a cheap metallic dress and her wig doesn't fit. She is drunker than anyone else in the room and she is prodding at Arthur on Edward's behalf.

"But you've only *been* sailing once and *once* is no fair indication. Look, Arthur, honey — look, lotsa people are sick, are sea-sick the first time out, but . . ." she belches wetly, "that doesn't mean they're gonna be sick *again. You don't hafta be seasick!*" she almost yells. "You gotta give the sea a chance't. You hafta give it a chance to work ya."

Arthur is searching the room above her head. Carol Careless clutches at his lapels and hangs there like a baboon.

"Listen," she says. "Doesn't it *mean* anything to ya? Doesn't mean anything that a man like Edward *has* a sailboat? *Owns* one? Hunh?" Then she looks up, squinting through entangled lashes and beaded mascara. *Arthur is not paying attention!* "You shit!" she says. "Who the fuck do you think you are?"

"Now, Carol." (Smiling)

"Don't you now-Carol me, you cocksucker." (Arthur is ashen now; fainting with horror at the epithet, heard by all and so . . . "Jesus, Carol!" . . . appallingly unfair, untrue and . . .) ". . . all he wants y' to do — all he's askin' y' to do is take a ride in his goddamn *boat!*"

Arthur has ceased to listen. And he is now afraid, utterly afraid of this hideous woman. Her hair smells of seaweed and she will not let go of him, won't release his lapels, and he is certain they are going to rip, be torn, destroyed. He tries to fight her off, but she is very strong, in the way of drunks and ladies in metallic dresses.

"Carol, will you please let go of my coat?" (Oh God, will You please get me out of this corner?)

And then she is mustering all her height and, suddenly, letting go of him, she rears back, as if on rockers, and spouts in his face: "You crapless creep!" and she falls straight down to the floor, striking her head, which bounces.

Arthur adjusts his tie. No damage done. Carol rises to an

elbow — to a knee — to both knees — to her ankles: to the bar.
It is over. Arthur sighs. He hopes Alicia has not heard what
Carol Careless has called him, and he wonders where Alicia is,
where his *wife* is — something he only wonders at parties.

Ishmael went down and sat in the dark at the top of the steps
with Professor Dinstitch, who was seated on the bench there,
waiting for his sister to retire.

Neither one spoke. The old man rested both hands on the
crook of his cane and Ishmael's hands were deep in his pockets,
fiddling with the lint. Here he was, in Cheeverland, with the
inventor of the atomic bomb, and neither one had anything to
say. It was the crickets who burred the air and the tree-toads
who sang, and the records, the music, that provided the words,
and the two men just sat. The flowers smelled, the cut-grass
smelled, and the waters, curling in from mysterious darkness,
and the breeze and the air itself and the cement — all smelled
of summer coming.

Ishmael knew he was being watched. He was not sure from
where, but he knew he was being watched. And then Professor
Dinstitch got up and coughed and went away. That was the
end of *that*. Clickety-click: the cane went up the path and along
the sidewalks and under the poplars and onto the porch and
into the house and beyond the door and was gone.

Ishmael waited. There was someone else.

"I've never seen you before," says Dennie Baker, emerg-
ing, looming up through the darkness of the steps below.

Ishmael could not quite see him.

"I've never been here before," he says.

"Well?" says Dennie, as if that meant something.

Well *what*? but Ishmael is silent. He wants to see this person
before he goes on.

"Who sent you?" says Dennie, not moving, not coming further up.

"No one," says Ishmael (appallingly naive, he will think, in
retrospect). "No one sent me. I came here on my own."

"Oh." Disappointment? Chagrin? Even . . . anger?

And then: "Listen, I'm sorry, but . . . would you do me a

favour and go away?'' Dennie's voice is a child's voice now.
Appropriate.

"Sure,'' says Ishmael, rising. "Is anything wrong?''

Dead silence. The waves below them.

"No. But . . . I got to meet someone and . . . I have to wait,
you see?''

"Alone.''

"That's it.''

"Okay,'' Ishmael is backing off, not knowing where to go,
but going. "I'll see you 'round.''

"Yeah.'' Pause. "And thanks.''

"Not at all. I hope . . .'' But Ishmael did not know what he
hoped, what to hope for the boy (for it was obviously a boy,
with that voice). "I hope you don't have to wait too long.''
And went away.

Kileys' dog is standing out in the middle of the road with its
tail between its legs and its head turned over its shoulder, looking back towards the corner where the Kileys live. The expression on the dog's face is no longer eager or merry or friendly; it
is frightened. It appears to have experienced some sort of shock
and to have just escaped with its life. For a moment, as Ishmael
watches the dog standing in the moonlike glow of the street
lamps, it seems like a creature in the wild — like a photograph
he saw once in the National Geographic, of some wounded
beast surrounded by its enemies, standing there waiting to be
killed. It eyes the lawns and the shadows of the hedges with a
kind of forlorn terror — as if dragons were lurking there, ready
to finish it off.

Ishmael wonders what he can do to help. Perhaps the dog
has been hit by a car — though he hasn't heard any cars. He
approaches the dog slowly, holding his hands behind his back
so they won't seem threatening.

"Here, dog. Good dog . . .''

The dog wheels round, its neck and head leaning up in the
direction of the looming stranger, who appears to have no arms
— no hands. It whimpers and pads over onto the sidewalk near
a driveway, where it can see that nothing is behind it but a
large, blank house. It sits down.

"Have you been hurt?" says Ishmael.

The dog just stares.

"If you'd let me come near you, I could look at your collar and see where you live."

There isn't a collar.

Ishmael thinks: well, it moved, so there's nothing broken . . .

The fact is, Ishmael is somewhat afraid of the dog. Its behaviour is so strange, he thinks it might attack him if he tries to touch it.

"I wish I knew who you are," he says. "But I'm sure you must belong somewhere and maybe, if I leave you alone, you'll find your way home."

Having said this and having retreated slowly onto the other sidewalk, Ishmael goes his way, leaving the dog staring after him. When he gets to the corner, he notes the Kileys' door (though he doesn't know it is the Kileys' house) is wide open and that all the lights in creation seem to be burning inside. The only sound is of a radio giving an account of a baseball game. Just as Ishmael is passing, Tommy Agee of the New York Mets hits a home run and the crowd in some distant stadium leaps to its feet with a roar you can hear as far away as the middle of the Sound.

Down the street, Kileys' dog throws back its head and begins to howl, but his howl is lost beneath the howling of the baseball fans and the lapping of the waves. Now, it is truly night and the moon makes its move to the centre of the sky.

Arthur sees Alicia, spied by chance through a hole in the dancing, and she is seated in a chair, with a glass in one hand and the other hand held out, as if to touch someone, but the someone unseen, unrevealed, and Arthur stands on tip-toes, trying to see, but failing.

He averts his gaze, not wanting to admit he is furious, even remotely upset. Probably Alicia has a lover. Well — why not? People do these things. They live in a civilized world. She's an *artist*. It can't be serious. Certainly they aren't going to *bed* together, whoever this man is and Alicia. That simply wouldn't make sense . . . After all, he'd *know*, he could *tell*:

she'd be . . . different. When you have a lover, there are certain new things you learn, and Alicia had learned nothing new
for . . . years. Not since she'd had that affair with that man
Crosley — *who's here tonight, with someone else, I see.*

Arthur starts to scan the room, hoping to see that Addie has
arrived, or Ishmael, or anyone new. Anyone. New. But there
are so many dresses, bodies, faces, arms, and legs — dancing,
he presumes — that it's impossible to sort the people out.
Everything and everyone is swaying about the floor, falling
back and forth between the walls, but Arthur cannot hear the
music above the aviary of voices and the clinking of ice in
glasses. Idly, or trying to make it appear so, he glances through
the windows to a view of the terrace where his gaze is confronted by a man who is urinating in full sight of the whole
room. *Oh well — what else is new?* Arthur thinks, and is just in
the act of turning away, of looking away and shrugging, when
a fat hand flattens his backbone against the wall, holding him
almost off the floor.

"What the hell's the meaning of your turning down my
invitation, Anderson?" The face is very ugly, screwed up,
desperate: not unlike its telescope counterpart of the afternoon.
This is Edward: Edward Kiley, owner of the odious sailboat,
husband of the luscious Emmaline — and lover of Carol
Careless. The strength of his wrist is amazing, sustaining
Arthur against the wall without the slightest trace of weaken-
ing. "You coming with us tomorrow, or not?"

"Not," says Arthur, choking only slightly, wishing he had
gone home ten minutes, half-an-hour ago. Wishing he had not
come at all. "They're nice people, the Powells," he
remembered saying. "You'll like them." And now he realizes
he hasn't seen either Powell the whole night through — only
the monsters they'd unleashed. "Put me down, Edward," he
says. "I can't breathe."

But Edward does not put him down. He grinds him further
into the wall.

"Why does it have to be *me* that goes sailing?" Arthur
whines. "What have I done that it has to be me?"

Edward looks blank. He doesn't know. He can't remember.

Arthur. Arthur Anderson. Yes. It has something to do with a
telescope and Arthur Anderson. And Emmaline. Arguing.
Fighting. Trying to kill him in the boat. And Arthur Anderson
seeing — watching — seeing. "You've got to come," he says.
"You've got to. It's got to be you."

Arthur is now on the point of passing out. His trachea feels
pulverized by the weight of Edward's grip. The shouting, the
breaking of glass, the violence of everyone's odour seems to
have gathered exclusively in this small corner of the room
where no one seems to be paying the slightest attention to the
fact that he is dying — being murdered up against the plaster.
With a desperate effort he brings his mind into focus and his
knee up into Kiley's middle, thinking as he does so: *Isn't it
strange? I haven't seen Emmaline all evening* . . . and then he
pushes, but before he can push all the way into the gut, Edward
Kiley has smashed his jaw, which is probably what he had in
mind in the first place.

Falling, flying, floating to the floor, all that Arthur is aware
of is the ridiculous fact that, at long last, he can see to whom it
is that Alicia has given her hand so lovingly.

It is Lydia Harmon: and Arthur is paying attention, at last.

Mrs Baker sits on the sofa at one end of a very long room, staring off into the shadows where her favourite son Neddy has
fallen asleep watching television. The Late Show is over and
now there is nothing but a white screen giving off noise. Mrs
Baker toys with her false fingernails and tears them off one by
one, thinking: what an unfortunate choice of colour; thinking:
this silver-blue fad will wear off, surely, after a while; and then:
wondering why they never got back to the lovely *old* reds and
oranges — the tangerines and fuchsias she remembered from
the war. How long ago all that seems, with the men all in
uniform and the women — all the women with their hair up
and all those ghastly shoulder pads that kept on slipping forward until the forward sloping shoulder was forced to become a
style in itself and a grace to be admired.

She looks up. Her husband is moving about the floor above
her head, going from one room to another, never pausing —
lights on, lights off — probably wondering where she is and

why she isn't where he wants her. Or has he forgotten I'm
here? Perhaps he's forgotten. I haven't *seen* him for days. When
was that? Tuesday? Monday? Oh well — I saw him in the hall.
Wearing that bathrobe Sister brought back from the Bahamas.
And *Dennis* . . . I haven't seen *him* in a month.

She looks across at Neddy and smiles. The movie had been
lovely. How Neddy had laughed and loved it — dancing with
his feet. It had been from the war years, Betty Grable and John
Payne — and why did one ever want to sleep with *him*?

Upstairs Mr Baker stops. Has she spoken aloud?

Afraid to tell her husband of her whereabouts, afraid to wake
her son, Mrs Baker places her bitten nails against her lips and
sits forward, reaching for another cigarette. Tyrone Power had
been more her speed. And that John *Payne*: what perfectly
awful posture, and she had always wondered how it was he
avoided being drafted to the Navy. The Airforce was simple:
no one that big would fit in an airplane. And the army had all
the *other* stars. So the Navy needed someone and John Payne
should have been in the navy; but wasn't. Hasn't been. Oh
well, it is over now, and Tyrone Power, Betty Grable,
Veronica Lake, and all the others — they are dead and she is
alone. Without them. Even Alan Ladd is dead. . . .

Alice Faye has said it best, she figures. What in? What was
that in?

Mrs Baker gets up and carries her glass and her cigarette and
her fingernails to the far end of the room, looking down at her
son, asleep in his father's chair, which his father never uses.
She tilts her head to one side and thinks: it is said of most men
that when they're asleep they look like little boys. Tyrone
Power looked 'little-boy-asleep' in dozens of films, but . . . my
son Neddy, when he lies here asleep in this chair, that's the
only time he looks like a man.

I remember. Yes!

And sitting down on the floor beside her son, she begins to
sing: "You'll never know just how much I love you. You'll
never know just how much I care. . . ." But she can't
remember all the words and the song degenerates to humming
and the humming to a sigh and the sigh to a sleep and the sleep
to morning.

On the beach — two figures. Three o'clock a.m. One figure in a white dress — Mexican silver chains. The other — a tank-top, blue, and a pair of white jeans.

"Are you the man?" says Dennie.

"I'm the man," says Addie.

"Jesus — I thought you'd never get here."

"I've been here," says Addie. "I've been here. But you're not here alone, you know. You're not the only kid I carry." She opens her shoulder bag.

"You wouldn't lay any Lipton's on me, would you?"

"Don't be so dumb. Come on — here . . ." She holds out the bag.

Dennie won't take it: "I don't know who you are," he says.

"Look, the last time I was here you weren't on the route. So come on. Take it or leave it. I've got to get off this beach."

"But how do I know who you are?"

"Mr Dixon sent me. Okay?"

"Okay, then."

Addie puts out her hand and, taking the bag, Dennie pays her. She counts the money, puts it in her shoulder bag, and turns to walk away. "Will it be you the next time?" Dennie calls.

Addie stops on the bottom step.

"That depends when the next time is," she says.

Then she climbs out of sight.

At 4:00 a.m. Dennie stands on the Bakers' terrace and stares in through the windows at his mother and his brother asleep. The room is filled with television light and is strangely beautiful. The walls, the furniture, and the figures on the floor and in the chair are aglow with the flicker of white-fire. Dennie leans one arm against the glass and presses his forehead to the arm. Neddy's mouth is open. Mrs Baker's false blue fingernails are scattered across the rug like confetti and the cigarette with which she fell asleep has burned a hole in her skirt. Upstairs, Mr Baker has seen his son on the terrace and has called the police. He will not be stolen from; he will not be robbed; he will not tolerate that anyone — that *anyone* — should take from him the precious view of his wife asleep. Not even through glass.

Ishmael is not in his room.

Still holding her shoes, not yet put on, Addie stands in the doorway waiting for the sun to come up. Her shoulder bag is empty now and droops from her wrist. She is chewing gum.

Her eye scans the room. A person's things look so lonely, she thinks, when there's no one there to be with them. A toothbrush especially, lying on a window sill.

She crosses to the bed and sits. She will wait. He will come. She likes him. In the room there is a special stillness and just the beginnings of light. And then the breeze, through the windows, begins to lift the corners of the magazines and there are

Pictures.

Downstairs one floor, Alicia lies at last in her bed, returned from the hospital; her beautiful black dress, soiled and bloodied, arranged against the back of the door. She can not close her eyes.

For sailing. For a sailboat ride. All over a sailboat ride, a ruined chin, a broken face, and — god — whatever would become of their film? Arthur will be in there for a month.

Don't smoke in bed.

But he won't press charges. Whether because he can't talk, or can't think, or is afraid, he won't and hasn't pressed charges. And Edward Kiley has walked away from the party, Carol Careless on his arm, saying Arthur has insulted her and that was why he's beaten him. Oh, it doesn't make sense. And where is Emmaline? No one has seen her. Emmaline has disappeared. Or perhaps just gone to another party. At any rate it was Carol Edward has defended. Carol Careless. Lydia thought she was tarty and probably didn't wash. She called her a 'blue-movies-lady' and wondered where Edward Kiley found her, not knowing Edward Kiley found her adrift in a rowboat one Sunday off the Buckleys' point. But that is all . . . immaterial. The thing is. . . .

Lydia.

Oh.

But no.

And the clock ticks and far away, in another room, another clock is ticking, but not in time and this is maddening. Maddening. *Maddening*. And here — I've left my rings on, every damn one, and my fingers are swollen — and I can't get them off. Hah-hah! *I can't get my fingers off!*

Oh.

And Alicia reaches for the glass that sits on the bedside table, filled to the brim with her special whisky, pieces of mint and ice. She chews on the mint.

Don't chew on mint in bed.

I must forgive someone. But who?

She ponders, wonders, turns. The windows are bright with the morning. Any minute now the sun would be nailed to the sky and that would be the end of sleep.

Oh.

Lydia.

No.

And she nuzzles the lip of the glass and she feels the liquid either of tears or of whisky softly soaking the pillows and she blinks and she blinks and she blinks: *that hat thing was funny, wasn't it?* And she sees it in her mind, the way it flew across the lawn and across the street and up into old Professor Dinstitch's trees and everyone racing out of all the houses to catch it, to catch Alicia's hat, and all at once, she snaps up in bed, nearly choking on the mint leaves and saying aloud: "It's him. It's *him!* It's *him I'll forgive!* Professor Dinstitch, yes!"

And, lying back, she begins to concoct the scene. At church, perhaps, or on the sidewalk under the cherry trees, under the poplars or over by the steps, with a view of the sky and the thought of the sea. And I'll say: "Professor Dinstitch, no one has ever forgiven you. No one has ever forgiven you for what you've done. But *I* forgive you. *I* do." There.

And Alicia sleeps.

Ishmael enters. There is music in his room as he approaches up the stairs. He is wary. He has not left any radio going. He is tired. His trouser legs are caked with mud. He opens the door.

Sunlight.

It takes him a moment to see that what he sees is what he

sees. And when he sees it, he vomits. Right there, on the threshold, throwing up supper and lunch and anything left of breakfast. Over and over he retches until there is nothing left in his stomach but burning bile of a dark brown colour. Coffee-coloured, sour beyond all hope of sweetening.

And then both hands to his mouth, to his chin, to his nostrils, he sags against the door-jamb, feeling his testicles rise and a wretched tightening of his anus.

All over the walls —

The walls —

All over the walls, every way he turns, wherever he looks, all over the walls, all over the ceiling, over the floor, on every surface, every table, chair, and curtain there are pinned and pasted, glued and plastered each and every page of picture, torn or scissored, ripped or razored from his twenty or thirty magazines — each one staring at him — every eye on Ishmael: eight hundred and fifty-two women, fingered, licked, explored, and spattered from every conceivable position. But there is nothing now left to bring up — either from his stomach or from his scrotum.

"Come in."

"I can't move."

"Of course you can. Come in."

"I don't want to come in."

"You *must* come in. Come in."

Ishmael reels round beyond the door in slow motion.

"What have you . . . what have you done?" he asks, beginning only now again to hear the music. "And *why*?" he weeps.

Addie is seated on the bed with a pair of scissors, her white dress mingled with the sheets.

The song is something John Lennon sings called "Imagine."

"Don't be afraid," says Addie and throws the scissors through the open window. "I want you not to be afraid."

Ishmael seems stranded in the middle of the rug, on top of Charleen Cheri's face and jutting tongue — as if she would lick his toes.

"You're standing on someone's face," says Addie, looking down.

Ishmael crosses to Felicity Fellatio, his heels on her thighs.

"Where were you?" Addie asks, lighting a cigarette and blowing out the match, which she holds in her fingers, letting the sulphur kill the stench of the vomit.

"I was out."

There is a pause. He does not know where to look or what to do and he has to exercise the most stringent control to prevent his fingers from reaching for his crotch. The pictures, being themselves, bring on this automatic, auto-erotic response.

Then, cutting through the music, cutting through his desire to drop, Ishmael hears Addie's voice, which is oddly tender and strangely sympathetic: "So you were 'out'," she says: "And did you find anyone?"

He waits and straightens and shakes his head: "There isn't anyone," he says. He looks at the floor, or what was the floor and is now a paper whorehouse. "Where *is* there anyone? I don't know. . . ."

"Right here," says Addie. "But you have to promise me something."

Ishmael lifts his eyes only, to see her.

"You have to promise me you won't pretend I'm someone else."

He can't do that. He knows he can't do that. But he doesn't say so. Instead, he half turns away.

"Oh, why have you done this to me?" he says, and scuffles through the pages to his suitcase and his vodka.

Addie holds her knees in her hands.

"A paper love-life isn't much," she says, and wishes to God he would laugh or would smile. Maybe she means it as a joke, but she knows now she can't say that. "Maybe I. . . ."

"Maybe you just don't understand," he says and sits on top of Caroline Caress.

"I guess I don't," she says.

There is a moment in which Ishmael drinks with a shaky hand — in which Addie stares from the window and then, not turning around to look at him, she hears herself whisper, either to him or to herself, she is not sure which: "I don't know why you want to live."

It is more than evening, not quite night.

Addie has gone away and all afternoon Ishmael has been in his room, not even daring to look from the window. Suddenly she went away in another taxi, watched by Miss Dinstitch across the road, and the leaves all seemed to turn in her direction as she went. Ishmael only heard the closing doors and the wheels.

Alicia has telephoned the hospital and discovered that Arthur is under sedation. It is pointless to go there, nothing can be done or said. She has called up the stairs to Ishmael, but since he has not answered, she presumes he is out, and she goes to the den where she plays the cello.

And now it is evening, but not quite night.

Ishmael ventures to the door, to the stairs, to the door, to the walk, to the sidewalk, to the steps — but not to the beach. He wears his white sweater, white jeans, white socks, and his white shoes. Even his cigarettes are white and the coffee mug with his vodka.

It begins to darken and the lights begin to falter across the water. Miss Dinstitch on her porch, Mrs Baker on her terrace, Ishmael on his step, and the man who whistles Beethoven in his garden, all listen to the cello.'

It plays and plays. And then it stops.

On Monday, Rosetta comes up coatless in the early morning. All through the weekend, the fires where she lives downtown have been smouldering and giving up more victims. Soldiers have been standing on the corners of the streets, their rifles slung with a crazy nonchalance across their backs. Most of the soldiers chew their gum and watch the smoking ruins through slitted eyes, like people who have sat all night to watch a horror picture marathon. Nothing moves them but the thought of bed. Rosetta, too, is tired, not having slept a great deal. Clyde has told her they are standing at a crossroads. "This is the end of us," he said to her, looking out at what the fires had done. "Either that or the beginning. I can't say which. It's just a moment in between a life and death . . ."

Now, Rosetta stops herself cold at the foot of the Andersons' walk. There on the lawn, with something between its paws, is Kileys' dog.

"Hi, there," says Rosetta — who knows the dog well.

The dog returns her greeting by wagging its tail and, indeed, the entire rear end of its body. Its eyes are bright again and merry. The thing between its paws is sticking up like a butcher's bone — all red at the top and ragged.

"Watcha got there?" says Rosetta, stooping to bring the object into focus.

Kileys' dog displays its prize.

Rosetta suddenly finds that she is sitting on the ground unable to move or to speak. The thing before her slowly conjures up its name.

It is a human hand and the dog, at last, is complete as Rosetta and the world around her fade.

Losers, Finders,
Strangers at the Door

Some lives
are only seen
through windows
beyond which
the appearance
of laughter
and of screaming
is the same.

. . . . there are no beginnings, not even to stories. There are
only places where you make an entrance into someone else's
life and either stay or turn and go away.

She cursed the day she'd hung the cages — strung them so
high, out of reach — cursed every time she had to pull a chair
across the room to reach them — cursed every time she didn't
think to check them — cursed every time she did. They were a
curse. But, then, in those moments, roars of laughter filled her
— when she'd said: those cursed cages are a curse! Whenever
she turned, to hear this laughter of her own, however, it was
always gone: either lost, unechoed, or had never been.

As now.

Damn them. So high up, she said aloud, all of them so unwatered: wanting. Expecting me to do it. Me to always do it for them. *Why can't they do it for themselves?* she bellowed, filling the house with sound at last. And then, as well, with laughter.

How could geraniums possibly water themselves.

It was perfect.

Madness.

Still he hadn't come: arrived. No matter how long she waited. Even if she didn't wait, he didn't come: arrive. Perhaps he wouldn't. Ever. And that would be a blessed relief. Or would it? No. That would be wrong. Was wrong. After all, he wasn't arriving of his own volition. He was being delivered. Sent. Dispatched. Like a package. It was wrong to refuse him. Wrong to turn him away at the door, the way one would send something back from Simpsons or Eaton's. *No, I've decided against that, today. Take it back.* Besides — she hadn't ordered him herself. Her husband Arnold had. This parcel will arrive. From Arnold. C.O.D. — this package, person, parcel — in her husband's absence.

What would he be like?

And where the hell is my pocketbook? I still can't find my pocketbook. Or glove. One glove. And — oh — I loved them so: that pair. And now I've only one. But, where's my pocketbook? My pocketbook? Not anywhere. Nowhere. Yes. I've looked. I have. I have looked.

HAVE LOOKED!

Everywhere.

And now it's — what? What is it? Four? It's already four in the afternoon. And dark. Already dark.

Or darkening at least.

And she wondered what he'd be like. *If he ever does arrive.* Can manage to arrive. He's probably some dumb fool, too charming to arrive on time. Or an idiot — always getting lost.

Just like my glove. And pocketbook.

She looked at the plants. Geraniums: *gerania.* Dangling, all bright and red and thirsty above her — just out of reach. On purpose, of course. In their iron cages, if they weren't out of reach, we'd all be banging and bashing our heads against them. Every five minutes. Wouldn't we? Even me. Why — even me — who am so very small.

Now, there's a laugh:

Like me — who am so very small.

It sounds like Christina Rossetti.

Or some other darling of the death-set.

Well — the point is — water the plants.

But, I can't do that. I can't. I mean, it would be a scream — just simply crazy — if this person, this package from Arnold were delivered to the door and found me falling off a chair with a watering can in my hand. In one hand. And this

empty glass in the other.

No. The plants can go hang . . . but, of course, they're already hanging. Hanged.

And the laughter came again.

Some day, I'll hire someone special. Someone just to come and water plants. And me.

No. What I'll do is this: I'll fill the glass and then I'll put on music — just a little music. Then I'll phone the airport — check on the plane's arrival — see if it's arrived or not and then. . .

She filled the glass, put on the record. Walked the room. Gin and Mahler. If he comes, I'll be a lady. Hah. A little lady — all the way.

I'm having a little gin, she planned to say: and tonic. What will you have? Brandy? (Of course.) Of course. What else? Who does he think he is? Don't you love it? Oh! What a *scene* it's going to be. That? — she would say — oh, just a little Mahler for the afternoon. You know the one — where all the children die and go to heaven. . .

Then, brandy-snifter in hand, she'd cross the room — impeccable, unparagoned, with slightly swaying hips, passing beneath impeccable, unparagoned gerania, with her Lana Turner smile, her Chanel suit and her impeccable, unparagoned hatred of this package-person drawn, revolver-like, snub-nosed and lethal. And then

she'd shoot him. Right through his goddamned C.O.D.

Yes! She'd really let him have it!

Politely, of course, because she is a lady. And every nuance will make him cringe.

If he ever gets here.

And then she imagined him arriving: Arnold's package, already cringing. Herself looking down and saying: take it back, I can't afford to pay for any other voyage but my own. Oh God.

And then she knew. Exactly where the glove was. And the pocketbook. Exactly where she'd left them. Dropped. Forgotten. Lost. And when she thought of this — remembered — she was standing in the dining room, standing well beyond the shadows of the cages — even beyond the reaches of the shadows, since the light was fading faster now, the shadows leaning out to touch her and she turned away to look beyond the lovely windows, into the darkening garden, into the secret garden out behind the house . . . this room, these windows: this was her favourite place.

And then she turned away and wondered what to do about the mess she'd made on the dining-room table with her paints. (This was her painting room, because the windows were so high. Much higher than the ones out front.) And the table was spread with papers — newspapers, wrapping papers, packaging papers — spread to protect the veneer beneath. And over the papers, scatters of broken brushes, seemingly moving in the moving light. Old bits of rag, as well. Even a handkerchief of Arnold's, daubed with magenta and blue — its large embroidered A almost obliterated with a single, still-wet spasm. . . green. Also, there were little tubes of colours: oils, acrylics, water colours; toy pastels and children's crayons. And a stack — a dozen high at least — of *Paint-by-Number* sets.

But this was really to have been the scene about the glove; the pocketbook.

She dialled.

A glove is a glove. They fall, she thought as she waited. Sometimes they fall and even crawl across the floor. Just to get away from you. I had a glove that even climbed up trees to hide. . .

Hello. Yes. Who are you? I want to know your name. Tell me. Don't argue. Don't talk back. Just tell me your name. Imperious son-of-a-bitch. If you don't tell me your name I'll have you arrested.

A voice at the other end of the line delivers its name.

All right. Now listen. This is Daisy McCabe: Mrs *Arnold Mc-Cabe*. So, I warn you — stand way back. (She pauses. Drinks — to let the name sink in — the only knife she has. And then goes on): I took a ride in one of your goddamn cabs this afternoon and lost a glove. And I want it back. Another pause. The voice attempts to reply. But Daisy interrupts:

a brown, suede glove. A driving glove. A very *important* driving glove. I want it and I want it now. So, while you go and check, I'll hold. . . (a question from the voice: just one) *McCabe*. I told you that. And don't pretend you don't know who I am. I know you know, because you have my . . .

glove

(my pocketbook: oh God. . .

she stares at the cages, with their shadows reaching down around her — dry and red and whispering

. . . and, in it, me)

So find it: FIND IT. Send it to me.

NOW.

The doorbell rings.

The package has arrived.

Daisy hangs up without good-bye. The doorbell rings again. Mrs Rosequist is out: so

Mrs Arnold McCabe must answer the doorbell herself.

The boy is what we call a boy in this society, but he is 25 years old and not a boy at all. Taller than Daisy by almost a foot (and she is five feet tall) he seems to hang above her, off the floor.

He removes his overcoat, revealing an out-of-season suit: summer. In the hallway, sitting near a table, all of what he

brought from the plane remains withdrawn and out of sight.
The rest — the bulk — will be delivered later.

His eyes, perhaps, are blue: in the present light it's very
hard to tell. But his hair is definitely pale, the shade of white,
fine sand — the sort that drifts.

Daisy is steadfast, refusing absolutely to take away or even to
indicate his overcoat. There is not a single gesture of regard.

Mrs Rosequist isn't in the house, right now, she says: I'm
drinking gin and tonic. You'll have a brandy. Yes?

Thank you.

My husband has a man — a valet — who travels with him.
But, of course, you know that.

Yes.

Tell me. . . (pouring the brandy) when you last saw Arnold.

Yesterday evening.

(The music is the one about the children.)

Was he fit? Did he seem to be bearing up? These executive
. . . (smiling) excursions can be so tiring. . . (turning — Lana
Turnering) for a man of Arnold's age.

He was absolutely fine.

(Now the impeccables, unparagonables: the swaying hips,
the Chanel suit, the L.T. smile; the hatred, snub-nosed, drawn
beneath the cages. And the shot. Right through the C.O.D.)

(holding out the brandy-snifter) I have a rather silly confes-
sion to make (he accepts the brandy: thanks her) I was at a
party once and . . . would you mind? (she flashes a cigarette to
her lips. He flashes his light, but she goes right on speaking,
just as if it wasn't there:) I was with my brother and his wife
and these people came across the room. It's quite immaterial
who they were. And I started to introduce my brother, when,
all of a sudden I realized . . . isn't this a crazy thing to tell you?
. . . all of a sudden I realized I couldn't remember his name.
(She laughs) My one and only brother! And I couldn't
remember his name! (And now, at last, his having held it open,
flaring for her all through what she's said — she bends toward
his light and takes it in a single draught.)

Looking up, she releases the smoke very slowly — so it

throws a momentary veil across her face. When it clears toward the cages — Daisy is standing with her lips apart; with her teeth clenched; with just the vaguest hint of laughter hanging in the silence.

Now — she says — you tell me who the hell you are. And what the hell you're doing here in my house? Because, you see, I seem to have forgotten you already.

They sit, not facing one another, near a table in the living room. The food Mrs Rosequist left before she left herself is almost gone; not quite completely eaten.

Daisy sets her fork aside, sits back and stares at the flowers above her, while the young man finishes his lobster.

Caleb, I suppose, is what you'd call a Biblical name?

Yes, ma'am.

She shoots him a look: servile is as servile does, she says; you needn't rehearse in front of me. All I want is answers and information.

Daisy stands up. She collects a cigarette and rather pointedly lights it herself. She refers, with a gesture, to the flowers, whose heads bend down toward them — scarlet and thirsty.

Were you aware, she asks, that flowers are the genitalia of plants.

No, ma'am — (with his mouth full of lobster) — I never heard that, Mrs McCabe.

Well — it's true. They are.

She reaches up and plucks the nearest dangling head.

I just castrated that geranium. You see? And, there's a theory, also . . . (she twirls the scarlet head between her fingers, rolling it back and forth) that if we only had microphones sensitive enough — the picking and cutting of flowers would produce an unbearable scream. (She pauses.) Fascinating. Yes?

No answer.

Suddenly, Daisy throws the genitalia across the room, where they land — if only approximately — in Caleb's lap.

Quiet. Isn't it? All at once.

Somewhat later, Daisy stands over near the living-room windows, just before she pulls the curtains.

I hate these windows, she says — without, for the first time, any malice toward him. I hardly ever stand here, or look out there down the Mountain. At night, I suppose one has to admit, it's a very beautiful city — with all its curving lights and falling streets. But — not to me: by day. Never by day. And certainly not from here. It's always from here — beyond these windows — that Arnold goes away. Either walking down the hill in his beautiful suits and overcoats — or driven away in limousines. This window always makes me think what hell it is to be rich. To have so much that it locks me in behind this glass — and — oh — a dangerous anonymity, I guess. I can't explain. But, whatever it is that drives him down that mountain — holds me here, in all these lovely clothes with all these goddamn flowers. (She laughs: it is graceful, for once — and not a shout.) Where does he go, in all those airplanes? Where is it I don't go? (Her neck straightens.) Well: I do get away, from time to time. In taxis. Cabs. I get a cab and go out riding. Just around. I don't know where . . . forgetting who I am. (She holds — then sighs a little laughter.) . . . maybe I do it just for the hell of it. Or should I say — (she turns) just for the non-hell of it, Caleb?

Daisy draws the curtains and sits in a chair that is cornered, shadowed: slightly removed from the scene.

Caleb has been watching her back with interest, but now she's turned around he looks away.

Are you shy? she asks.

He doesn't answer right away.

Afraid? she asks.

At last, he shakes his head — his answer dies: I just. . . I guess I haven't much to say.

Well, tell me about yourself.

Nothing to tell.

Don't be ridiculous.

No. Really. Nothing. Nothing.

What about your father? Tell me about your father. Is he living?

Sort of.

(Laughter.) There! You see. A fascinating answer. Tell about him.

There's nothing to say.

Like father, like son?

Caleb smiles at this (at least): you see — my father doesn't know. . . we have nothing in common. Nothing. He doesn't. . . understand.

What? Understand? What?

What . . . I do.

Oh.

He's just a very ordinary man.

And your mother? Tell me — (smiling) does she understand?

She's dead.

Unh-hunh. And when was that?

I think I was fourteen. Sometime. Then. Around then.

What happened?

An accident. An airplane that crashed.

Like ours just did? said Daisy, smiling.

I beg your pardon?

Nothing: just — I guess — an intellectual joke. I never know what they mean myself. But — sometimes — someone laughs — and then I think I understand. But — you didn't laugh: which means that neither of us, sitting here, will ever know exactly what I meant. Go on.

She'd been away. And she was coming home to us. From Rome.

You're Catholic?

Mother was. I guess I am. But — no. My mother was. I'm not. I'm nothing.

Nothing.

Yes. It was Marian year. My mother's name was Mary. And — among all the others — she went to be blessed by the Pope. . .

Arnold. Arnold has been blessed by many Popes. By three, in fact.

He said so. Yes, he told me that.

How could he help it? Daisy smiled. Go on. Your mother. Mary.

The Pope refused to bless her when she murmured she was separated from my father. And then . . . she begged it of him, saying she would reconcile: be reconciled. And he — it being the Marian year — gave in, I guess —

And so she kissed his ring. I can see it. Genuflected; let him bless her; got on the plane. And was killed. I see it. Yes. I see it all. (A pause:) What happened? To the plane, I mean.

It struck an Alp. And there were no survivors.

None?

Not any. No. And they still don't know what caused the plane to crash. No storms; no calls for help; no indications either plane or pilot was in trouble; no malfunctions. Nothing. And there were 242 persons on board. Persons. People.

Persons will do. I think of myself as a person from time to time, she smiles. And then . . .?

At the graveside we stood with a lot of strangers. No one knew who anyone was — or had been. What they buried — what there was was just a lot of boxes: just a lot of half-filled boxes, all without names. And we stood together. And we stood together — all the mourners — strangers — knowing we would never know who stood by whom; who lay with whom; or what was buried. I think. . .

Yes?

I think that was very hard for my father. Very hard. Because he hadn't seen her — even alive — my mother — such a long, long time. (Caleb taps his finger against the edge of his plate. His fingernails are very hard.) And then we went away. Except — I do remember one more thing.

What's that? Daisy is squinting at him — darkened, in her corner.

I was standing — standing there, thinking I stood beside my father, but — in fact — we were separated, somehow. And — some other person took my hand. And held it. All through the service. Very hard, I remember: holding me very hard. And then, when the service was over — letting go. And I looked up and realized it hadn't been my father.

Who, then?

I don't know. A man. Some other man.

A pause: a hold, while Daisy blinks. And then she says: how long ago was this?

Eleven years. Or ten.

Daisy takes up another cigarette. Caleb rises, crossing, already flashing his light and lights her darkness with it — almost meanly, so it seems to Daisy.

And you remember her? Your mother? Mary?

No. (The light goes out. He crosses back to the empty plates.)

Well — anyway — the Pope died, too. (A beat.) She got him in the end. (Another beat.) Or someone did. . .

Then: laughter. Daisy rises from the corner.

Laughter, someone once said to Daisy, *is braver than silence.* She thinks of that, now, but — looking at Caleb — knows she mustn't say it. That would be another intellectual joke that — if he didn't laugh — she might lose faith in. And she needed it: no, not the joke — the faith. She gets herself another drink and looks across the room. You don't understand me, do you? Sad. How sad, she says. And to think I once had a face — like yours — as beautiful as yours: every nuance lovely, innocent and lovely. (A pause.) And sinister. (She turns away, dropping ice cubes into her glass.) Then, one day, in the mirror, the loveliness — the innocence — is gone. And only the sinister remains (she faces him): as I'm sure you can see.

I'm a loser. Loser of things, I mean. I mean: lose things. *Lose* them. Always. Nearly always. I am nearly always . . . things. Some people find things. Find them. Finders. In the street. In taxi-cabs. In other places of inconsequence. The difference isn't losers-winners: it is losers. . . finders. Caleb? Where was it you found Arnold — he found you? Where are these places one may be a finder: *find.* . .? What is it one must do? Or *be*? To find things for oneself?

(All of this — of the above — from *I'm a loser* down to *for oneself* she wants to, means to say aloud: but can't. Instead — aloud — she says what follows:)

I'm glad you're here. I'm glad. And, when Arnold returns, I shall be very glad. (A pause.) I have a friend — a close friend, very close — whose name I do remember, by the way, but which I won't divulge, because. . . Because. At any rate, this friend whose name I won't divulge, is married: down the Mountain — and her husband has a penchant for — (she watches Caleb now, to see what he will do — to see if he will cringe, or curl) are you wondering what I'm going to say? Thinking — is she going to say this husband of her friend has a penchant for horses? Goats? For Germans? Men in raincoats? For the Dutch in wooden shoes? What are you wondering, I wonder? Well. To kill suspense — I'll tell you: tell you what the penchant was (or is) . . . This husband of my friend has simple, very simple tastes. He likes to be beaten (watching) half to death.

Caleb doesn't stir an inch. His hands just dangle down between his knees. His mouth is closed. But, across his brow, the drifts of hair begin to catch — are held by beads of sweat.

Beaten. Half to death. Imagine. Think where he had to go in order just to find someone — someone he could trust to beat him only *half* to death. Someone who wouldn't kill him. Think. Imagine. Where he had to go. And what he had to do. The care with which he had to . . . choose. And think what his wife went through, until he was returned: came back, returned, as from the grave — a happy man, but . . . beaten half to death.

Daisy takes a drink and almost chokes. On laughter:

hah! When I told this story to another friend — a certain Mrs Bresson — when I told this story to her, she said a very witty thing, I thought. *Which half?* she said. Oh — (laughter under ice cubes) which half? I think it's just a scream.

Caleb, in his chair, begins to stir: begins to lift his hands — to try to find some other place to put them, one by one — one here, one there, one here, one there — but all they do is sag again — fall back between his knees and dangle, where they were, as helpless now as then, before he tried to get away and hide.

You're tired, says Daisy: tired. Oh do forgive me: this is

unforgiveable. Look at the time. It's nearly midnight, now —
and you have had a long, long flight — and I just go on talking,
while you must be nearly. . .

OH! I nearly said it. Nearly said: half dead. . .! Half dead.
Why — you must be half dead!

Caleb doesn't budge. Not even the corner of a lip is moved.

Attempting to sober — to escape her laughter — Daisy says:
you're tired, forgive me. That's all I meant to say. Okay?

Okay.

Now: to go on — to get on with this story I was telling you.
The wife of this man (the wife being my friend) — you must
attempt to feel her panic: think of how she worried, what she
went through when he went away, was gone. Such long periods
of time, sometimes, he'd go away — you must imagine how
she felt, how ill she was: became. Because she knew that,
needing what he needed, he must find and frequent the darkest
places — places in the dark: and dangerous. And always, she
knew, he must be so careful to select the most delicately poised
and . . . balanced of perverts (She waits a moment, thinking
about this herself — and then she goes on') and then he must
exit with this man . . . this boy . . . this man . . . and find with
him some room, somewhere and brave out that dark with him

be brave

brave out that dark, together with a stranger, having whatever it was he needed so carefully applied — having it applied,
so neatly and so carefully — with instruments and implements
I dare not mention; think of. . .

and survive it all

intact.

The silence that follows this surveys the house from end to
end.

Well.

My friend knew one day it must follow that her husband
would not come back: return, or be returned; that he could not
be always returned to her intact — alive. That is — she knew
that he must die — be killed —

by a stranger. By some strange man — or boy — whose

name would not be known: whose face would not be known to
her. And this she COULD NOT BEAR — (the silence fled the
house) because not knowing who she was herself, she could not
bear another stranger in her life — who could — who would
deprive her life of
   what?
   Its *name*.
   Silence. Caleb, at last, knows where to look. He looks directly at Daisy. At her face; her hand that is frozen to its empty
glass; her other hand that reaches up to touch her hair.
   Then, Daisy speaks and says: she wanted, at least, to be able
to gaze on the stranger's face and say, *I know. I understand. I
know.* She wanted to . . . forgive him. Fold up her own identity
inside of forgiveness. Do you . . . do you understand?
   I think so. Yes.
   Anyway, at last unable to tolerate her anguish any longer,
my friend decided she must say to her husband — (and did — I
mean, she said it) *at whatever the cost to me and whatever the cost to
you, for God's sake go and find someone and bring him here.* (Daisy
pauses and then, in the other woman's voice, her friend's, goes
on:) *Bring him. Bring him here. To live with us. To be with us.*
   TO BE WITH US.
   And so — he began to go away less often less and less and
less; until, one day — a young man appeared at the door. And
has been there ever since: in the curious phrase of my friend —
they have been there all together, ever since. And
   (now she turns and looks at Caleb. Tears. Without mascara.
Tears. Just tears and she smiles at him — putting out her
hand)
   and so — that is why I am so glad you're here. At last. So —
very glad you're here.

   And when Arnold returns — I shall. . . No: there is no *gladder*,
is there. Nothing better than very glad. So that will do,
whenever he comes.
   If he does.

   Before you go to bed: before I show you where it is — will be —

where you'll sleep, would you get a chair and water all the
plants? You can see how small I am. You can see that, without
Mrs Rosequist, Arnold or his valet, all the plants would die.
Would perish. So high up. They should never have been hung
— been hanged — so far above us. On the other hand, if they
weren't, we'd all be banging and bashing our heads — why,
even me, who am so small. So, if you wouldn't mind; before I
show you where it is you'll sleep — be sleeping from now on. . .
You do believe me, don't you? That I'm glad — relieved —
you're here? You do believe that, don't you?

   Yes, ma'am.

   Good. Done and over. Finished. The parcel is safely
delivered: the package has been accepted. C.O.D. The flowers
will be watered. What is there left to say?

The Book of Pins

A Friday 2:15 p.m.

The old hotel still smelled the same and it gave off the same
gold light. In the lobby, the dark oak panels shone with the
same deep glow of oil-of-lemon wax and the smoky mirrors
reflected still the same old women in the same brocaded chairs.
Nothing changed. The people were changed, perhaps, but
never their image — never the basic reflection of what was
there.

When Annie Bogan came out of the Bar and Grill, she noted
that the woman behind the magazine counter must just have
come on duty. She was putting away her handbag, eating a
humbug; jangling her bracelets, staring around the lobby, fix-
ing her lips. Annie continued to watch the woman's assemb-
lage from over by the elevator doors. Fifty-five, perhaps, or
more; with a thin, French mouth and jaw-breaker eyes, way in
behind her glasses, the lenses of which were encased in tortoise-
shell and lacquered beads. Her hair was faintly mauve, with a
rinse; and her pale blue smock had a pointed crest that read:
L'ÉTOILE.

Annie thought of her, then, as Star — as Mademoiselle Star,

who shone in the lobby of the old hotel. The lobby was her place. Her fame was *to be there*.

Good. That pins another one.

The elevator came. Two men got off and, thank God, no-one else got on. Turning to face the front and reaching for the button, Annie saw, with some panic, a pair of feet in flapping galoshes, charging through the revolving doors and over the carpet towards her. Quickly, she fumbled for her floor and pressed eighteen instead of twenty-two. But, still — that didn't matter. The main thing was the doors had closed and Annie had achieved her goal. She was going upstairs alone.

2:20 p.m.

She rarely stayed in hotels, but, whenever she did, it was always at the pinnacle: the top. Twenty-two floors, or ninety, or ten — it didn't matter how high or low — she always had to be the farthest away the hotel could offer. When it couldn't offer the top, she went somewhere else. She might even go to another city. But, over the years (she was now approaching forty-two) the old hotels of her choice had come to enjoy her patronage and, mostly, they gave her what she wanted. Fame, in its way, had these advantages: rooms you liked; private tables in the Bar and Grill; a man to open doors and get you through unseen; a certain separation from the race the totally unknown could not afford. Who else but the famed could refuse the company of strangers — the touch of hands?

Annie's room was the last on the left, with windows facing both east and south. Her views were of the park and the dark cathedral; of streets slipping down to the town and the river itself, the black St. Lawrence: oiled by ships in transit; arched by bridges; strung with lights. It was autumn and the leaves had fallen: the very best time of year to see in all directions, including down. She had always preferred the November streets, alive and wet with snaky neon; reflections everywhere; and everywhere, the bent, unseeing eyes of passers-by. The very best time of year. In every way.

The telephone rang.

"Annie Bogan, please."

"Mademoiselle Bo-gan n'est pas ici, M'sieu'."

"Uhm-oh." (Whoever it was could not speak French, she supposed. All the better to keep him at bay.)

"Eh? S'il vous plait, M'sieu'? Un message pour la?" (Dead silence.) "M'sieu'?" (More fumbling silence: a sort of sigh.) Annie now amused herself by adding a sing-song tone: "Okay! A vo'service, M'sieu'. Bye-bye. . . ." and had all but completely hung up, when the voice came through with a shout:

"You bitch! Is that *you*?"

The voice now had a certain familiarity, even held at arm's length. She brought the phone back up to her ear.

"Qui va là?" She smiled. The standard *English* greeting in Quebec, since Wolfe.

"It's me, you dumb-assed broad."

"Hughie?"

"None other. . . ."

"Come on, now. Don't get smart," she cut him off. "Where are you now? Are you *here*?"

"Of course I'm here. I live here. Christ! You don't remember nuttin'. I always said you was nuts. So — what's ya doin'?"

Hughie Gates. And, suddenly, she didn't want at all to see him. Two seconds before, when first she'd recognized his voice, her heart sort of leapt up — but, now, his collegiate gaiety had brought her down with a bang. She remembered him real: as he was.

"I'm busy," she said, too fast. "You know I'm very busy these. . . ." she went on, trying to string it out so it wouldn't sound unreasonable. "And just how *did* you, by the way, find out that I was here?"

"Claire. She knows everything." (Hughie's wife.)

"Really!" (I'll kill her.) "And how are *you*?"

"Hating it."

"Hating what? Montreal?"

"Teaching, dumb-ass. English. You know: *an-glais*." Roars of laughter. God — he thought he was a bloody scream. . . .

No. She did not want to see him.

"Hugh, listen, what can I do for you, hon? I really am quite busy."

He paused. He was obviously thrown. Mostly, she was glad to see him: when she saw him. Over a year, but not quite two. A long way off and a long time ago. In Toronto.

"I thought we might have a drink," he offered.

"No." She had to say no. "It's just this trip. I'm really kind of pressed."

"Okay," he said. And he came right down to the Hugh she had liked, the one she could abide, with his own voice: "I'll tell you the truth; there's a problem. . ."

Jesus. She didn't need a problem. Not someone else's problem. Not now: but, still. . . .

"What is it? Is it Claire?"

"Come on, Annie: don't be so crass. I thought you had more imagination than that. Jesus! A man says he's got a problem and everybody jumps right in with 'your wife, of course!' " (He was using his voices again.) "It is not my *wife*, dumb-ass: it's. . ."

Someone was talking off-stage at Hughie's end of the line. Annie waited. She might as well hear the worst and then hang up.

"Are you there?" she said.

"Yes, yes. Hang on. . . ." More voices. Claire's was one of them — and, then, one other: indecipherable.

Annie watched herself waiting in the mirror across the room. She was wearing red. Her face was absolutely white and her eyes were absolutely black. She was Irish, but her long, white face, black hair and vivid mouth had a way of making her image Japanese. Her wrists were Japanese — and her hands, with beautiful, cultured nails like pieces of elegant shell, were Japanese. And the red. She surrounded herself with red: all kinds and every shade of red, from pink through orange. And black and white. Kabuki. F.N. Thompson even called her that: "Kabuki Bogan: the Lady of Words." And his letters always began: "My Lady. . ."

"Yes?"

"Well, you see — we have a visitor. Who sort of wants to see you."

No. "Who's that?"

"It's Frannie."

Annie caught her breath. She was lost in the mirror. Too bad: the pause would be telling. Still, she couldn't help it. *Frannie*. Jesus-and-Teresa. Why? "So what's the trouble?"

"Trouble?" His whimsy had returned.

"Don't be dense, Hugh. I've already said I'm busy. And I could hear all those voices. Ergo: trouble. Now — come on. Tell me. Stop horsing around. There isn't time for cute. . . ."

"Well — fuck you, too!" He was serious, now: and angry. "Christ! You pick up a few reviews and a bit of money and you go all grand on everyone. Screw that, Bogan. Good-*bye*." And he hung up. Just as suddenly as that. He was gone. And with him, why ever it was that Frannie had been so desperate to see her. She felt as if someone had pinned her.

4 p.m.

The phone didn't ring again. And she couldn't, even though she'd gone so far as to look up the number, really telephone him. Not Hugh. Not after the past — and the present. No.

She'd tried to take a few drinks. But never — they never worked. They were not the same. It was not enough. Nothing but all the way was enough. And she thought of her arms — and the needle and just how long it had been since (careful) yesterday. And, well: it was now . . . it was sometime, now, in the afternoon. And she walked, had walked to the window and looked, had looked all the way down. It was twenty-one window-ledges down and she looked, had looked at the street. And then it was now. It was now in the afternoon and, yes, she would have to. Yes, she would have to. Yes. And she did.

She crossed the floor and drew off the dress and was still in red, because the slip was red and then she went and locked herself in the bathroom. She locked the door, because the locking of the door was a part of the process: always had been a part of the process. And always would — and always would — and always would be. Even locked in behind a thousand doors, she would always lock that final door. The farthest door. The furthest door. Farthest and furthest.

Farthest is place, she repeated: *furthest is always in the mind.* . . .

And then, in twenty minutes (four o'clock) she came back

out and lay on the bed. Her arm, which was sore, was across her face and her eyes were closed. In a moment, it would not be bad: so bad. And then it would slowly get better. And better. Until it was all all right. And the needle took effect.

She wished there was music. Music was always nice. Or Frannie. Or something. Later on, she might — she just might, yes, go out and see if there was something. Somewhere. But, now (she got up) a drink: a drink would go down very nicely, very nicely, thank you now, my love.

And she lifted the dress and she floated, all in red, across the room toward the windows — gathering whisky all the way. The Lady of Words was pinned against the glass. If only F.N. Thompson could see her now. His Lady. Laugh.

11 p.m.
Le Bistro was slowly filling. Annie felt late. She always felt late in the rush.

There was music here — and that was good. Helen Reddy was singing a song called "Time." ". . . carry me on . . ." she could hear, as she raced, or seemed to race for a place, alone, at one of the tables. She sat. Her coat was a weave of red and orange: and, above it, her face was powdered, over-white and she wore her deep green specs, the ones with the silver frames and her gloves were as long as giraffes and her shoes were like tongues that could taste the floor.

Here was a haven-place. A home. Relaxed: "A Pernod, s'il vous please." Amongst the true companionship — the anonymity of peers. Of peer-sons. Wow! She breathed. She sighed. The Lady of Words who hadn't made it out the window yet. Tonight.

Off with the gloves, then: one by one, expose the nails; one by one by one by one; the Pernod fluted into frame; the boy who brought it beautiful; the waves of Helen Reddy's singing one by one *and when I* one by one *go home my heart like a* one by one *stone: will they* one by one *call me their own when I* one by one *go home?*

Her fingers, laid out in neat array at last upon the zinc, were very pale and shell against the grey. She was mirrored, now:

and waited. She counted up her muscles, thinking: here are poems: *here are my poems: my desperation in repose.* . . .

It was good. It was written: published — and good. Even Hugh had thought it was good — in his back-handed way — even in anger, good. And, here was freedom — if someone would come.

The faces scattered round the room were English, French, *Canadian*, some above leather, some above dumpy-wool and duffle. And their feet all leaned so easy on the floor. It was lovely to watch their feet and to wait. There were faces she knew and some she did not. There were shoes she didn't give a damn about and some she longed to hold between her teeth and suck. Some shoes had even come across and said hello. It was getting early now — and the earlier it got, the more she thought: if someone doesn't come, I'll have to let some one sit down. She was cast adrift: anonymous, and yet they knew her. Her specs were a ruse against the dangerous light — and a signal of respect for friends. And every one of them who stayed for words was good about her book: no flattery, just pleasant praise, acceptance, gratitude that she'd survived. The pleasure of her peers, who knew you survived, or did not survive, a book. And then. . . .

There was Frannie.

She could see him beyond the glass refractions and he had to break through the Gauloise fog to reach her.

"Hello," he said. His hands were in his pockets.

"Yes. Well. You didn't phone, you see. And I thought you might have telephoned when *he* hung up — and then I got unbusy and . . . I drifted over here. Sit down."

He did not sit down.

She watched him — sideways, while he watched the room. He did not look well. He did not look sane, somehow.

"Sit down. It *would* be nice. You draw attention, when you stand."

"Maybe I want to draw attention."

"Frannie. Shit. *Sit down.*"

He sat: a sort of glide to the chair, his hands still deep inside his pockets, shoulders hunched, his hair across his face.

Annie smiled.

"Here we are," she said. She reached for a cigarette and held it tight between her teeth. "I'd like a match, if you have a match," she said.

Frannie fumbled around in the depths and hauled out a Zippo lighter and flicked it open. He struck the flint with his thumb and placed the flame at her disposal. The waiter came. Frannie ordered a bottle of wine and Annie held her glass up, empty. Frannie and Annie.

The waiter took the glass and went away and they were left alone again.

"How come you're in Montreal?" she asked.

"I'm writing a screenplay," he said. And he gave the word a smell as he said it.

"Film Board?"

"Yes."

She knew he hated it. "It's a living," she said.

"So's dying," he said, "by comparison."

Annie smiled. "Remarks are not literature, Mister Hemingway," she said.

"And you are not Gertrude Stein." He finally turned and fully faced her. "Thank the Lord Jesus."

The waiter brought the wine and a glass and Annie's pernod. Frannie began to talk.

"It's rained four days," he said. "It will rain for one day more — and then it will snow." He poured his wine. "This place is nice: I've always liked this place. The table-tops are *zinc*. They're French, you know. This whole idea is French. The whole idea of *zinc* is French."

Annie watched him, feeling careful: moored, not quite adrift.

"You zinc zis isn't Frenzh. . . ." he rapped the top of the table. He was trying to smile. It took a long time. And it never quite came.

Annie locked her hands. *Please, Frannie: don't be dumb,* she tried to say, but couldn't. And then she looked up and Frannie was weeping: soundless, immobile. "What's wrong?" she asked in the gentlest way she could. "What is it, Frank?"

"For Christ's sake, pay no attention." He got out some
rainy wads of Kleenex and a pair of old, blue gloves and set the
gloves aside while he blew his nose.

Finally, he said: "It's good to see you, Ann. I'm glad. I'm
very glad you've had success."

That did it. "Come off it, Frank," she said.

She bit her lip and looked around the room. She'd pin him,
if he wasn't careful. And then she looked right back. "I'm
sorry," she said, and meant it. She was. She knew he didn't
need another hurt. "You want to go?"

"I haven't finished my wine."

Annie laughed. "You're a hopeless drunk."

"I know."

"And you think that's attractive?"

"No. What *is*, these days?"

Anger: "*Christ!* I was only *kidding*, Frank. Jesus! *Hopeless!*"

"I'm not complaining about my hopelessness. Don't you."

Annie sat silent. She looked around for someone to pin. It
didn't matter who, just someone. She began to feel a chill and
she wove her coat around her shoulders, drawing on the long
black gloves. With a terrible sense of foreboding, she felt the
floor return beneath her feet. Her face began to freeze with a
desperate poise. I'm here: she thought. I'm here, goddamn it.
I'm here.

Frannie began to finish his wine. It took him almost an hour.

Annie thought: I wish F.N. Thompson would come. I want
to be carried out a Lady.

The Saturday 3 a.m.

In the room, they lay on the bed, in the dark.

"Funny," said Frannie: "how we talk in voices, like Hugh
— and terrible puns like me and French, like you."

"Funny? Why funny?"

"Dunno. Just funny." He drew on his cigarette and made
an orange firefly. Bang. It went out.

"Do that again. It was nice."

He did it again. And then he began to make it dance around
in the shifty dark above the bed. "My father used to do that."

"Yeah?"

"Yeah. He used to sit on the other side of the room, when we were going to sleep as kids. My brother and me. And Dad would make these zippy fireflies all around the room."

A pause.

She could feel him shake.

"What is it, Frannie?"

"Oh shit. I don't. . . . I really don't know. I've been crying like this . . . waking up, even *waking up*, crying. Weeks. I don't . . . I really don't know why."

Annie put her hand out: felt his naked stomach with her fingers, slowly rubbed his stomach — side to side — her fingers arched. The weeping vibrations slowly ebbed and her hand lay still: "Go on," she said. "Finish about your dad."

"Oh. He used to read — recite us stuff. Christ. He used to do us a number called 'MacCrimmon comes no more.' In the dark. It was electrifying."

"Yeah."

"And hymns. He used to do us hymns. He wouldn't sing: he'd just . . . it was just the words. There was one — you remember: 'Who would true valour see, let him come hither. . .?' "

"Yeah."

"One here will constant be, come wind or weather. There's no discouragement — shall make him once relent — His first avowed intent — to be —"

"A Pilgrim. Yeah. I know."

Annie rolled onto her back. She got off the bed and went across the carpet. Somewhere, she found the whisky and brought it back.

They drank. And Frannie went on, propped up, with his legs beneath the sheet: "He wanted to be a poet, you know. My dad. And so did I. But, I ain't. Films, for Christ's sake. Fucking screenplays. For creeps without assholes. . . ." The crying began again, but now it was only tears and his voice: "Do you know the last time I stayed in this hotel? When I was . . . after I was married. Here. Downstairs somewhere — we had our honeymoon. Someone and me. Marian. Me. In this hotel. And

I'm queer, for God's sake. Queer. But, I got married. Yeah. I sure did. Loaded with integrity. That's me. All because — why? I don't even know.''

Annie didn't speak. She felt like ice. She drank — and sat at the foot of the bed, with the extra blanket round her shoulders.

"And the latest is," said Frannie, "I fell in love with Hugh." After the silence, he laughed. "A married man? You believe?''

"I believe."

"What does it, Annie? Eh? What does it to us? Eh? What *does* it to us?''

Annie didn't speak. She was thinking: "us."

Frannie went on: "I never have time to write. I mean, I never have time to *write*. I never do. And I think — keep thinking — if I could just get out of this rut: if I could only write — if I could only find some nice, queer kid and fall in love, if I could only be my. . ." (whispered) *"self.* Be *me.* But — it's been so long. Such a long, long time since I was . . . *any*one. Ann. You know? Since I was *anyone.*'' He laughed — but it was cynical. "And I *am* a hopeless drunk. And I . . . .''

"Frannie?''

He drew in his breath. "What?"

"Shut up.''

Annie got off the end of the bed and came around to the side.

"Shut up about your goddamn self and shove it. Go to sleep.''

She yanked the sheet and got underneath and threw the extra blanket down around her feet. Her back was to him: solid. He could see the shape of her shoulder and head.

He sat very still. But, all at once, she reared on her elbow and shouted at him: shouted — over her shoulder: "And you cry one more goddamn tear and, so help me Teresa, I'll throw you out my fucking window!" And then she lay down, flat — and was gone to him: useless, unhearing. Stone.

Frannie finished his cigarette and gulped several times from the bottle. But he didn't cry again. He sighed, instead, just once and then got up and went to the bathroom.

When he'd gone, Annie lay there thinking — wide awake: cold sober: afraid. She couldn't understand what he meant.

She understood *him*, but not what he meant. His breaking —
but not his being broken. *I mean — he's F.N. Thompson, for
God's sake; F.N. Thompson. He has four books. Four books — and I
just don't understand. He can't not know who he is. He can't. He calls
me Kabuki Bogan — and My Lady and he used to make me laugh.*

She listened. She heard him pee — then silence. But, he
didn't come back.

And she lay there, thinking now, well — I guess I've pinned
another one I didn't want to pin. And me? I was only . . .
(drifting) waiting for someone.

She watched the windows: heard the rain, she saw the sky. It
would be all night, before it would be morning. All the whole
night; and then, just another day.

She drifted all the way, against her will, to sleep.

4:15 a.m.

In the bathroom, Frannie sat on the john, drinking whisky
from the bottle. The light was obnoxious white, unshaded. Still
— he refused to sit in the dark.

It was odd: being drunk, so terribly drunk, stark naked,
sitting on the john, in this, of all hotels. He hadn't even
thought of Marian for years. She was married again, now:
happy, with kids.

He guessed he really had upset Kabuki Ann — surprised,
because he'd thought, he really had, that Annie was riding
high. Of course, she was always riding *high* but. . . . Joke. Bad
joke. Bad. Bad joke.

Jesus: oh Jesus; why did they have to speak in voices when
they meant their hearts to break?

He rose. *Go to bed.*

He crossed to the sink. He set the bottle down. He opened
(God knows why — he wished forever after that he hadn't),
opened the medicine-cabinet door and found the whole of her
mystery: staring at him, flashing in his face. Her collection.

Of razors.

The Sunday 11 a.m.

Frannie had left her sleeping, Saturday morning. All day
Saturday it rained. And all day Saturday, she stayed in her

room and wandered between the windows and the bathroom. She had a little food sent up, but hardly ate. She gave herself the needle: 4 p.m. and went again to sleep, without the pause of thought.

Now, it was Sunday. Down below in the church there'd already been one Mass and now they began to arrive for the next. And Frannie, he'd been right: quite right. It snowed. The park was full of ghosts.

Annie made herself sit still. She was dressed. Erect. Immensely real. The mirror told her so, far off across the room. And now, she truly waited.

Music. That would have been nice. And then it was. There were bells. Obtrusive. Making her count. *Don't count.*

The shells at her finger-ends were resting on her knees. Behind her, on the bed, the razors waited, laid in their boxes — some on velvet, folded.

She lifted the book from her lap. Open.

"I have made razors of my life, my words," she read "because my life, my words have razored me. . . ." and closed it over, flat and open, cover up on the bed, in hand.

She rose in one step to the windows.

There.

Jesus and St. Teresa: here.

And she flung the book to the street.

And she waited.

And she waited.

And she waited.

2:15 p.m.

Kabuki Bogan came out of the Bar and Grill and noted the woman behind the magazine counter, coming on duty: late again. There she was; pinned: her handbag; humbugs; jangling bracelets; lips and lacquered beads. And her pointed crest: L'ÉTOILE. The Star.

By the doors to the street, Annie paused. The man stood ready to let her through, unseen. She smiled: "Merci." And was gone, till, maybe, some other success she'd engendered overtook her by surprise, and brought her back.

And the old hotel still smelled the same and gave off the same gold light. In the lobby, the dark oak panels shone with the same deep glow of oil-of-lemon wax and the smoky mirrors reflected still the same old women, the same brocaded chairs. The people were changed, perhaps: but never their image. Never the basic reflection of what was there.

Daybreak at Pisa

For William Hutt

This is a scene from a work-in-progress: a play about the poet Ezra Pound. The characters are self-explanatory; but perhaps it should be said that the cage referred to is the cage in which Pound was kept at the end of the Second World War by the American military authorities while he was being detained in Italy before being sent to the U.S., where in time they would attempt to bring him to trial as a traitor. In the end he could not be tried because he was found to be legally insane. — T.F.

Pre-dawn: and Ezra burns in his cage, caught in the white hot glare of a searchlight.

He wears his overcoat against the cold — its collar turned up next to his ears. His mad, electric hair appears to be standing on end. His hands are in his pockets, as far into the depths as they can get. But the whiteness of the light and its intensity prevent us from seeing the features of his face. There is nothing there but a white paper mask with burn holes and beard. One of the burn holes — down near the bottom — slowly opens, spreads, and issues words.

And Ezra says: "That moon of yours is a travesty, my friend. Your sense of subtlety is worse than mine. . . . Might I suggest a filter of cream and gold? Old Ceres' moon, with honey dripping from her lips. . .? And a bowl, with a spoon if you please. . . ."

There is no reply.

"I'm hungry, damn it!" Ezra says. "A person's stomach knows when morning comes. If you could just turn out that light — I bet you'd find the sun could find the sky all by itself. . . . It doesn't need your help, you know. It's not a moron, boy. There is a track it follows every day." He raises up his hand and points. "An old, well-beaten track. With breakfast at one end and supper at the other. . . ." His finger traces the track across the sky. "Eh, boy? You hear me? Yes? If you put out that light of yours — who knows? The hen might lay her egg and we could eat. . . ."

Ezra withdraws his hand from the air and puts it back in his pocket: cold. "You want me to starve out here? You bastard, boy! Put out that God damn light!"

An egg sails out across the stage and breaks on Ezra's cheek.

"You fascist pig!" a voice calls out from somewhere in the wings. "Soo-soo . . . you piggy-pig!"

More eggs are thrown, and slops.

But Ezra stands his ground.

The walls behind him, of the cage, are spotted with garbage, some of it making scarlet blotches on the stones.

"Sooey-sooey-sooey! Piggy-piggy-pig!"

The climax of this outrage comes when a pail of muck is emptied through the lattices of Ezra's roof onto his head.

But, though he cowers against the wet of it, he straightens once the streaming ends. And then — the movement slow, deliberate, precise — he lifts his fingers to his cheek and wipes away the egg, placing his finger-ends inside his mouth and sucking them clean.

When this is done he reaches out towards the light and raises up his fingers: one, and then another.

"You there, with the arsehole," he says. "I dare you to sit on my breakfast now. . . ."

The light goes out.

The sky is all pale blue, seen through the lattices of Ezra's roof.

There is a slow and careful fading-in of insect noise — and faraway a dog, and further still a cock, and further still, beyond them all, a bell.

Ezra — dragging an old grey piece of sheeting from his pocket — starts to clean himself, with spittle when he must, but he pauses now and listens. "You've left out the birds again . . ." he calls into the wings. "You hear me? Where are the birds?"

Silence.

"What? You do this every morning and you still can't get it right?" says Ezra. "Insects first: then *birds*, you dolt! And *then* the dog, the cock, the bell! Dear Jesus Christ. . . .!" He looks at God. "You know what you need down here?" he yells. "You know what you need down here, you *ditz*?" And he points into the wings. "What you need is a new stage manager!" Ezra shakes his fist — his piece of sheeting at his imagined enemy. "You pea-eyed priapus! GET IT RIGHT! INSECTS — BIRDS — then DOGS. . .!"

Dorothy enters, falling up the steps from the auditorium; carrying her little folded chair and table; crawling carefully through the wires that are stretched between the stage and the house. She also carries — as always — her knitting bag, her old cloth shopping bag, and her parasol. Ezra hides in the furthest corner he can find.

All at once the birds begin to sing.

Dorothy says: "Good morning, Ezra," setting her things on the ground. Ezra, as usual, does not respond. Dorothy surveys the mess in his cage.

"Looks like the birds have been at you again," she says.

"There are no birds," says Ezra. "All the birds are dead. Save one. . . ." He glowers. "Good morning, Dorothy."

Dorothy gauges the distance between herself and the cage with a practised paranoic eye and sets her chair in place accordingly. The length of her husband's reach is known by heart: just as the depth of his thrust was known in earlier times. In youth. There had always been a part of her, inside, he could not reach. And now — when the reach is all external — she is determined each of the visible sanctuaries must remain inviolate: her wrists; her eyes; the nape of her neck; and, especially, her lips. She will never let him touch her lips again — as once she had — lest some unwilling word be drawn into the open and revealed.

Looking up at the latticed sun — the lattices of other bars than Ezra's — Dorothy unfolds her small tin table, placing it beside her chair.

"So what have you brought this morning?" Ezra says.

"Tea," says Dorothy. "Same as always."

"Tea?"

"That's right."

"Tea stands for Traitor. . ." Ezra snarls. "How dare you?" he roars.

"Ezra. . ."

"Every day you bring it here to taunt me! Tea! Tea! Tea! For Traitor. . . .!"

"Nonsense," says Dorothy, shaking out her handkerchief and watching it drift down towards the table — Dorothy's tea-cloth, unembroidered, neat and square and clean.

"I only told the truth. Tea-tea for Truth!"

"Be quiet. You want them to come?" Dorothy lifts her chin towards the wings, where danger lounges, dressed as soldiers, barely visible to those of us who sit beyond the wires and watch. Ezra leans up close against the bars and reaches out with both his hands towards his wife and whispers at her, vehemently; "*Aiuto, Dorothea. Aiuto. . . .*"

She ignores him, fearful of his languages, never quite certain which of them is real — and, if they are real, never quite certain of the meaning. Her shoulders tell us this: the way she turns away and produces from her shopping bag her cup and saucer, jar of milk, and thermos bottle. Also biscuits, each one wrapped in a separate piece of paper, each one very dry and thin and old.

Ezra squints and watches every item making its entrance into the growing light. Finally Dorothy lifts the cup and blows the dust from its rim.

"Me," says Ezra. "I had an egg for breakfast."

"That's nice," says Dorothy, and lifts the thermos bottle

up, removes its cup, and pours a long bright amber stream into her cup while Ezra, watching it, recites his litany of teas for "treason. . . traitors . . . tortured . . . trapped. . ."

Dorothy sets the thermos bottle aside and replaces the cap; after which she reaches out for the jar of milk.

But.

Ezra suddenly stands in the centre of his cage and roars at the top of his voice: "I AM NOT I THAT WAS BUT I THAT AM!"

Dorothy sits. And sighs. And is afraid. She sits with her back to her husband — looking at us, tired. She knows that now the soldiers will come. And they do. And Dorothy folds her hands in her lap and waits for whatever might be going to happen next.

Three of the soldiers come this time. And one of them bangs his swagger stick against the bars. "Shut up, in there, old man. . ."

"I am shut up in here," says Ezra. "Fool!"

"I mean your mouth — shut up!"

"I'd rather shit in yours than shut up mine," says Ezra, calm.

But the soldier to whom he speaks is enraged and heaves himself against the bars. "I hope they hang you by the balls, you fascist creep!"

The other soldiers pull the maddened one away.

"You mustn't. Mustn't. Don't. He's crazy. And he doesn't know the meaning of his words. He doesn't even know his name. . ."

"Ezra. . ." Dorothy whispers.

"What?" says a soldier, not having been aware she was even there.

"Ezra," she says. "His name was Ezra Pound."

One of the soldiers, fairly decent, motions the others away and stands there looking at Dorothy.

"He was a tall, great man," says Dorothy, looking past the wires at time: the past. "With a great red head of snakes for hair and his eyes were green, like glass. He gave off heat. I'd never felt such heat. But his shadow . . . in his shadow I was cool. He loved the sun. . ."

"I was the sun," says Ezra.

"Yes," says Dorothy. "He was. The sun."

Ezra walks away into the shadows.

Dorothy looks across at the soldier. "Can I help you? Is there something I can do?" she says.

"No, ma'am."

"Then you could leave us — couldn't you."

This is not a question.

"Yes, ma'am," says the soldier, turning to go. But before he goes he takes a final look at Ezra in the cage and mutters with amazement; ". . . *was*." And goes.

Dorothy pours her milk from the jar, Ezra turns to the sound of it. Dorothy now undoes a biscuit, folds the paper, nibbles at the biscuit, drinks her tea.

Ezra looks along the bars and takes a little walk, then stops and adjusts his posture, watching his wife as she feeds along the biscuit edge.

"Fifteen bars, this cage," he says. "How many teeth have *you*?"

Dorothy, not replying, fishes deep inside her bag and withdraws an envelope of raisins, nuts, and figs. "If you had to choose a death," she says, "would you rather hang — or be shot?" She sets the cup aside and frees the saucer, carefully pouring out a ration of the nuts and raisins onto its gleaming surface.

"Fifteen bars," says Ezra. "And sixteen spaces."

"Seventeen," says Dorothy, and sets the saucer down on the ground about six feet away from her chair, towards the precipice dividing them from us.

"Sixteen," says Ezra. Adamant. Time for another outburst.

"Seventeen," says Dorothy, taking her place again in the chair, lifting the strand of figs and beginning to unbraid them, laying the braid in her lap and each unbraided fig on her handkerchief, her tea cloth. "One space runs along the top," she says.

Ezra looks. It is true.

The fifteen bars are set in cement at the bottom; but across the top there runs another bar, and this bar is set at either end

in the walls. Between this bar and the lattice roof of Ezra's cage
there is a space at least six inches deep.

"All right," he says. "There are seventeen. But only
because you're a woman. There's always the lateral for
women, isn't there? Always the God damn lateral. . ."

"Apparently, yes," says Dorothy, still unbraiding figs.

"Whereas for me — for men —" says Ezra, running his
hands up and down the bars "there is only the vertical.
Hunh?"

"Only if you say so, Ezra," says Dorothy. "But my mind
tells me there was a time when every thought you had was
horizontal."

"God damn right there was a time!" says Ezra. Then he
thinks about it. Youth. "And I was splendid — lying down.
Splendid," he says. "Recumbent. Rampant! *I*. . .!"

"Yes," she cuts him off. "You. Recumbent. I . . . looking
down." She puts a fig in her mouth.

"What?" says Ezra. "You looking *where*?"

"Looking down," says Dorothy, trying to finish the fig. And
then: "I only ever saw you from above — when you were lying
down."

"You lie!" he shouts. "You lie!"

"Oh, yes. I'm always 'lying' aren't I? Just as you were
always 'lying.' *Down*."

"Bitch."

"Trouble is, I never did know who was underneath you,
there. . ." She eats another fig.

"THE EARTH WAS UNDERNEATH ME THERE! Cow. . .!"

Dorothy swallows the fig.

"The earth?"

"You're God damn right it was the earth. You're right.
THE EARTH. IT WAS ALWAYS THE EARTH!
ALWAYS! ALWAYS! THE EARTH. . .!"

Dorothy lifts her fingers to her mouth.

The sound of all the insects dies.

The dogs, off stage, lie down.

The ants are terrified: immobilized.

A raisin falls.

The flies, parading in the saucer, rise into the air and disappear. And Ezra's gaze rises after them. . . .

"Aye. . . ." His voice is a long thin whisp of sound. "I would fuck the sky if I could. . . ."

He looks at Dorothy.

Her back.

"Your tea is cold," he says.

Dorothy lowers her hands into her lap; her chin dips down toward her breast.

And Ezra says: "You mustn't be afraid." He wants to make her laugh. She won't. "The *sky* is not afraid," he says. "I shout at her all day — and look how calm she is. And not a cloud in sight. . . ."

But Dorothy just sits. And then she says: "The sky cannot hear you, Ezra. She has no need to be afraid."

For a moment both of them are still, till Ezra says: "I should rather, then, be hanged than shot. . . ." He looks at the sky. "So I could be up there with her: silent. Yes. . .?"

Dorothy takes a biscuit from the table, slowly unwraps it, blows it clean, and stands.

"Ezra. . .?"

"Yes?" Still looking at the sky.

"Are *you* afraid?"

He looks at her.

"Yes."

Dorothy turns and walks toward the cage. Very slowly she offers him the biscuit through the bars. "Thank you," she says, "for telling me the truth. . ." and watches him. He eats. "What does it mean?" she says. "What you said before: *aiuto*?"

"Help," he says. "In Italian. Help. *Aiuto*. . ."

"Oh."

Then Ezra smiles. "Don't turn around," he says. "Don't move."

"Why not?"

"There's a bird in your saucer," he says.

And there is. It is feeding.

Out of the Silence

Prose scenes from a play in progress.

Tom and Vivien were married: always, it seemed, had been married, still would be married even when Vivien died. Tom said afterwards, in many different ways (and most of them oblique): "A death once started never seems to end." And it was clear he meant her death would not be over till his own had taken place.

Tom was a writer; Vivien was not. Not that it mattered, should have mattered. But it did. Both, at first, were equally fond of silence. Out of the silence Tom made words and put the words on paper. Seeing the words on paper, Vivien caught the first disturbing intimation that the silence they had shared had not, in fact, been shared at all. Tom had been raiding her dreams, her privacies, even her nightmares. What was on the paper was her own, not his. Stolen. Worse: it was as if her voice was in his pen and unreclaimable. What might he do with the rest of her, then? Unless she got him first.

"Are you alive, or not?" she used to say. "Your self, I mean. Are you living yet, or not?" Always speaking down towards the top of his head (Tom always seated) or from somewhere off across the room: this woman wearing white, in shadows; hating any other light that did not emanate from her. "Speak to me. Speak," she would say. "Tell me what *you're* thinking. Tell me what *you* think. . .," blowing out the candles; turning off the lamps: making out of darkness a new kind of silence through which to hear and then denounce his words. "You are not even *you*!" she cried at him once. "Look at you, sitting in the dark."

"I didn't make the dark," he said, trying not to say *you did.* Succeeding, because he knew in his heart she had not really made the dark, only its counterfeit: the turning off of lamps.

Slowly, over time, she tried to obliterate the shape of words from forming in her mind, tried to avoid their presence in the house, said to Tom she had forgotten how to read. "Please don't leave your work about. I'd rather not. . . ." ("remember what I think," she didn't say.)

Daylight became so harsh she had to shield her eyes, pulling down the blinds at dawn. Afternoons were blotted out with pills, sometimes injections: anything narcotic, even, towards the end, with other "Light," said Vivien — saying it to her doctor (later, the doctor saying it to Tom) — "is noise. Always, I want to stop my ears."

"What sort of noise?" the doctor asked. "Tell me what it sounds like, please."

Vivien waited, wanting to be precise — forgetting, because she had worked so hard at forgetting how to be precise. But finally she said: "The noise is of someone bursting through the glass."

"What glass?" the doctor asked.

Vivien did not answer.

Tom, when the doctor told him this, sat very still. Vivien, twilit in her pallid dress, stood in his mind before her bedroom mirror, staring at herself. And he knew she was waiting for the bursting to begin. White, he thought, must be the loudest noise of all. And her wardrobe, now, was exclusively white.

Two days later, Tom had Vivien committed.

After the great dark car had driven away and the papers had all been signed; after the doctor had said, "You may sit over there, if you like" and Tom had seated himself in the straight-backed wooden chair; after the Matron had been told to wait outside; after the April afternoon was safely shut away behind Venetian blinds; after the noise of all the lights was dimmed; after the pause containing all these things had passed, Vivien began to speak, not quite aloud at first.

"I see two doors," she said. "But if I walk across the room, I know that only one of them will open."

Tom put his knees together, sitting as the chair demanded, letting his ankles touch — one hard bone against the other — his mind already ticking over, knowing that one of the doors indeed was locked, but the other would open. For him.

"This — the other door — is mine," said Vivien. "The only difference is, it has a key." She looked at Tom. "Someone else will open it and someone else will close it. You can still put out your hand and turn the knob: a gesture, with so many others, I must now renege." She made a fist and opened it and made a fist again. Twenty years of opening doors and twenty years of marriage. Gone. She opened the fist and let them fall away. Tom even noticed that she wiped her palms on her skirts. He was thinking that she should have said, "A gesture I must now renege *upon*. . . ," that she'd left out a word, that her language — sense of language — was dying, dead.

"Doorknobs and fountain pens, eh Tom? Two ways of getting out. Two ways of pushing up the lid. Buried alive, we all want out. . . ."

Tom looked down at his feet: the April mud on the edges of his soles.

"Me," said Vivien. "Me, I was buried in you. I even lost my voice in you." Now, she looked at the doctor pointing with her semi-fist at Tom. "Buried alive inside that man. *Me*." She smiled and made the fist complete. "And when he leaves this place, you know what he's going to say when he gets in the street?" She looked at Tom — Tom now looking back — and she raised her fist above her head and shouted, "*Lazarus. Me.* I have come back to tell you all!" She looked away and dropped her fist. "In my voice." (Whispering) "*My* voice. . . ." (Weeping, silent tears and open eyes.) "Mine. Because it's me that has to die. Not you." And then she looked at him again. And shook her head and tried to smile. "Oh, no. That isn't what I meant to say. That isn't what I mean. . . . If I had come in here to die, then I'd be lucky, wouldn't I. . .? If I had come in here to die." (To the doctor) "Can you promise me they don't kill people here? Because, if they do, you should make him stay and let me go."

The doctor slowly shook his head. "We don't kill people here," he said.

"You take them somewhere else to die?"

Tom stood up.

"Sit down," said Vivien.

Tom sat down and wondered if it was force of habit, fear or both. That fear itself was force of habit.

Vivien said, "All we have to see is what there is. Yes? And you can't deny we've seen it, all of it, together, you and I. I have gone mad . . . your word, not mine . . . and *you* have not. Gone mad. Or, so they say. Or so that open door implies. Yet, all we've seen is what we've seen *together*, you and I. Years of silence. All those . . . *wonderful* years of silence shared. Which you betrayed. Betrayed, because you never said to me, you never said *to me*, 'We have seen what we have seen together. You and I. Landings, stairs and doors. Curtains, carpets, tables, chairs. Leaning out along the window sills, walking out along the streets. Cats and garbage cans and the sound of singers singing in the summer rain. . . .' " (Here there was a pause: alarm that all the words had rushed out, bidden by forbidden memory, trampling down the sedation rampant in her bloodstream, streaming out in defence of her terror that the open door was not for her. Then, slower, drugged by the counterweight of what she had become, perhaps by choice . . . choices she could not remember: longings to sleep; longings to be forgotten; left, bereft of self in the safety of absolute anonymity, not to be Vivien any longer. Not to be Vivien, either Tom's or her own.) "You betrayed me, Tom. You betrayed me. Not because you put me down on paper but you didn't put me down on me. Out of the silence all you had to do was write

across my forehead, scribble on my arm, print for me somewhere here. . ." (she pointed at her breast) ". . . I *am*. That's
all. Just *me*. That I was here inside this body-flesh. In me and
not in you. 'Cause all we saw and all we saw and all we
saw. . . ." She was winding down, sagging near the wall, and
the doctor rose and went and held her up. But Tom was afraid
to go: he couldn't cross the room. "All we saw and all we
saw. . .," he was thinking. "All we saw, and all we didn't
see."

He looked, as best he could, at his collapsing wife, watched
as the doctor called the Matron through the door (the other
door), saw how they put her gently in a chair, folding her arms
and arranging her hands, the Matron pulling down the skirt
that had ridden up, unseemly, in the final slide towards the
door.

Vivien, he thought. In white.

Shouting. Silent. Sleeping in nightmares, waking into
dreams.

Yes: it is true, all we have seen is what we have seen
together. Yes: it is true, I never wrote across your heart *I am*.

No: it is not true that you lived and died inside of me.

You lived and died inside yourself. And you will leave your
life and death with me as if I was your safe deposit box. Damn
you. Well, I will go home now and do the one good thing I
think that I can do. I will turn on all the lights in memory of
you. And listen to them sing. No death should go without its
song. And when I've learned the song — your epitaph — I'll
write it down.

Dinner Along the Amazon

For Robin Phillips

Perhaps the house was to blame. Once, it had been Olivia's pride; her safe, good place. Everyone else — including Michael — found it charming. Prestigious. Practical. North Seton Drive was a great location. Running out of Rosedale down toward the ravine, all its back yards were set with trees and rolling lawns. Autumn and spring, Olivia could happily walk or ride her bicycle to Branksome Hall, where she had been teaching now for six years. She really had no right to complain. Number 38 was handsome enough — its glass all shining; its paint unchipped.

Recently, however, Olivia had begun to balk at the physical act of arriving there; of being on the sidewalk and turning in toward the house, admitting that she belonged on that cement and was meant to walk through that front door. There was always something lying on the grass she would not allow was hers: a torn, wet *Star* or a bit of orange peel — (*I didn't put that there!*) — something left by a neighbour's child or someone else's dog. And even, once, a sinister pair of men's blue undershorts.

Inside, the house gave off the smell of discontent; of ashes in the sink and slippers prowling through the halls at night; of schisms rusting like a set of knives. Also the odour — faintly underarm — of Michael's petulance and Olivia's silence hiding in the closets. *Boo . . . .*

Today, on the twenty-eighth of April, Olivia entered the house with her arms full of flowers at five in the afternoon. The flowers were done up in green paper cones, but still the smell of them was rampant under her chin and she stood in the middle of the hall not speaking — only listening — dizzy with the scent of freesia.

Michael was in here somewhere. Up in the sun room, probably. Drunk. Conrad's car was in the driveway, rubbing its already damaged bumper up against the garage. This could only signal they would both be drunk: not only Michael but Conrad, too. Old friends and empty bottles. Poor deadly Conrad, dragging the unwelcome past with all its frayed address books and stringy love affairs behind him, had come to "visit for a while" — i.e. to crash until he'd pulled himself together. God damn old friends.

It could not be borne. There wasn't time for the past in their lives. Not now. Not ever. All it did was crowd you into corners and turn out the lights. Then it rattled you with guilt and regret and left you inarticulate and incapacitated. Who needs that? *I'm taking enough of a beating from the present, thank you very much*; Olivia thought. *Damn you, Conrad. Much as I love you, if you hadn't come, I could talk to Michael. Now. Tonight. I could tell him and get it over with.*

No I couldn't.

Olivia peered to her left, into the dim shuttered light of Michael's den. She tried to imagine the thing in her belly running through that doorway into those shadows to find its father. It was impossible. He would slam the door in its face. *Get out!*

She knew this was only a coward's excuse. Michael didn't hate children: he hated the future — and that was different. He hated anything he couldn't control: he hated anything he didn't know. Certainty was the only ally you could trust, in Michael's books. Certainty and literature. History — (maybe)

— and a few poems written on the backs of envelopes. He *wanted* children, but he didn't want their lives to run beyond his own. He couldn't bear to inject them into the future — only into the past. Michael would like it best if his children had preceded him. Then he could say to them; "Everything I told you was the truth. I have never lied. It is all borne out by what you have seen: the known — the safe." The future was his enemy.

In Michael's den, there were piles and piles of notebooks and reams of paper. These were his diatribes — some of them four or six or ten years old. They were covered with marmalade fungi and peanut butter mushrooms. Olivia smiled. The rug was stained with his solipsisms. She had listened to him roaring there, amongst his books — knocking over his drinks — jabbing his fingers at her: "Just you wait, Olivia! Every word I say is true. . . ." Then he would have to verify every word — dragging down all the pertinent books, drawing out all the pertinent pieces of paper, going crazy — ranting — when he couldn't find what he wanted. In its way, it was a sad, dead room. Echoes hiding in the curtains. The roll top desk had pigeon holes that smelled, Olivia swore, of pigeons: all the pigeons flown away with their messages — the words that Michael couldn't find. In a bowl, he kept all his paper clips attached to rubber bands — ready to fire at the passing parade or at any rash intruder who brought the future into his presence: man, woman or child . . .

No. There could be no child.

Olivia turned towards the kitchen, leaning her ear in the direction of the stairwell, hoping to hear the sound of sober conversation. Even of laughter. But there was nothing. Only the silence between drinks. Up there, sitting in the sun room, they were probably holding their breath: Michael and Conrad, hiding from Olivia. *Don't give away our secret, Connie.* Mustn't let her know we're only ten years old, when she thinks we're twelve, at least.

Olivia took a deep breath that left her gasping for another.

It *was* the house: its airlessness; its *culs de sac*; its bear pits waiting for the bears. It had lost its capacity to generate dreams. All it reflected, as you moved from room to room, was the tidy horror of what was really going to happen.

As Olivia entered the kitchen, the sun room made a creaking noise above her head. She looked up, thinking; *they're walking on tiptoe. How ridiculous. Two grown men . . .*

She crossed to the sink, making sure her heels could be heard as she went. Still clothed in all her outer garments, her tweed coat; her three layers of scarves; her soft, rich sweater; her wool lined boots — she set her briefcase on one cutting board and the packets of flowers on the other. She turned on the tap for a glass of water and reached to the left for a thick, red tumbler with a crack in it. Habit. It was always there, the last of its kind. There had once been eight — a gift from Conrad. Pinned to the curtain above the sink was one of Mrs Kemp's inimitable notes:

> Mrs Penny I done the back room up for Mr Fastbinder and put a towel and a wash cloth on his burow. You run out of blue sheets so he only got one and the other ones yellow. Grennel is loss again. Hiden.

Olivia, reading, was holding the tumbler under the tap.

> I could not find no more OLD DUTCH so have put down OLD DUTCH on the list. 4 large ones please as the bathroom really eats them up. Mr Fastbinder near creamed the garge. Dont let them tell you different. I will be in tomorrow to clean up after.
>
> Lilah Kemp.

The cold water ran on Olivia's hands, comforting, numbing.

> Ps   Prof Penny did not eat his sandwhich. Toona if you want one.

All the usual digs at Michael were intact. Mortal enemies —

Michael Penny and Mrs Kemp. And Grendel. Grendel was Michael's beloved dog and, like his master, he always hid from Mrs Kemp and her dreaded vacuum cleaner and her dreadful tuna sandwiches, the edges of which she always left in Grendel's dish.

Olivia set aside the tumbler and took down the note, threw it into the garbage pail and replaced the pin in the folds of the curtain. As she drank her water, she wondered where the dog might be this time. Lying poisoned, perhaps, in someone's flower bed — the victim of Mrs Kemp's "toona." The detritus of neglect. Poor old Grendel.

Poor old Grendel had a habit of lying dead in other people's flowerbeds, but his favourite place of all was in behind the curtain of the shower stall, where he portrayed with alarming veracity the corpses of his master and his mistress — one and then the other. Michael and Olivia, dead.

Olivia's hand went down to rest on her belly and the red tumbler, in the other hand, shook. *Michael first and then Olivia — dead.* I am not a murderer. Not. I am doing what is right. The only right thing: the only possible thing.

She began to cry — (*oh why am I crying?*) — her gaze shifting sideways, awash — (*please: it's so shaming*) — toward the flowers — (*and stupid: stop*). What had the flowers been for, she wondered, setting the tumbler aside. To get her past the front door without throwing up? Not that. No. She could tolerate the tension one more week — so what had the flowers been for? Perhaps, she decided, they were for Grendel, always "dying." Or for Michael, still alive. Or for the undug grave in her belly. Pick a card — any card. Now put it back in the deck. Just don't tell me which card it was . . . .

"Hallo."

Olivia grabbed the sink and nearly fell before she turned.

Standing in the doorway was a man she had never seen before. A man — a "boy." He was in his early twenties.

"Yes?" she said.

His arms were full of brown paper packages.

"Who are you?" he said, with casual, inbred impertinence.

Olivia was flabbergasted. "I'm . . . Olivia Penny," she said.

And this is my house, she almost added. But didn't.

"Are you Professor Penny's sister, then?" The young man barged completely into the kitchen. The brown paper packages were clinking suspiciously like future toasts, and the young man was trying not to spill them before they could be proposed.

"No, I am not Professor Penny's God damn sister. I am Professor Penny's God damn wife," said Olivia, stepping aside to avoid being trampled. "And who the hell are you?"

"I'm with Conrad," the young man said. He laid his loot — eight bottles of wine, four bottles of scotch — beside and on top of the flowers and turned to smile at Olivia. "You're a scream," he said, and put out his hand. "Conrad didn't tell me you were *funny*," he added. "I'm Rodney Farquhar." (His grip was like the proverbial vise.) "Or should I say I'm Conrad's God damn lover?"

"Why are you here?" said Olivia.

Rodney Farquhar's face was emptied of all expression. Perhaps he didn't know the answer to the question.

"You've just set all your things on top of my flowers," Olivia continued. "Would you please find some other place?"

Rodney moved in on the bottles and began to shift them, two by two, onto the kitchen table.

"Why are you here?" Olivia repeated.

"I was sent to get the booze," he said. "I've just come back. . . ."

"I can see that. Booze for what?"

"For the party," said Rodney. His back was to her.

Party?

"What party?" said Olivia. Her eyes had narrowed. Her blood was rising.

"Conrad's party," said Rodney.

"Conrad is giving a party? Where?"

"Here, of course."

Olivia ground her teeth and was speechless for a moment. Then she said, "Am I invited?"

Conrad was lying in the bath. The bathroom was full of steam and the steam was scented with Conrad's favourite cologne:

Chanel 19. Michael was seated on the toilet, the lid down — its grey fur cover slightly damp beneath him. Conrad could barely be seen in the fog.

"Aren't you going to boil yourself to death in there?" Michael asked.

"Never," said Conrad. "The heat is wonderful. It spreads the alcohol faster through the system. Give me another . . . ."

Conrad's hand, with goblet, appeared from the steam.

Michael poured more scotch and the hand withdrew and then Michael poured more scotch into his own Waterford goblet and took a great, raw mouthful; "ahhhh . . ." He set the goblet on the floor, fingering its cut design. "Always drink the best from the best," he said. "So, who have you invited?"

"Fabiana Holbach," said Conrad.

"Yes. And who else?"

"Who cares who else? Fabiana Holbach. That's all that matters."

"So I gather," Michael sighed. He lighted a damp cigarette, with a damp recalcitrant match. "Are you sure this is really a good idea? Inviting Fabiana after all these years?"

"All these years number precisely three," said Conrad. "Give me a cigarette."

Michael handed over the one already lit and lighted another.

"You realize, of course," he said, "she's married, now."

"People can always be convinced their current marriages don't work," said Conrad.

Michael muttered 'yes' and 'amen' to this, but not loud enough for Conrad to hear.

"What's her name, now?" said Conrad.

"Mrs Jackman Powell."

The bath fell silent. Not a ripple.

"You don't approve, I take it," said Michael.

"It's neither here nor there," said Conrad. "Truth is, I always thought that *Jackman* had to be the most pretentious name a man could have. Isn't his brother's name plain old Tom?"

"Yes."

"Maybe their mother's name was Jackman."

"No. Their mother's name was Tompkins."

Conrad laughed. Then sobered. "Son-of-a-bitch," he said. "So she married Jackman Powell."

"That's right." Michael was watching all he could see of Conrad — the arm that lay along the rim of the tub; the shape of the neck; the thrust of the head as it bent to the glass to drink; above all, the tension in the hand that held the cigarette so hard against the tub, the cigarette broke and the lighted end of it fell to the floor. Conrad didn't even notice. All he did was mutter: "sons-of-bitches."

"Who?"

"All of them," Conrad said with a kind of vehemence Michael had never heard from his friend before. "All of the God damn Powells. God damn sons-of-bitches." Conrad sat disconsolate, still barely visible.

What, Michael wondered, could have happened to Conrad — usually so resilient and now, apparently, defeated by the mention of a mere name. They had spent all their school days laughing. Not that a person could go on laughing forever. Michael was perfectly aware of this and of the darker things that had affected Conrad's life. But this was something new; unknown. As if the laughter had escaped and Conrad could not locate it.

"I suppose," Conrad said, "this means Fabiana will actually bring him with her. Jackman. I suppose this means I'll have to face him . . . stand there and actually shake his God damn hand."

"I suppose so. Does it matter?"

"Yes. It matters."

"Why?"

"Won't go into it. Later, maybe. After they've gone. Not now. The son-of-a-bitch . . . ."

"You've said that. Several times."

"I know I have. Leave me alone."

"You know I can't leave you alone, Con . . . ." (Michael was using a swishy, sibilant voice — the one he always used to tease Conrad.) "I adore you."

"Don't," said Conrad. "This isn't funny."

"I'm sorry." Michael lighted another cigarette and handed it through the mist to Conrad. Ever since Conrad's father had died, three years ago, there were things you couldn't talk about. Not always having to do with Fastbinder senior (whose name had been Karl). Sometimes with mysteries Michael wasn't privy to. The causes of Conrad's silence: the long sojourn abroad in Italy and Spain; his sudden reappearance; Rodney Farquhar; Fabiana Holbach Powell. . . . God knew, any or all of these things could and should be the centres of conversation. But, more often than not, they were the cause of snapping jaws and bitten tongues.

"Change the subject," said Conrad. "Help me understand what's wrong between you and Olivia. Give me something to laugh about."

"You think we're going to laugh about *that*?" said Michael.

"Maybe," said Conrad. "Is there another woman?"

"No," said Michael. "I wish there was."

"What do you mean? Is there someone you love?"

"Yes."

"Someone you can't have?"

"Yes. I suppose you could put it that way."

"Who?"

"Olivia."

"Oh." Conrad drank from his glass and took a drag from his cigarette. "Have you ever seriously thought of falling in love with me?" he said.

"I wouldn't know how to behave in bed," said Michael, trying to be funny: failing. "What *do* you do with Rodney?"

"I admire him, dear," said Conrad. "He adores it. I tell him he has the most beautiful pudendum known to man or boy. A palpable lie of course. But Rodney believes it. Sometimes I pull it for him."

"Don't be so God damn crude. That's disgusting."

"Well — you asked."

"It's so childish."

"Precisely. And Rodney is a child."

"And you? What do you get out of all this?"

"Notoriety. Open doors. Rodney's connections are quite

spectacular, you know.''

''But you don't need open doors, Con. Every door is open to you.''

Conrad was silent. Then he said: ''*was.*''

''You mean to tell me you've taken up with that young man just to get through a few doors? It's grotesque.''

''How the hell else am I supposed to get through? Who else would take me? I'm a forty year old faggot without a cent to my name.''

''That's only temporary, Con.''

''You're damn right it is. Any minute now, I'm going to be a forty-*one* year old faggot without a cent to my name. And stop laughing! Rodney's getting restless. The young always do. They wake up one morning and they *see* you. That's why I always insist on separate rooms. Never let your lover see you, Michael. It's death.'' Conrad held out his goblet. ''If anyone turns up here tonight, it's only going to be because Rodney Farquhar asked them. I may be the attraction — but it's Rodney's circus.''

Michael said, ''That's ridiculous'' and poured more scotch.

''It's not ridiculous. Alas,'' said Conrad, lying back in the bath. ''I overheard him on the phone. *Do come and see old Conrad again. He's so amusing. Tells such wonderfully funny stories. Even gets drunk and falls down . . . but never loses consciousness. I tell you, it's a scream. He once had a whole conversation with the Princess of Rheims lying flat on his back in the middle of the floor. The whole room flocked to him. People were actually introduced while he lay there. The footmen brought him drinks and got on their knees to serve him.'* I heard him, Michael. He could sell tickets. But I can't. I'm the one they all come to see, lying down on the rug. You do have a rug, I hope.''

Michael could see Conrad, now. The steam was beginning to dissipate. His skin was alarmingly pale; his arms and shoulders lacked entirely the tension of muscles; his neck was like a girl's, stretching to hold the tremulous chin in place and the large, round head with its dank, stringy hair seemed unable to contain his skull which pushed against the skin like a swollen melon about to burst. His hands were almost ridiculously fine;

waxen, beautifully shaped and manicured . . . .

"Please stop staring," said Conrad. "Tell me about Olivia."

Michael did not say all of this that follows. He only said the parts he could articulate. The rest — the precision and the syntax — were in his mind, but silent under a cloud of scotch and daydreams. Downstairs, he could hear Olivia setting the table in the dining room — telling Rodney she didn't have anything that matched by way of crystal and china — all because Mrs Kemp had her own definition of the word 'set': "*break eight and leave four.* . . ." Rodney could also be heard on the telephone, ordering food from Fenton's. Grendel was found in the hall closet and came up the stairs to lie outside the bathroom door.

Michael said: "When you said you always insisted on separate rooms, I understood. Our bed — Olivia's and mine — is divided down the middle by the Grand Canyon. We might as well live in separate hotels."

Conrad glanced at Michael, huge and majestic, just a shape in the steam: backlit — hovering on the toilet seat — holding both the bottle and his goblet — his head turned sideways, looking for the words. Michael was six foot four and he had a club foot that no one ever talked about. It affected his walk, of course, but not outrageously and on the occasions when it pained him, he would remove the boot and rest the foot on a table or a chair. He was resting it now on the edge of the tub.

She's gone away somewhere, Con: gone without going, of course.

Conrad waved his hand in the soapy water, watching it vanish.

Now what am I? A sort of bachelor, living in her house; always on the periphery of Olivia's life. "Goodbye, Michael." "Goodbye, Olivia." "I'm going to the other end of the sofa, now." Gone. Like that.

I saw a movie once. One of those "Nature of Things" on the CBC. It was a film about some tribe in Borneo. One of those primitive tribes — still living almost a prehistoric existence. Ceremonial killings. Sexual segregation. Ritual circumcision. Unbelievable savagery. The way they treated one another — slaughtered their animals — slaughtered their enemies. Three things stood out: three I will never forget. One was the pig thing.

The women with children lived in special houses — groups of women and children — until the children grew to be a certain age. And they had these pigs, you see, as pets. The women and the babies and pigs all lived together and, the way it was shown, they seemed to be quite happy. Then the men would decide it was time to have a nice feast of pork and they would come and drag away the pigs and they would kill them. The women's pets, you see. The children's pets. But it was only the men who got to eat them. Pork was supposed to induce some special kind of magic. So off they went — the men — to their bachelors' quarters where they'd roast these pigs and sit around having magic dreams.

Another thing was the women killing their babies. But only their boy babies. Only their boys. But it wasn't always . . . I mean, they didn't necessarily kill every boy.

What you have to know is, the women did all the work. The only thing they didn't do was hunt. But everything else was left up to them and they had to do it all with their babies on their backs and their children dragging along behind them. You could see it must drive them mad; all these children and all this work and, all of a sudden, there would be this moment when one of them would take off down to the river. Where she would drown her baby son. Not quite dispassionately — certainly with anger — but suddenly: coldly — methodically — without remorse. It was awful. You knew it was revenge for how the men had made them live and for what the men had done to their pigs.

And then there was this other thing — the third thing I remember.

This is about the bachelors. Even the husbands were 'bachelors.' And they moved in and out of the women's lives — mating with them — not 'making love' but truly mating, animal style. And stealing their pigs and watching the women — always from a distance. There were these huts — retreats — high up in the mountains where the bachelors went. Also, there were these compounds where the growing boys were kept. Not just kept with the men — but, really, kept apart from the women. And this was some kind of privilege. Different, you see, from the dowdy huts and the little, crowded farmyards where the women lived with all the pigs and babies. The men and the boys had contests. They played games and laughed. They created a culture of male totems . . .

"Why?" said Conrad.

"Fear," said Michael.

That was the basis of it. Fear. Partly disgust and a sort of mystical distrust of the women because of menstruation. But also a childlike fear of the power of women to give birth. And this fear was real and so tacit that, even though the men had segregated the women — even though they had succeeded in debasing them and disinheriting them, the women taunted the men. And they got away with it. They stood on the hillsides in groups and they laughed at the men in the compounds and they dared the boys to come out and have sexual intercourse. Dared them with all kinds of lewd, graphic gestures and always laughing. And, of course, the boys wouldn't go. They were afraid. They backed off. They hid. Or else, they came outside the compound in an army and they'd kill the pigs. Sometimes, too, they made war on their neighbours. Anything, rather than go to the women.

"Are you sure it was really the women they were afraid of?"

Michael did not answer this.

Conrad pulled the plug and the water began to surge toward the drain. He lay back watching it ebbing, revealing his pallid, hairless body.

"Anyhow, that's how I see myself now," Michael said. "A kind of ritual bachelor, living in retreat. Taunted from the hillsides. Being watched and listened to. But silently . . ."

"What about her pigs?"

Michael thought of the yelling matches and the slamming doors and the undone, promised things. He also thought of the silence with which Olivia seemed to be rebuking him. "I guess I've killed a few," he said. "But I haven't had the benefit of any God damn magic dreams."

The last of the water drew away with a great, loud sucking noise and was gone. Conrad lay there in the empty tub, with his goblet in his hand and his toes sticking up.

After a moment, he spoke and he said, "This is how they found my father. Just exactly three years ago. The twenty-ninth of April. With his wrists slashed."

"Today's the twenty-eighth," said Michael.

Outside the bathroom door, Grendel threw up the remnants of Mrs Kemp's toona sandwich. It was now 6:45. The guests would arrive at eight and still no one knew — but Rodney — who they would be.

"Conrad wants an egg."

"But we're going to eat in an hour-and-a-half."

"I don't think he wants it to eat," said Michael.

"He's going to throw it at someone, is that it?" Olivia was undoing the boxes from Fenton's and setting the contents in bowls and souffle dishes. Rodney was arranging her flowers in crystal vases on the cutting board.

"All I know is, he wants an egg."

"He wants it to lift his face with," said Rodney. "If you have a pastry brush, you'd better send that up, too. And a nice little dish to separate the egg in."

"Has he been doing this long?" Michael asked.

"About a year," said Rodney. "And only at parties. It makes him look Chinese."

"All we need," said Michael. "The Empress of China."

They arrived in the first warm rain.

There was a girl whose name was Louellen Potts who had once been one of Michael's students. She was now out taking care of other people's children in a daycare centre, wasting her talents as a first rate critic. She had come, this evening, ostensibly as Rodney's "date" — but she seemed to have an ulterior motive: at least, in Michael's view. She was one of those dreadful women who hound you with their beauty while they beat you with their mind. Michael cringed from the thought of what lay ahead: Louellen attempting to best him at every turn in the conversation, opening one and then two more buttons of her blouse and thrusting her breasts into the lamplight. If only she were less attractive, he could be sure of winning.

Olivia rather liked Louellen Potts. She was one of perhaps six students both she and Michael had encountered in the classroom and the lecture hall over the years. What Olivia instilled from *Heart of Darkness*, Michael destroyed with *Frankenstein*. Kurtz and the Monster, walking hand in hand: *that* was the future, according to Michael.

When Fabiana Holbach Powell arrived, she was not with her husband, but her husband's brother Tom and Tom's wife Betty. Fabiana's husband, Jackman, was enigmatically "abroad." The word "abroad" was delivered by Tom, while Fabiana looked the other way.

They had drunk for half-an-hour, waiting for Conrad to come downstairs. Michael put on some passable tapes (acceptable to everyone, that is, except Louellen) and the atmosphere was actually bearable. Under the influence of Cleo Laine, things loosened up a bit. The sailing voice cut through the dreadful, early chit-chat and very soon people were asking freely for "another scotch" or another glass of white wine. If only Louellen would stop exposing herself, life might be endurable.

Tom Powell was a cold-eyed blond who had just come back from Nassau. He had one of those infuriating tans and an even more infuriating physique. He didn't say much. The eyes said it all. They never left Fabiana, unless they were turned on Michael (perhaps '*through*' Michael would be more accurate) during the course of such questions as: "When was the last time we saw you?" and statements, such as the patently ridiculous: "You're looking well, Mike."

Betty Powell just sat on the sofa and rummaged in her pocket book for something she never found.

Fabiana, on the other hand, was radiant — as always. She carried with her — just as she had as a child — that wonderful and wondrous sense of someone always on the verge of imparting the secret of life, if only she could remember the wording. Her gaze would drift away towards the answer — beautiful and oddly heartbreaking — only to return yet again with the words; "no — that's not it . . ." implicit in the wounded, blue confusion of her eyes. She had once been kidnapped and the ransom had been a million dollars. Lucien Holbach, her father, had refused to pay it — even though he had sixty millions and his wife twenty millions more. Fabiana had escaped, unharmed.

Or had she? Michael wondered.

At any rate, she had escaped and, shortly thereafter, she had been married to Jackman Powell — who was currently "abroad." She claimed to have never seen her captors, having been forced to wear a blindfold the whole time. It was when, after hours of silence, she had discovered she was standing in the middle of an empty house that she made her escape. All of this had happened in Jamaica: a place to which Fabiana had never returned.

Years and years and years ago — when they were children — Conrad Fastbinder had fallen in love with Fabiana Holbach and, for a while — in later years, before the kidnap, it seemed that Fabiana might return his love. But three things had happened in rapid succession, dashing all those hopes forever: until now. Fastbinder's father had died, leaving him penniless: Fabiana had been kidnapped and Jackman Powell — ("that son-of-a-bitch!") — had married her.

Tonight, through some fortuitous twist of fate, she had turned up in Michael and Olivia Penny's living room without her husband — and only her brother-in-law ("that other son-of-a-bitch!") to watch over her.

Conrad waited for Cleo to begin singing "*Traces*" before he made his entrance.

"*A faded photograph,*
Covered, now, with lines and creases . . ."

Fabiana claimed not to recognize him.

Michael, never having seen his friend in lacquer before, tended to agree with Fabiana. Conrad, decked out in summer whites and with his hair plastered back, looked like someone trying to escape from a Somerset Maugham short story. His tie was a florid pink (admittedly, in fashion, if you glanced at the right magazines) and he reeked of Chanel 19. As for the face — it was true. Conrad Fastbinder had descended from the upper reaches in a Chinese mask.

The trouble was, he couldn't speak — whether because of all the scotch he had drunk in the afternoon, or because of the strictures of his 'face-lift' or, perhaps, because of both. As a consequence, he merely bowed over Fabiana's hand, and kissed it — after which, they all went in to dinner.

Michael sat at the head of the table, leaning back in his chair. He was turned to one side in order to accommodate his foot which increasingly troubled him as the evening wore on. He watched his guests — or rather, Conrad's guests, through a haze of pain and liquor.

Far off, he could just make out Olivia seated at the other end of the table. She was smiling — oh rare event — and, though the smile was somewhat fixed, it appeared to be genuine. What could she be smiling about? Michael regretted he had not begun to count as soon as the smile had turned up — just to see how long it would stay. It was rather like a visitor: another guest at the table: a stranger. He should keep a little book, like Hamlet: "My tables — meet it is, I set it down . . . Olivia smiled today for twenty seconds."

Why?

Michael looked around the table.

See who's here; he thought. All the bachelors. This is a bachelors' dinner. Rodney, Conrad, me. And Tom Powell — *he's* a bachelor. So's his wife. Look at them! I bet they touch each other with tongs. Or perhaps they wear gloves. Louellen Potts is a bachelor. (Damn it.) So is Fabiana.

So is Olivia.

Every damn one of us, living alone.

Here we are on the hillside — having killed the pig — and about to fall beneath the spell of the magic dream, perhaps.

Louellen Potts was sitting beside him: green eyed and green in tailored tweed. Breathtaking: youthful. Budding. Hair that falls — every hair in place and smelling of skin and flesh, no perfumes, only air and apples and sitting with one hand near his own, turned up — so innocent — or was that innocence? Maybe it was disdain. Knowing the harmless impotence of pockmarked hosts in their cups . . .

Not pockmarked. No. Do not go cruel into that good face. Be kinder. Kinder to yourself. Be kind.

Then, on the other side of the table, next to that blazered booby — Rodney Farquhar, pal and pudendum to the fallen Conrad — there was someone weeping.

Fabiana.

Was it true? Was she weeping?

Tom had told the tale at dinner — the dinner just finished, the one whose little bones were scattered under the grape seeds even now mounting on the plates as the bachelors lingered over their wine.

Tom, without saying so, had made it clear that Fabiana was waiting for a divorce. Her husband, his brother Jackman, had disappeared. He was a civil engineer — or something — and, though Fabiana's lawyers (working, of course for *him*) had told her he had "left her" and had gone somewhere, they would not say where. Not precisely. Only "into the Amazon region." That was all. That was how they had put it to her: "Jackman has gone" — into roughly speaking one million square green miles of rain forest. Now, he had been gone eight months and the lawyers had said, "he is probably not coming back."

So she could not get a divorce. She could only wait the mandatory seven years, after which she could declare herself a widow. Not that Jackman would be dead. He had gone there with her money. It was the money that was dead.

There was more, of course. Money. Enough for Conrad to cultivate, if he'd only take that egg off his face.

Michael watched Fabiana.

Just as Olivia's badge was neatness, Fabiana's badge was a restless wrist — her left — which she constantly massaged with her right hand, adjusting her watch and her bracelets and her bones, while the wrist turned slowly, this way and that. She also never looked at whoever was speaking, but set her eyes on those who were listening, watching perhaps for some clue as to the importance and meaning of what was being said. Now, it was Olivia who was speaking and Fabiana was watching Betty Powell, her sister-in-law. Betty Powell was cutting up an apple with a knife and there was blood on her napkin, of which she seemed to be entirely unaware.

Olivia was still smiling.

The subject under discussion had been famous mistresses and who had performed that function best in history. Olivia had just said something startling and amusing and even Michael was laughing.

Olivia had suggested that Antinous, the beloved of the Emperor Hadrian, had been the world's greatest mistress.

"Why?" Louellen Potts had asked.

"Because," Olivia had answered, "he couldn't bear children."

"Do you mean he couldn't stand them?" Betty asked. "Or just that he couldn't have them . . ."

She was ignored.

It was then that disaster struck, as it will out of silence.

Thinking he spoke in a confidential tone, and being quite drunk, Conrad turned toward Michael and reached out his hand as if to emphasize his words. As a result of the gesture, he knocked over Betty Powell's glass. Wine and blood and an apple core.

But that was not the disaster. The disaster was in what he said.

What he said was, "There's your answer, Michael. You and Olivia should have a baby."

Michael said; "Thanks for the advice and shut up."

Conrad said; "Oh, I see . . ." and he laughed. "You're afraid Olivia will kill it."

For a moment, there was only the sound of dripping wine and of someone breathing and then Louellen Potts turned down the table in Conrad's direction and said, "Do you think that's funny, Mr Fastbinder? Do you really think that's funny?" Then she turned to Michael and she said, "Why don't you hit him? If I were you, I'd hit him."

"You are not me, Miss Potts," said Michael. He was looking at Olivia, who looked away.

Now, Louellen turned to her and she said; "Mrs Penny? Don't you want to be defended?"

Olivia didn't answer her. She was looking at her napkin.

"Really, Professor Penny," Louellen said — still standing — "I think it is outrageous. And if you won't hit him, I will!"

"Sit down, Potts." (Michael)

"I will not sit down! This appalling man has just said the most appalling thing about your wife and . . ."

"SIT DOWN!"

"Michael . . ." This was Olivia. "Leave her alone."

"I beg your pardon," said Michael, alarmed, his voice rising. "I beg your bloody pardon?"

"You heard her," said Louellen — somewhat tipsy herself. "She says you're to leave me alone."

Michael said, "You condescending green-eyed bitch!"

"Michael!" said Olivia.

"Don't you 'Michael' me — you down there in the dark! What the hell right has she to put herself in my shoes?"

"She's only expressing her feelings, Michael. And whether or not they're valid, she has a right to express them."

"Not at my table, she hasn't!"

"This is our table, Michael. Not your table. Ours." Olivia did not even raise her voice.

Michael snapped. "Well she's sitting at my end!"

And Louellen said, with great vehemence, "*Standing*!"

And suddenly, everyone was laughing. Everyone, that is, except the Powells. They did not seem to know what to do in the presence of laughter.

Louellen Potts sat down and there was then a second, but minor disaster. Her hand had fallen onto the table rather near Michael's. And now, unthinking, Michael took it — merely as a gesture of forgiveness. Except that he did not let go.

Louellen looked at the table, not quite focusing on her up-turned fingers resting under Michael's hand. Her main awareness was of Olivia's eyes.

Michael felt the reverberation and he, too, became aware of Olivia's eyes. He turned his hand away slowly and withdrew it all the way back to his head, where he pushed back his hair.

"Conrad," he said.

"Yes, sir," said Conrad.

"Tell us about the time you got lost in that hotel and ended up in Princess Diana's bedroom."

In the living room, Conrad was lying on the rug, smoking a cigarette and staring at the ceiling. Michael, limping as unobtrusively as possible, was going about the room and bestowing second brandies into upheld glasses, including Conrad's.

Beyond them, the dining room glowed in the flickering light of its guttering candles. The table was an ordered ruin, with its eight distinct place settings, each distinctly destroyed by a separate pair of hands; the eight plates marred with the elegant parings of apples and cheese and pears; the wine glasses emptied to an exact degree, each one a signature; and the napkins, folded or thrown down and the chairs pushed back, reflective or violent or simply dispensed with — and the low, silver bowl of freesia, the flowers drooping as if they had been assaulted — and the mirrors that reflected mirrors that reflected mirrors — each one holding its perfect image a further remove, like sign posts down a road that led into darkness.

Rodney was playing the piano.

Otherwise — silence.

Olivia returned from the hallway, having opened the front door to let in some air. Outside, there was a spring rain and the strong smell of budding. She picked up her glass — allowed Michael to fill it — touched him with her pensiveness as he passed — and leaned against the door jamb, neither here nor there.

It was warm — and Fabiana's wrist was moving.

Slowly — it was imperceptible at first — as if a butterfly had entered the room and caught their attention only by degrees — Fabiana began to talk. She began in the middle of some interior monologue that perhaps had occupied her for some time — which yet seemed pertinent to the monologue of each of the others; one long sentence describing their mutual apprehension, whether it be about the past or the present or the future; arising out of that common literature which is the mind, peopled with common characters, moving over a common landscape, like a book they had all read — from which now one of their voices began to quote aloud:

". . . I know he went there without me in order to escape me. And yet I never bothered or pursued him. I was always standing still, it seems. I hadn't wanted him at first; but only let myself be wanted. The way a dog will let itself be wanted, not understanding why, except that out of being wanted — wanting comes. And out of being chosen — choosing. And out of being longed for — longing. Con knows. I never gave my loving. Never trusted myself to give. Never let it happen. I was always the little sister — sitting in the front seat, watching in the mirror. Until I met him — Jackman Powell. He was like a drug you take at a party, for fun. And then you wonder what it was. And then you ask for more. And then you realize you're hooked. And you never stop to think they've hooked you on purpose. You only think what a lovely feeling it is — and all you want is more. Until one day, they refuse. *There isn't any more.* Or worse, *there is — but I'm not going to let you have it.* And then they hold it up — they keep on holding it up where you can see it — and saying to you: *no; no more, Fabiana. Never any more.* And then they shoot it into the air, they waste it before your eyes. And they walk away — and they leave you with this empty syringe — and nothing to fill it with. And nothing to fill your veins with. And they haven't told you what it was — so you don't know how to ask for more. Because it was unique; it was *theirs* — they grew it, manufactured it or conjured it out of the air. And then they get on a boat and they don't even wave good-bye. And they're gone. And then you get a message — telling you they've disappeared forever."

Nobody watched her while she finished.

Instead, they each one welcomed the anaesthetic that prevented, if only for the moment, the idea that hope itself — anticipation — had disappeared for all of them into the Amazon region along with Jackman Powell.

Michael looked with a dreadful panic at Olivia.

Louellen Potts — the briefest of his dreams — got up to leave the room.

"It's time to go," she whispered, having lost her voice in

Fabiana's recitation. "Late," she said. And went upstairs to collect her coat.

3:00 a.m. and Grendel made a tour of the house, making his presence known to all the mice and to all the ghosts who haunted the dark, including the dark at the edge of everyone's dreams. Finally, he settled at the foot of the stairs, intermittently waking to stare out the open door through the screen at the sidewalks sparkling with rain — and to listen to the droning in the den, which to Grendel was like a cave, inhabited by bears or perhaps by giant, cave-dwelling birds whose wings were lifted in constant repetition, casting their immense shadows across the floor towards his paws. Michael's curtains. He eyed them with a careful wariness. He never completely slept. When there was thunder, the piano would echo its dying reverberations and the cello, in its corner, would hum a low, solemn note. The crystal prisms that hung from the candlesticks also sang and the dying fire in the grate made another song and the floorboards creaked in the faraway sun room and the windows sighed all over the house.

His ears hurt — chewed in a week old battle — and his gums were tender, having been torn. All along his back, he ached. No position was comfortable.

Everyone had gone upstairs — and he was alone. All the food — anything of real interest — was locked away. Except . . .

One bone, he remembered — put down by Michael under the kitchen table.

Grendel got up and fetched the bone and brought it back to the foot of the stairs. All through the next hour, he held it tenderly between his paws and wrecked it — very slowly — with his chipped and broken teeth.

The sound of gnawing — bone against bone — was all that could be heard. That, and the sluicing of the rain. And Olivia's voice, as she lay in the bed with her gaze on the patterns running down the walls.

"Michael . . . ?"

She was smiling.

Far in the Amazon region, a pin dropped.